# Out of Tune

by

D.C. Greschner

Science Fiction

FriesenPress

One Printers Way
Altona, MB R0G 0B0
Canada

www.friesenpress.com


First Edition — 2024

This book was 100% Human Made (no AI was used)

Cover design and illustrations by Helen Burger



ISBN
978-1-03831-195-5 (Hardcover)
978-1-03831-194-8 (Paperback)
978-1-03831-196-2 (eBook)

*FICTION, SCIENCE FICTION, HUMOROUS*

Distributed to the trade by The Ingram Book Company

# Acknowledgments

I would like to thank the following supporters, whose generous contributions have made this publication possible:

Jennifer Bayne
Kayla Bowyer-Smyth
John Callahan
Rob Christison
Shannon Clark
The Cunninghams
Geoffrey Davidson
Deanna Delaney
Shannon Demers
Conrad DeWitt Newell
Claire Doherty
Jaimie Dunbar
Ivan Elieff
Dave Ewoldsen
Andy Greschner
Sue & Ron Greschner
Aaron Jamieson
Ashley Kereszti
Tisa Komadina
Amelita Kucher
Becca Lamb
Heather Lee
Nicolas Lemieux
Clyde Loggie
Amanda Lunny
Robert Millington
Tricia Mowat
Kindra P. Ormiston
Robyn Peirce
Todd Powell
Jeff & Eden Poynter
James Rees
Sean Rousseau
Joe Scheubel
Francesco Tehrani
Beverly van Druten-Blais
Kori Weinwurm
The Wilde Clan
Peter Wootton

# Table of Contents

# FIGURE 1. PHYLOGENETIC TREE OF LIFE

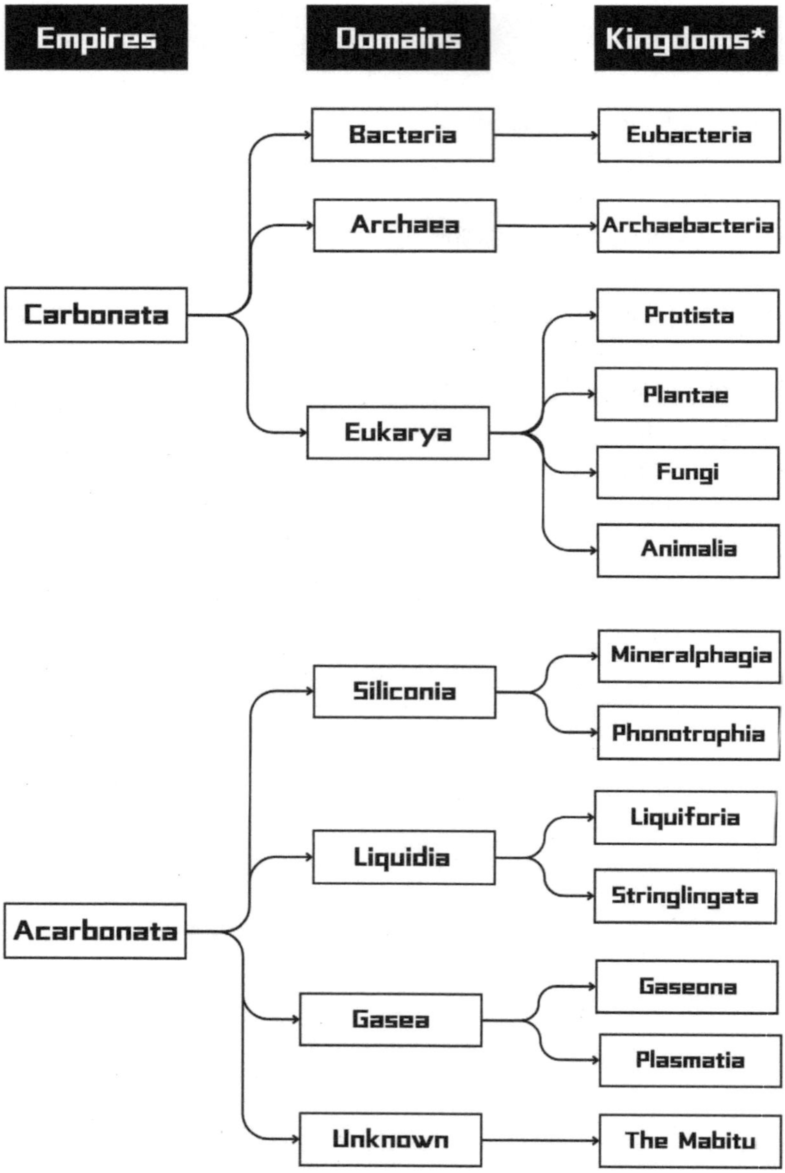


*Note: Figure 1 does not include all kingdoms of life, only a select few examples.

# PROLOGUE

The tank-like doka bug[1] wheeled over the snaking roots and loose soil of planet Orn with an air of pomposity. Its heavily-armoured body easily bulldozed through the rough terrain—rough for a centimeter-long beetle-like insect, anyway. Unlike an Earth beetle, the doka bug had evolved specialized appendages that acted as toothed wheels surrounded by a membranous tread, allowing it to plow easily through the ornian landscape. Its exoskeleton consisted of several layers of chitinous plates, which offered nearly perfect protection against predation. Because of this, the doka bug roamed around with complete confidence—some might even say arrogance.

True, it was blessed with evolutionary gifts that rendered it highly adapted to the natural environment on planet Orn. However, the environment had changed dramatically in recent years, and perhaps the doka was not quite as well-evolved as it thought. In fact, there was a distinct possibility that its inflated ego was no longer merited. Oblivious to this notion, the doka bug trundled along, hoping to happen upon a suitable mate. It had been trundling for quite some time—forty-two days to be exact—nearly the entire life expectancy of the tiny creature, and in all that time, it had not come across a single specimen of its own genus, let alone its own species. It was running out of time to pass on its superior genes to a brood of lucky offspring. Of course, the doka bug's simple nervous system did not enable it to form such complex thoughts, but its instincts hinted at a vague sense of urgency.

Perhaps it was this sense of urgency that motivated the bug to venture impressively far from the habitat of its hatching, unaware that the stalks of treep[2], normally about the size of a pond reed, were growing larger and larger. So large, in fact, that even the doka's perfectly designed tread was beginning to struggle over the thick roots and runners. It was only a matter

1 *Mesoarthropoda doka:* Empire *Carbonata,* Domain *Eukarya,* Kingdom *Animalia*

2 *Phragmites ornean:* Empire *Carbonata,* Domain *Eukarya,* Kingdom *Plantae*

of time until the bug got stuck, and that is precisely what happened. Wedged between a root and a stalk, the doka found itself unable to continue forward. It tried several times to spin its wheeled appendages, but the root was too smooth, and the tread spun around in circles, unable to gain traction. But would this genetic feat of motility be so impressive if it could only move in one direction? Certainly not. Once it accepted its inability to move forward, the doka began to reverse, and was delighted to find that the tread caught, and movement was once again possible. Proud of its accomplishment, the bug continued in the reverse direction as if to show off its conquest over nature.

It wasn't long before its overconfidence backfired. As it were, the bug had been reversing up the stalk of a very large treep plant and was getting further and further from the safety of the ground. The size of the stalk was such that its normally tiny protrusions were large enough to be gripped by the doka's tread. However, as the doka climbed higher and higher, the stalk began to taper, as did the size of the protrusions. Eventually, it reached a point where they were too small for the tread to grip and the doka lost traction. Before it could process what had happened, and with the force of gravity on Orn being similar to that of Earth, the bug began to slide down. Reflexively, it stabbed the stalk with its proboscis to hold itself in place. Normally, this behaviour would have been yet another useful adaptation in the doka's arsenal, but things had changed on Orn and the giant treep was no product of natural selection. The instant the proboscis pierced the outer layer of the stalk and contacted the plant's inner juices, the bug's tiny body, armour and all, disintegrated instantaneously.

*That makes seventeen today*. The farm worker[3] had watched the entire scene unfold through his hermetically sealed biohazard suit. He kept a running tally of doka bug evaporations to occupy his mind during the long, strenuous days in the treep fields. The juices in the stalk of the treep plant contained an enzyme called Alphasigmoidal Globulase, ASG, which destroyed most types of organic matter on contact. The doka bug's adaptations paled in comparison to this deadly defence mechanism. Wild treep only contained trace amounts of the enzyme, and its juice was only strong enough to deter grazers from taking a second bite. But when the scientists at AntiPro™ discovered its

3 *Macroarthropoda ornean:* Empire *Carbonata,* Domain *Eukarya,* Kingdom *Animalia*

effectiveness in weight loss products, they selectively bred treep plants with the highest concentrations of ASG and patented the new strain. The results: an exceedingly profitable product, as well as the untimely deaths of many an exploding doka bug and countless other critters that had the misfortune of coming into contact treep juice—farm workers being no exception.

The farm worker compulsively checked the tape that sealed the gap between the gloves and the sleeves of his biohazard suit. He did not want to become the next victim of treep exposure. Last month, he had witnessed a co-worker lose two of his hands. He had been warned about the dangers of treep juice, but nothing could have prepared him for what he had seen. He couldn't shake the image of the rapidly dissolving flesh. One second his co-worker's hands were there; the next, they were gone, bone and all. It had happened so quickly. Thinking about it made his wrists tingle. He pushed the image from his mind. He was paid by the kilogram, and he couldn't afford to waste time dwelling on the frivolity of workplace hazards. He checked the tape one last time, and then grasped a cluster of long stalks in his upper two hands. With his lower two, he hacked away at the base with a dull sickle, spraying the deadly juice all over his biohazard suit, which suddenly seemed much too thin. He looked for another doka bug to occupy his mind while he continued his work.

The worker had almost managed to stop thinking about dissolving hands when a drop of hot liquid materialized on his forehead. It trickled down and stung his eye. He froze in panic. Had the treep juice breached his suit? He had checked the seal around the wrists, but not the head piece. How could he have been so careless? Images of his wife and six children flashed through his mind as he waited in terror for his head to disintegrate. The terror vanished as quickly as the doka bug when the liquid reached his mouth and he tasted the familiar saltiness of his own sweat.

The worker laughed out loud, partly in relief that his head was not dissolving and partly at his own stupidity. He knew better. If the liquid had been treep juice, he would have been dead long before his brain could interpret the signal from the sensory receptors in his skin. It had been a long day, and he was just tired. He shoved a handful of stalks into the burlap sack slung over his left shoulders and continued on to the next bunch.

Once the sack was full, the worker hauled it to the weighing station to determine whether he had harvested enough to pay for his weekly food ration. If not, he would have to return to the field and reap one more back-breaking row. The scale beeped as the measurement stabilised. The scale attendant gave him a quick nod to indicate that he had amassed an acceptable amount. He let out a sigh of relief, tossed the sack into the back of a transport, and then headed to the decontamination shower.

The transport carried the day's harvest of treep to the spaceport, where it was loaded onto a massive astrobarge and shipped to the refineries on the moon Ydna. Here, machines crushed the stalks and collected the potent juice in large glass vats. The raw juice was heated to a temperature that partially denatured the ASG enzyme, making it safe for consumption. A sample of the batch was sent to quality control to undergo a series of rigorous tests to ensure its safety. After passing the tests, the refined juice was bottled and shipped to a factory planet in the Triangulum Galaxy. Here, the partially denatured ASG was extracted and manufactured into powdered form. The powder was packaged, labelled, and ready for distribution. This particular batch was headed to a small planet near the edge of the Milky Way Galaxy. The human beings of planet Earth were some of the leading consumers of AntiPro™'s magic diet powder. By sprinkling it on their food, they could eat as much as they wanted without absorbing a single calorie.

The worker limped with exhaustion from the transport station to his shack. He had a vague notion of the destiny of the crop he worked so hard to harvest. He had overheard other workers whisper about the hoomans and laugh at photographs of the fat, fleshy beings who consumed to excess. A low grumble rose from the depths of his empty stomach. It had occurred to him once or twice that the circumstances were rather odd. He worked so hard and could barely feed his family, and yet the hoomans were paying a hefty price to actively *prevent* caloric uptake. When he tried to express the absurdity to his wife, she had assured him it was just gossip. Everyone knew that treep juice had life-saving medicinal properties, and he thus risked his life every day for a noble cause. She sounded just like the company's upper management. Long days in the treep fields had always rendered him too tired to press the issue, but after today's scare, he found himself unable to turn his mind off. When he finally did fall asleep, he dreamed of doka bugs exploding in the treep fields, except they weren't doka bugs. They were the scale attendant, the suit manager, the site supervisor. Instead of feeling horrified, the worker laughed wholeheartedly as, one by one, he watched AntiPro™'s higherups vanish into nothingness.

Three weeks after it was packaged, the batch of AntiPro™ arrived at a warehouse on Earth. It was then loaded onto a truck and delivered to several supermarkets around town. A woman with absurdly tall hair and a purple blazer paid more than the ornian's weekly salary for a single 250-gram tub. Meanwhile, the farm worker clocked in for another day's harvest, only this time, he veered slightly from his usual routine. The previous night, he had returned home from work to discover a brood sack forming on his wife's carapace. She was pregnant. Again. The worker had become hysterical. He could barely feed their family now—what were they going to do when several more children were born? An ornian female's brood sack could carry up to fifteen young, and he had praised his lucky stars when she only had six the first time around. It was too early in development to guess how many were forming now. His wife, upset with his negative reaction, had insisted that he would need to get a promotion. "But no ornian has ever received a promotion," he had argued.

"What about Snyeild" she'd retorted. "His wife was bragging to everyone that the company had accepted his request to move up to scale attendant."

"And look how that turned out," he said, referring to his colleague who had lost his hands the previous month.

"Well, who got his promotion then?"

"No one, as far as I know."

"There you go! They must be looking for someone else to take his position. That someone should be you!" The worker had not responded. Instead, he had fantasized about his boss exploding like a doka bug. Then a thought had occurred to him. Maybe he *could* get a promotion. Maybe if he worked as a scale attendant, he wouldn't have to go through the decontamination showers and would be able to sneak some treep juice into the main office building, and then . . . He could picture all his problems evaporating in the blink of an eye. Accidents happened all the time in the field, why not inside? The company would have to replace all the pencil pushers with someone. He had sat in silent contemplation while his wife had rambled on about how he would need to do something to get noticed by his superiors. This morning, he set out to do just that.

Instead of sauntering to the dressing room in silence, he spoke to the suit manager behind the desk. He had spent the entire transport ride figuring out what he would say and had decided that the best way to get noticed would be to show them that he was in on the company gossip. "It's a good thing no hoomans work here; they would never be able to fit into these suits," he said awkwardly to the suit manager and let out a nervous chuckle. Without so much as acknowledging that he had heard him, the manager selected one of the more well-used biohazard suits off the rack and passed it to the worker. The worker took the suit, thanked him too enthusiastically, and continued into the dressing area. He told himself that the suit manager must be having a bad day, and he would try using the same line on someone else. Perhaps the scale attendant would be more receptive.

He set off into the field wracking his brain for more ways he could get noticed. Maybe if he exceeded his daily quota of treep, he would be praised for his hard work and offered a promotion. It would be difficult, given the immense effort it took just to gather the minimum amount. He surveyed the field and headed toward the row with the tallest, thickest plants. He grabbed a large handful of stalks and slashed at them with his sickle. It was getting late in the harvest and the stalks were especially turgid. With each slash, the pressure caused more spray to burst forth from the stems and soak his suit. He worked quickly, shoving the stalks into his sack before they could lose too much of the precious juice, unaware that late-harvest treep was even more potent than usual. The longer growing season allowed the plants to produce more of the deadly enzyme, building up its concentration in their fleshy tissues.

The worker fell into a rhythm: grab, slash, bag. Grab, slash, bag. Instinctively, he started to sing to the rhythm. He sang like his ancestors before him who had farmed these lands for centuries, long before AntiPro™ had bought up all the fertile land and used it for ASG production. Back in the days when the ornians grew a variety of crops that sustained their population and no one went hungry. Back in the days when treep was no more dangerous than a strong onion. As he sang, the flexible material of his hermetically sealed biohazard suit vibrated from the sound waves, creating a delightful overtone. He sang all the way down the row and then into the next, his face shield fogging up with each note he sang and clearing with each inhalation.

Approximately half-way down the third row, the worker noticed something sounded different as he sang. In fact, it felt different, too. It felt as though he could breathe more easily. He could *see* more clearly. The suit stopped vibrating along with his voice and the face shield was no longer fogging up. He sang louder in hopes of recreating the overtone and continued to hack at an especially engorged stalk.

A tiny drop of liquid landed on his forehead. This time, it was not sweat. This time, there was a breach in the worn-out suit, which was two years past its expiration date and knowingly kept in rotation by upper management to "reduce unnecessary expenditures." The contents of the worker's head splattered across the inside surface of his face shield. The small slit between the face shield and the hood fabric had allowed enough treep juice in to dissolve down to his second set of shoulders. His first set of arms remained mostly intact in their sleeves, severed from the rest of his body, hands still clutching the stalks of treep that had suffered a similar fate a split second earlier. The afflicted body parts, now a fine red mist, escaped through the same slit through which the treep juice had entered, leaving behind no evidence that the upper quarter of his body had ever existed. He did not have time to think of his pregnant wife or their six children. A lone doka bug was the only witness to the horrific display.

# CHAPTER 1

## Linda Pumpernickel

*Homo sapien*
Empire: *Carbonata*
Domain: *Eukarya*
Kingdom: *Animalia*

Linda Pumpernickel awoke with a start to the sound of a large vehicle speeding past her bedroom window. She nearly jumped out of her leathery skin as the back end of the truck collided with the curb and crashed down to the pavement on the other side. She felt around blindly for her thick glasses and caught sight of the AntiPro™ delivery truck just as it lurched around another corner, again failing to dodge the curb. Linda was almost certain she saw a piece fly off, although she could never be *too* certain these days, what with her declining vision and increasingly vivid imagination. What she was certain of, however, was the odd feeling of empathy gnawing at her amygdala the same way each street corner gnawed at that poor truck's undercarriage. She envisioned more pieces of machinery flying off the vehicle as it careened helplessly down the road, destination unknown, unable to slow itself down. It could survive quite a few dings, the loss of its headlights, a wiper blade . . . but what would come of the poor beast when its motor was inevitably penetrated? What about its tires? A tear formed in the corner of her left eye as she pictured the truck struggling to continue forward, slowing down, engine sputtering, coughing up vital fluids until it could go no further and stopped lifeless and abandoned at the side of the road.

She snapped out of the daydream and lifted up her glasses to wipe away the tear before it could drop. She scolded herself for relating so strongly to an inanimate object, remembering what had happened when her great uncle

Theodore had done the same. Linda suddenly became aware of the throbbing in her temples and the burning at the base of her esophagus. Her back creaked as she reached for the bottle of antacid that lived on her bedside table. She took a swig and almost choked when she noticed the time displayed on her antique two-dimensional alarm clock. Had she really slept in until ten o'clock? She really was letting herself go. She felt a pang of guilt for wasting the morning, but what else would she have done? She didn't have any important business to attend to. She didn't have much business at all. Since her retirement nearly five years ago, the amount of business in her life had decreased dramatically.

*Much like the air in the truck's tires.*

*No!* Linda told herself, determined not to slip back into her fantasy land. She forced herself to stand up slowly, waited for the headrush to pass, and then shuffled to the bathroom to splash her face with cold water. She looked into the mirror and cringed at the sight of the old lady staring back at her. She pulled her glasses down to hide her crow's feet, but the powerful lenses only magnified the dry canyons that formed a vast network around her eyes. In an act of futility, she dabbed lotion into the crevices until her skin could absorb no more. She felt a jolt of arthritis in her wrist as she screwed the lid back onto the tub of anti-aging moisturizer. "False advertising," she said to her reflection. Her eyes moved from her crinkled face up to the wiry baby hairs that stood upright along her hairline like antennae. She dampened them with water from the sink, knowing very well they would spring back up in a matter of minutes. Constantly dyeing her hair in an unsuccessful attempt to hide the gray had clearly caused some damage. Her most recent colour experiment had resulted in an unnatural orangey-yellow colour that she despised only slightly less than the gray. It was a losing battle. She sighed and tied it back into a small flop of a ponytail, and then wrestled with her bangs until they sufficiently hid the deep creases in her forehead that otherwise made her look perpetually surprised.

Exiting the bathroom, she shouted a voice command to turn on her holographic television. The artificial intelligence reminded her that shouting was unnecessary before displaying a targeted advertisement. Her living room momentarily transformed into the decadent dining hall of Spacay Space Vacations' seniors' getaway astrocruise. Linda paid no attention to it as she rummaged around her closet, struggling to find an outfit that wasn't horridly unflattering on her ever-widening waistline. She eventually decided on wide-cut jeans with an elastic waistband and a white blouse with a pink floral pattern. She laid the outfit on her unmade bed and searched her dresser drawer for matching socks. Not only did she require socks that matched each other, but socks that matched the whole outfit. Linda clung to the belief that a good pair of socks really tied an outfit together. It is unknown where she got this idea from, but it had caused her a good deal of stress whenever she lost a sock to the dryer gnomes. So much stress, in fact, that she had stopped putting socks in the dryer altogether and begun hanging them on a line. A logical person could see that this was a quite irrational stressor, as her socks were barely visible once hidden under her jeans and her shoes. Linda, however, was not what most would consider a logical person.

"Where are those blasted things?" she muttered as she tossed sock after sock out of the drawer. She was searching for a pair of socks that perfectly matched the light pink flowers on her blouse. She emptied the entire drawer and still no luck. She stumbled barefoot onto the balcony to see if the pink socks were on the line. She discovered too late that it had rained overnight and everything on the line was soaking wet, and now, so were her feet and the bottoms of her flannel pajama pants. She was faced with a dilemma: should she walk back inside with wet feet and trace footprints all over the floor, which she would have to wipe up? That seemed like a real bother. But what else was she to do? Stay outside?

"Screw it," she said, and removed her pants right there on the deck. She could use them to dry off her feet and avoid mucking up her laminate floors. She bent over and started dabbing her feet dry, completely unaware that her sizeable rump was in full view of her neighbour, Mr. Thompson, an eighty-something-year-old widower who watched in stunned silence from his rocking chair on the porch.

Back inside, Linda was now faced with a second dilemma: whether or not to go ahead with her chosen outfit in the absence of the proper socks. After several minutes of pondering, rummaging, and pondering some more, she went ahead with the original outfit. She decided plain white socks would do with this selection. Although the obsessive part of her mind was deeply distressed at this decision, the small rational part of her brain that remained was able to block it out for the time being.

After several more minutes of fussing about, Linda was finally ready to head out into the world. Whether or not the world was ready for her remained to be seen. She stepped out into the cool, late morning air and felt her sock anxiety dissipate. It was a lovely spring day. Air quality was tolerable. She estimated visibility to be about twenty kilometres, which was as good as anyone could hope for these days. Linda was in no hurry. Her only real commitment since retirement was singing soprano in her senior ladies' show choir, satirically called the Baffin Babes. Apart from her compulsive sock matching, Linda was quite laid back—at least that's what she told herself.

As she wandered down the street, she admired her neighbours' gardens and the tall palm trees that lined the road. It was hard for her to believe that this neighbourhood had once been arctic tundra, covered in snow and ice for most of the year. Nowadays, Baffin Island in Northern Canada was one of the few inhabitable places left in the world. Any closer to the equator, and it was simply too hot. On the rare occasion when solar winds temporarily cleared the layer of smog that surrounded Earth, space travellers could see the brown dust belt that encircled the centre of the planet. The dead zone, as it was called, covered more than half the total surface area of the planet, spanning fifty degrees north and south of the equator. The only creatures that could survive such barren conditions were extremophile bacteria and a handful of insect species. The occasional bird could be seen instinctually following a migratory path through the dead zone until the extreme heat either caused it to promptly turn around or drop dead.

Linda looked up to the overcast sky and spotted a carbon scrubber as it soared by. She had always liked the purple jet stream left behind by the scrubbers, which had been commissioned to remove excess carbon dioxide and other greenhouse gases from the atmosphere after the overuse of fossil fuels nearly destroyed the planet some years ago. She hadn't the faintest understanding of how they worked, but she thought the purple streaks were pretty. Today, they were also digging up feelings of nostalgia, as they reminded her of the clouds on planet Sagana. She had lived there and found work teaching English to the saganites during the great evacuation, which had lasted for nearly two decades. It had begun when extreme weather events and natural disasters rendered Earth unfit for human occupancy. Linda recalled the widespread panic and mass hysteria when people were forced to relocate to various sister planets so that environmental restoration could be carried out. That's when the carbon scrubbers were first commissioned. She never understood why some people were so resistant to leaving a planet that so obviously needed some time alone to recuperate. She had taken the move in stride and thought of it as an adventure. There was nothing wrong with a little change of scenery, and the scenery on Sagana was lovely.

Linda smiled as she recalled the incredible nasality of the saganite voice, and how it had caused them to struggle with English pronunciation. She had tried to use her knowledge of vocal technique that she had learned from singing in choirs to help them, but it was no use. Years later, she came across an MRI scan of the saganite larynx and discovered that it was located up in the nasal cavity, unlike the human larynx, which is down at the entrance of the trachea. It was physically impossible for them to *not* sound nasally. All her efforts had been in vain. The memory made Linda giggle out loud as she continued her leisurely stroll. A passerby saw Linda's far off look followed by her giggle and wondered if he ought to contact the neighbourhood psychiatric hospital to ask if they were missing a patient.

Linda had been reminiscing a lot in the past few weeks, which made her even more spacey than usual. The other day, on her way home from rehearsal, she was thinking about grade school when she was struck with a bad memory of a particularly nasty girl who had given her the nickname "Linda Plumpernickel." She had been so busy dwelling on this thought that she missed her bus stop and had to walk five kilometers to get home. *Serves me right*, she had thought. *I need the exercise.*

What was it that was stirring up all of these old memories and emotions? It was probably her upcoming milestone birthday: in two weeks time, Linda was going to be sixty-five. In fact, the main objective of today's outing was to begin preparations for her birthday party, but first, breakfast. Linda could smell the intoxicating aroma of freshly baked bread and pastries as she approached Daisy's Diner. She entered the small café to the ring of a bell and took her usual seat near the window. Daisy heard the bell and popped out from the kitchen. "Ah! My morning delivery of pumpernickel!" Daisy made the same joke every time Linda came in and laughed just as hard at her own wit as though it were the first time. Linda didn't mind. Daisy was old and borderline senile. Unbeknownst to her, she had acquired the nickname "Crazy Daisy" with some of the regulars.

"Good morning, Daisy. I'll have the usual." The "usual" was an apple Danish pastry and Earl Grey tea with milk and honey. Daisy made the perfect cup of tea every time. Linda didn't know how she did it, but the proportions were always spot on.

"Would you like AntiPro with that?" Daisy asked as she reached for Linda's favourite mug.

"Not today," Linda replied. She had given up that wretched stuff years ago after suffering a fainting spell caused by malnourishment, but Daisy could never remember. Linda thought it was obvious, what with her currently rotund figure. When her meal came, Linda savoured it. There was nothing in the world more comforting than a good cup of tea. It was like being hugged on the inside. She took a bite of her Danish and then a sip of Earl Grey, creating a delightful mush in her mouth. The best thing about Daisy's Danishes was that she baked them to perfection so that there were no crunchy bits of apple. Just warm, apple-y goo, through and through. The perfect Danish and the perfect cup of Earl Grey made for a divine combination. After she finished her scrump-diddly-umptious breakfast, Linda invited Daisy to her birthday party and tossed her napkin into the trash can on her way out the door.

* * *

Later that day, Daisy would take out the trash and toss it into the dumpster out back. The next morning, the garbage truck would come along, foraging through the streets like a giant beetle, pick up the dumpster with its steel pincers, and dump it into its cavernous abdomen. After completing its route, the truck would then drop its load at the nearest TRASH ejection station, located forty-five minutes away from Daisy's off Highway 78, just past the carbon scrubber launch pad. After being compressed and packed into a high velocity super-rocket (the disposable kind), the garbage, including Linda's napkin, would be launched into space. Four days later, give or take a day and a half, depending on the position of the Earth's orbit at the time of ejection, the rocket would reach the black hole H1821.

Unbeknownst to Earthlings of the time, the quantity of garbage that entered the black hole would become so great that it would develop its own gravitational pull strong enough to condense into a new planet. After several billion years, this planet would develop a molten plastic core, a solid mantle and crust, and an atmosphere consisting largely of carbon dioxide and methane. Eventually, life forms would emerge, and then evolve into a diverse ecosystem, from which a new species of sentient beings would spring forth. The sentient beings on the planet would harvest their natural resources, which were derived from the human-made wastes sent there billions of years prior and were composed mainly of plastics, rubber, metal alloys, and nuclear waste. They would use these materials to manufacture products like trees, soil, and rocks. The manufacturing process would produce incredibly harmful waste products, such as oxygen, nitrogen, and dihydrogen monoxide that would pollute their atmosphere and lead to a global climate crisis.

# CHAPTER 2

## Dr. Snodgester Slayneli

*Homo sapien*
Empire: *Carbonata*
Domain: *Eukarya*
Kingdom: *Animalia*

Linda woke from an afternoon nap just in time to catch the beginning of *Earth's Hour*, a subset of the news in which journalist Petunia Petals interviewed experts about various worldly issues. Linda only tuned in to gawk at Petunia's flashy fashion choices and then gossip about them at choir. The celebrity's altitudinous hairdo baffled Linda. She stared at the three-dimensional hologram floating in her living room for a minute, and then went about her errands. Linda left the 3D-TV on, half listening, as she tidied the kitchen and began dinner preparations.

"The study of sound energy in the universe is not a new field of astronomy. Cosmic microwave background radiation was discovered on Earth in the 1960s. Radio telescopes, such as the one located at the abandoned Arecibo Observatory in Puerto Rico, have been around for just as long. However, it wasn't until fairly recently that the significance of large-scale universal sound energy was viewed through a different lens." The charismatic hostess was particularly proud of herself for coming up with that line, which was made obvious by the flash of humour in her intense blue eyes and the slight raise of one corner of her brightly coloured lips. She wore a flashy purple blazer with dangerously pointy shoulder pads, which her producer hated. He complained that all the flashiness took away from the serious nature of the show. Just to spite him, she wore her hair even flashier by backcombing it until it was at least five inches high and filling it with multi-coloured ringlet extensions that occasionally wrapped around her shoulder pads, which "distracted audiences," according to her producer. But he tolerated it because he knew as well as Petunia that her outrageous fashion attracted a demographic of viewers that would otherwise be uninterested in the show.

After pausing briefly to let her lens pun sink in, the hostess finished her introduction. "I'm Petunia Petals, and this is *Earth's Hour*. Today's guest is here to talk about his ideas on sound energy and the universe. I'd like to welcome esteemed astrophysicist, Dr. Snodgester Slayneli."

The camera zoomed out, revealing an aging man with dark skin, a mustache, and a puff of salt and pepper hair that was beginning to recede at either side of his forehead. He had kind, dark brown eyes that sparkled with intelligence, as well as a glint of mischief. Peering into those eyes, one was immediately struck with the feeling that they hid a wealth of information no one else knew. And, of course, they *did*. He was a doctor of astrophysics, after all.

"Dr. Slayneli," the colourful hostess continued, "could you give our viewers some background information on the currently accepted hypothesis on how the universe formed?"

"Well Petunia, I think it's safe to assume that most of your viewers have heard of the big bang theory," Slayneli began in his deep, confident voice. Unlike many of his contemporaries, Slayneli was not camera shy and came across as well-spoken and engaging on television. "Most scientists now agree that the term 'big bang' is only a partially accurate description of what happened during the formation of the universe. Instead, we should refer to the 'big *bangs*,' plural, since there were many bangs involved in the formation of the universe. These bangs sounded like unimaginably large cannons being fired repeatedly in a predictable rhythm."

He turned to the camera to speak directly to his viewers. "Now, we all know that the universe is an immense, complicated place, filled with complicated life forms, so surely its formation was not as simple as cannon blasts. Indeed, there were many other sounds involved—sounds that were eerily similar to cymbal crashes, horn fanfares, and several other orchestral instruments."

"The cosmic symphony," Petunia chimed in.

"Yes, that is the term some scientists have used in their writings."

"So how does your research differ from theirs?"

"It doesn't differ, Petunia, it builds on it," Slayneli corrected. "I have simply analyzed all of the different sounds, translated them into audio patches detectable by the human ear, and assimilated them into one."

"Simple, yes," Petunia said playfully to the camera. Slayneli grinned in response. "And what did you find when you listened to all these sounds at once?"

"You aren't going to believe this," Slayneli said slyly, "but the resulting track bore a striking resemblance to Tchaikovsky's *1812 Overture*."

"You mean, the one that goes 'la-da-da-da da-da *da* da da'?" She sang the melody more or less accurately.

"Yes, that's the one!" Slayneli's eyes widened, but he tried not to look too surprised that the fashionable host was familiar with such a historical piece of music.

Petunia paused, waiting for the astrophysicist to crack up and let her in on the joke. He did not. Instead, he continued to describe his research, becoming more and more animated in his excitement.

"Perhaps our most ground-breaking finding has been that this music never stopped. It's happening all around us, every minute of every day!"

Petunia cocked her head to the side, listening. "I can't hear anything."

"Of course, you can't. It's much too broad for a single organism to hear all at once. It's spread throughout the universe, and not always at frequencies that we can detect." Slayneli saw Petunia's painted eyebrows furrow in confusion. "Think of it this way," he explained. "Although we do not consciously hear the sounds of the universe, we would certainly notice if they were to stop. It would be like when the furnace shuts off and you suddenly become aware of the silence."

"Okay," Petunia nodded, eyes closed in concentration. "But I can hear the furnace when it's on if I turn my attention to it."

"Here's another analogy for you," Slayneli continued. "A city creates constant noise, which is a result of all of the sounds happening in that city simultaneously: the rumble of car engines, the chatter of conversation, the rustling of leaves, and so on. You can focus your mind on two or three separate sound events, but the rest becomes background noise. I like to call it a 'buzz.' Your brain has evolved to only focus on sounds that pop out and could be potential threats. All other sounds, including the cosmic symphony, become part of the background buzz."

Petunia's blue eyes narrowed. "How does all this sound travel through the vacuum of space?" Surely this question would stump her guest. But Slayneli didn't miss a beat.

"If you imagine the universe from the perspective of a giant, each star, planet, and asteroid acts as the matter through which huge sound waves travel. Sure, empty space exists between celestial objects, just as empty space exists between particles of gas in the air. It's difficult for us to wrap our minds around the idea of such large sound waves, but spectral analysis shows evidence of wave-like movements of distant galaxies."

Petunia certainly could not wrap her mind around the idea, so instead, she wrapped a pink ringlet around her finger nervously. For the first time that she could remember, Petunia was speechless. Unable to think of a follow up question, she said, "It's time to take some questions from our viewers." The phone lines immediately lit up. "Caller one, go ahead."

"Hi there," the caller said in a thick southern accent. "Dr. Slayneli, are you familiar with the idea of entropy?"

"Yes, sir, I am."

"According to entropy, matter tends towards maximum disorder or randomness."

Slayneli was slightly offended that the caller felt the need to explain this to him and barely suppressed an eye roll. "That is correct. What's your question?"

"How can a universe that favours randomness produce sounds that are organized enough to be musical?"

"You mean the same universe that has produced cells, which are organized into tissues, which are organized into organs, which are organized into complex, intelligent life forms?"

The caller did not respond.

"Are you still there, caller one?" Petunia asked. He was not. "Okay, moving on to caller two. We're ready for you."

Both Petunia and Dr. Slayneli were caught off guard by the feeble voice that croaked through the speaker. It reminded Dr. Slayneli of his late grandmother. The old lady's voice asked, "What are the implications of your findings?"

"Great question," Slayneli said. "Such *organization* in sound patterns, as caller one put it, implies that there is some sort of significance to the phenomenon. It is my belief that the sound energy produced by the big bangs is vital to all living things, much like sunlight is essential to life on Earth. And just like life on Earth depends on a certain balance of the sun's energy—we would perish if there was too much or too little—so, too, does the structure of the universe depend on a certain balance of sound energy. Too much or too little sound energy would disrupt the balance, and that's what scientists mean when we talk about universal de-tuning."

"So, you agree that universal de-tuning is real?" the caller asked.

"Without a doubt," Slayneli said directly into the camera.

After a brief pause, the caller continued, "How are you able to focus such widespread energy into sound bites that we can make sense of?"

"Another great question," Slayneli replied. "We use a focusing sonoscope to quantify widespread 'buzz' noise. Much like a light microscope focuses light waves through a series of lenses into a field of view, the *f*-sonoscope focuses a broad range of sound waves through a series of tympanic membranes into a single frequency known as the consequent pitch. The consequent pitch depends on the scope of the sounds entering the sonoscope. Currently, the strongest sonoscopes can take in all of the sounds of an entire planet. For example, the consequent pitch of every sound happening simultaneously on Earth at any given time has a frequency of 392.0003 hertz and is perceived as G4 in the Western musical scale. Scientists have found evidence that Earth's consequent pitch has remained incredibly stable at G4, we think since the big bangs. Only in the past one hundred years or so has it begun to shift."

"What would cause it to change now?" caller two asked, stealing the show from Petunia Petals, who was becoming ever more distressed that a single caller was hogging all the airtime. Dr. Slayneli was too engaged in the conversation to notice her fidgeting.

"Graphs show the pitch shift beginning at around the year 2090. What major change occurred in the universe just prior to that?" Slayneli was purposely leading the caller to draw her own conclusions, much like a teacher would lead a pupil.

She thought for a moment, and then said, "The Second Space Age?"

"Very good! The Second Space Age was characterized by a marked increase in intergalactic trade and travel. For the first time since the big bangs, materials were being transported all over the universe much more rapidly than they would naturally."

"And the consequent pitch of a planet depends on the types and proportions of matter on that planet," caller two quoted Slayneli's Law to the lawmaker himself. She was having an epiphany live on television. "Which means that large scale imports or exports to or from a planet would affect its pitch!"

"Bravo!" Slayneli couldn't stop himself from clapping. "You've done your homework, caller two. May I ask your name?"

"Norma," the voice over the phone said smugly.

"Thank you for your call, Norma," Petunia interjected and closed the phone lines to focus attention back on her fabulous self. "Dr. Slayneli, could you tell us more details about the specific events leading up to the Second Space Age?"

Slayneli was disappointed Norma had been cut off. It was refreshing to speak with someone who actually seemed to understand the science, but he humoured his host. "Humans have been sending stuff into space since way before the second space age. It all started with simple rockets, spaceships, satellites, and probes. Then, in the 2020s, billionaires ran out of vacation destinations on Earth and decided to give space a try. This led to the evolution of the space tourism industry, which became affordable to the upper middle class in the 2060s. By the 2080s, the department of extraterrestrial relations had developed strong ties with several planets beyond our solar system. With Earth's temperatures becoming unbearably hot in most places, many people immigrated to our sister planets.

Petunia inhaled sharply in an effort to cut in, but Dr. Slayneli pressed on. "The popularization of intergalactic trade and travel also led to an influx of alien materials onto planet Earth. Substances that would have never formed naturally on the planet are now imported in abundance. One example of this is ASG, the active ingredient in anti-protein powder made by companies like AntiPro™. The importation of ASG to Earth began when the obesity epidemic threatened the existence of mankind, causing heart failure, as well as the inability and lack of desire to copulate. Oddly enough, this epidemic was actually beneficial to the Earth as a whole, as it temporarily halted the overpopulation of the planet. Then, the availability of ASG saved many lives from serious health conditions and re-established the ability and desire to reproduce, thus re-establishing the trend towards extreme overpopulation. However, the subsequent widespread use and abuse of the drug took, and continues to take, as many lives as it has saved, killing its abusers via fatal malnourishment. And so, nature continues its struggle to maintain balance."

Slayneli had done what he had promised Petunia he wouldn't do before the show went live. He had strayed off topic and started rambling about other issues he was passionate about. Even worse, he was speaking critically about AntiPro™, the show's largest sponsor. He saw Petunia throwing daggers with her eyes and the producer flailing frantically from behind the camera, so he changed the subject.

"And we can't forget about TRASH—Transfer of Rubbish and Sewage to H1821. This program was created and implemented by British astrophysicist William Sugarbaker, who won the Nobel Prize in 2099 for solving many environmental and physical space issues on the planet. Sugarbaker theorized that ejecting all of Earth's waste into the black hole would be a safe and effective way to solve many issues of pollution and overpopulation. It worked quite well, but neither Sugarbaker, nor any other human, could have predicted the long-term consequences of this mass exodus,"

Slayneli paused just long enough for Petunia to ask, "By 'consequences,' I assume you are referring to universal de-tuning?"

"Yes. That, and the fact that no one knows what happens to all of the trash once it enters the black hole."

Petunia raised her eyebrows in consideration. "I hadn't thought of that," she said.

"Not many have," Slayneli said. "I should also mention that I've only discussed the events that took place here on Earth. Similar trends occurred on billions of other life-sustaining planets throughout the universe, thanks to the ever-growing influence of the Intergalactic Trade Corporation."

"We have time for one last question," Petunia said in response to the producer's gesture to wrap it up. "According to the response on social media, our viewers are dying to know why we should be concerned about universal de-tuning. What would happen if the universe went out of tune? How far out of tune must it get to become dangerous?"

Slayneli took a deep breath, nodding thoughtfully. "It is predicted that the bogus oscillations caused by conflicting sound waves would interfere with gravity, eventually causing planets to be flung from their stars, and stars to be flung from their galaxies, and so on, in a butterfly effect of epic proportions. It is unknown exactly how this would affect the universe as a whole, but scientists believe it would cause incomprehensible devastation. The exact degree to which the de-tuning must occur to have an observable effect is also unknown."

"Unknown?" Petunia asked skeptically. Slayneli was ready with another analogy.

"It's like plate tectonics. Seismologists know that the plates are shifting and pressure is building up, but they cannot predict with much accuracy when an earthquake will strike. All they can do is monitor the seismic activity and hope for the best. Similarly, we can monitor the pitch change of a star system, but we do not know when it will start to cause problems. It is known with some degree of certainty that once the de-tuning reaches its limit, it will result in the extinction of all life in the universe. I wish I had a more definitive answer for you, but at this point, more research needs to be done."

Dr. Slayneli briefly debated whether or not to continue with what he was about to say. He wanted to bring up another controversial topic, but the producer was now vigorously signaling for them to wrap it up. The mischievous spark ignited Slayneli's eyes, and he decided to continue. "The main obstacle to furthering our understanding of universal de-tuning is that, for some reason, it has become a political issue. The problem with politicians is that they don't look beyond the scope of their term in office. It's not their fault, really; it's the system. It's also a flaw in human nature. We don't have the brain capacity or the foresight to think of the long-term consequences of our actions. Who would have thought that catching one more fish would lead to the extinction of that species, which would then cause a total collapse of the marine ecosystem? Who would have thought that driving gas-powered vehicles would cause eighty percent of Earth to become uninhabitable?"

Petunia opened her mouth to answer, but the question was rhetorical and Slayneli continued his lecture before she could make a sound. "Well, the truth is that everyone knew these things because scientists warned them, but they continued to do them anyway because of their inability to see beyond their own lifespans. And so they go about their business, day in and day out, worrying about more 'important' things, like, how much weight they've lost on the latest AntiPro™ diet, or planning their next cosmic vacation, unwilling to accept the fact that those things will contribute to their own extinction." If his mic were handheld instead of clipped onto his lapel, this would have been an appropriate time to drop it.

"Thank you so much, Dr. Slayneli. That's all the time we have for today's show." The panic-stricken host turned to the camera with eyes the size of saucers. "Thank you for tuning into *Earth's Hour*. Today's program was brought to you by AntiPro™ and the Intergalactic Trade Corporation. I'm Petunia Petals."

# CHAPTER 3
## The Baffin Babes

When Tuesday evening rolled around, Linda, too, rolled. She rolled off the loveseat, where she had been hand sewing sequins onto a costume while singing along with her choir practice track. She had been focusing so hard on the two tasks that the sound of her antique grandfather clock chiming in the six o'clock hour startled her right off the couch.

*Oh dear me! I'm going to be late!* In her best attempt to hurry, she jammed the needle through the stretchy fabric, stabbing herself in the process. She cursed loudly and went to the bathroom to search the medicine cabinet for her tube of liquid skin. She removed every single box and bottle and pill case from the cabinet but could not find the liquid skin. Instead, she found an old-fashioned bandage. It took her three tries to place the adhesive strips just right, so they weren't too tight or too loose. Once the bandage was placed, she saw the tube of liquid skin hiding in the mug that served as a toothbrush holder. Had she accidentally used the liquid skin as toothpaste? She vaguely recalled her teeth feeling strange the other day, but she didn't have time to dwell on that now. She shuffled into her bedroom to get her sheet music and glittery, lime-green pashmina and caught a glimpse of her dishevelled reflection in the mirror. *Drat. I can't go out looking like this.* Since this was Linda's only real social activity these days, she insisted on keeping up appearances.

Linda bumbled and Linda fumbled, and Linda futzed about. By the time she had found socks that matched her pashmina and hid her forehead wrinkles behind her bangs, she knew she would be half an hour late. Again. She also knew that she would be on the receiving end of the director's glare, and possibly even a lecture from Mary-Joe of the choir's board of directors, who was responsible for taking attendance, and who took her job way too seriously. *Maybe I can avoid her*, she thought as she boarded the sky bus. Then she realized that she had left her sheet music sitting on her bed, which meant she would have to sign out a copy of the visitor's sheet music. Mary-Joe was also in charge of the visitor's sheet music. Linda contemplated skipping rehearsal altogether to avoid the wrath, but she had to go to invite the ladies to her birthday party. No one had responded to her e-mails.

By the time Linda arrived at the hall, she had decided not to sign out the sheet music. She figured she had the songs mostly memorized anyway. She carefully pushed open the large door so as to not make a sound and tiptoed her way to the risers. She'd almost made it unnoticed when the door slammed shut behind her and everyone turned and glared. Linda suppressed her embarrassment as she clambered to her spot in the third row, not in the middle, but not on the edge, behind six-foot-tall Virginia. At five-foot-two, Linda could barely be seen by the audience, and she had all sorts of trouble trying to see the director. She had requested a new riser placement on several occasions, but the director refused, explaining that the current configuration was optimal for the blend of voices.

After nearly knocking over several singers with her booty, Linda found her place. It turned out that it was choreo day and she didn't need her sheet music after all. *At least one thing is going in my favour*, she thought. Judy, the choreographer, was busy discussing something with the director. At fifty-five-years-old, Judy was the youngest member of the choir. Linda took their discussion as an opportunity to whisper to Barb, who stood to her left.

"I'm having my birthday party this Saturday. It's at my house at four o'clock, or whenever you can make it. Any time after four."

"I'll check my schedule," replied Barb.

"I'm making appetizers and desserts. And my famous peach punch. All ASG-free, but you can bring your own if you like. I would love to have some Baffin Babes come so we can sing some songs. You can bring friends if you want, too. And, of course, spouses are also invited."

"Ms. Pumpernickel!" bellowed the director. "I think you've disrupted rehearsal enough for one evening."

Linda rolled her eyes. *Is this choir or boot camp?* she thought.

"Now that I have your attention," said the director, "we have decided to change some of the choreography for our fundraiser show."

There were audible sighs throughout the risers. Just when they had learned something really well, it was changed. This led to mass confusion and arguments about whether they were doing the new choreography or the old choreography and which was which. Most of the members were senior citizens and they had enough trouble learning it one way, let alone having it changed fifteen times. Linda was particularly inadequate at learning choreo, but she was totally oblivious to this fact. She danced all the wrong moves with absolute conviction. Linda completely zoned out during Judy's instructions and only snapped back to when the rest of the chorus started to run the song from the top. Linda poured her heart and soul into her jazz hands to the left, unaware that everyone else was doing spirit fingers to the right. She was off in Linda Land, having the time of her life. She had forgotten all about her shame for being late and interrupting rehearsal. The director and choreographer shook their heads in frustration. They simply did not know how to get through to Linda. And this was the real reason for her placement behind Virginia the Giant where her flailing was the least conspicuous.

Halfway through rehearsal, there was a short break and then announcements. This was Linda's chance to announce her birthday bash to the entire choir, but first she had to sit through the board members babbling away about uninteresting things. The last board member to speak was the treasurer, the most long-winded of them all, who gave them a detailed breakdown of the choir's budget. By the time she was finished, Linda had drifted off into the deepest depths of Linda Land and did not hear the president ask how the new costumes were coming along.

"Earth to Linda," the director said.

Linda jumped. "Huh? What?"

"Any news on costumes?"

"Oh, right, yes. The tops have all been made, I'm just finishing up the sequins."

"Will they be reading for a fitting next week?"

"Oh, yes, sure." In truth, Linda was behind schedule with the costumes. She would have been finished already if it wasn't for Beatrice going off AntiPro™ and gaining nearly a hundred pounds. Linda had had to re-sew her top three times. Good thing the material was so stretchy, otherwise she was looking at a fourth. “Speaking of next week, I have some news that’s not exactly choir related, if I may.”

“Make it quick,” said the director sternly. She was clearly annoyed with Linda wasting more of their precious rehearsal time. This only made Linda nervous, and when she was nervous, she had great difficulty finding her words.

“I, uh, I just wanted to tell you how very dear you all are to me . . . and, uh, it would be very special . . . er, it would make me feel special . . . uh, I would like to invite you to my house this Saturday for my birthday party. It starts at four o’clock, or five, or three . . . uh, you can show up whenever it’s convenient for you. I will spread out . . . uh, I will have a spread of appetizers and desserts to share.” Linda had begun to recite specific directions to her house when the director interrupted her.

“Linda, why don’t you just e-mail everyone your address? We can find your house with our map apps.”

“Well, I think there’s something wrong with my e-mail. I sent out invitations the other day and no one responded. I’ll try again.”

“Ok, great. Let’s review the new choreo again. From the top.”

Linda, feeling slightly embarrassed, but only slightly, slunk back up to her spot on the risers. It didn’t take long until she was back in Linda Land, dancing up an error-filled storm.

When she got home that evening, Linda sent six separate messages to the choir’s e-mail list. Each message contained three to five hundred words explaining in excruciating detail the directions to her house from various starting points. None of them included her address.

# CHAPTER 4

## Groodle Schmoodler

*Oodlean oodlean*
Empire: Carbonata
Domain: *Eukarya*
Kingdom: *Animalia*

*Moodle foodleoodlethfoodlel coodlengroodlegoodletoodleoodlen, Oodle thoodlenk yoodleoodle oodlegoodleoodlen foodler goodlethoodleroodleng boodlefoodleroodle moodle toodledoodley oodlen woodlershoodlep oodlef thoodle moodleghty oodle. Moodley yoodleoodle spoodleoodlek thoodle oodle boodleoodlentoodlefoodlelly doodleroodleng yoodleoodler coodlerroodlent loodlefoodle, soodle thoodlet yoodleoodle moodleoodle boodle bloodlessoodled woodleth oodlevoodlerloodlestoodleng joodley oodlen thoodle oodleftoodlerloodlefoodle.*

With a final "oodlemoodlen," Reverend Groodle Schmoodler concluded his sermon. His voice was deep and raspy, but not a dry raspy, more of a wet raspy, like someone who had smoked two packs a day for the past thirty-five years. It was as though no matter how much phlegm he coughed up, there was always more left behind, eager to escape the moist prison of his wide throat. He was a walking, talking, ever-filling goblet.

He made the O-shaped sign of the Oodle with his third and sixth appendages whilst closing his boodleblooble book of prayers with his fourth and seventh, and then stepped out from behind the oodletoodler altar using his first, second, and fifth. The congregation obediently echoed the closing to the prayer and returned the sign of the Oodle. The reverend looked out into his sea of followers with five of his eyes (the other two were watching where he was going) and was met with uncomprehending yet unquestioningly faithful stares. It was difficult for many of his followers to understand the sermon because they did not speak Oodlish. Here is a rough translation of the above passage:

> *My faithful congregation, I thank you again for gathering before me today in worship of the mighty Oodle. May you speak the Oodle bountifully during your mortal life, so that you may be blessed with everlasting joy in the afterlife.*

The reverend began to spin off the stage. Oodleans do not walk in a forward direction the same way as other sentient carbonites, such as humans or saganites. Rather, they spin. Their bodies are radially symmetrical, so they have no front or back or sides. Unilateral walking really only makes sense if one has a front and a back. The oodlean body plan exhibits seven-fold radial symmetry. As such, Groodle Schmoodler had seven tentacle-like appendages that radiated out from a central cephalothorax and seven eyes that encircled the top of his head and gave him a 360-degree field of vision.

As the reverend twirled away, the congregation of oodleans began their choodlent, a chant that would continue until their throats were raw and their voices were too hoarse to continue. The religion they were practicing was called Oodlism, as they considered the word "oodle" to be sacred. The oodleans believed that if they were able to utter the word "oodle" an infinite number of times during their lives, then they would be rewarded with an eternal afterlife. Of course, this is an impossible feat, but most oodleans are better known for their gullibility than their intellect. In order to maximize oodle utterances, the reverend spoke Oodlish during his sermons and the congregation chanted the choodlent for hours after the service. Some of the more radical oodleans even incorporated Oodlish into their everyday speech. This way, they were guaranteed to "speak the Oodle" thousands of times every day, thus increasing their chances of an infinite afterlife. Unfortunately, Oodlish is not a very efficient dialect. It takes around three times longer to utter a sentence in Oodlish and four times longer to comprehend than ordinary Ydlish. Most oodleans cannot even understand Oodlish at all. The omnipotent Oodle was a very recent concept to the oodleans, who were previously an atheistic race called ydleans. The very concept of religion was unheard of on their planet until Oodlism was introduced only forty years earlier. As a matter of fact, it was founded by Reverend Schmoodler himself.

Schmoodler was born into an unimaginably wealthy family and had the means to travel throughout the universe from a very young age. Throughout his travels, he observed all types of alien species. He had a keen attention to detail and was fascinated by many of the absurd cultural, social, and political practices of other planets. One of the most perplexing phenomena he had observed was religion. He was intrigued by the way that stories which had absolutely no basis in science and were impossible to prove or disprove could control billions and billions of beings. He watched entire planets destroyed in holy wars that were fought solely in the name of an unseen, unheard god. As a young ydlean, Schmydler (as he was then called) became obsessed with religion. He studied religions from several different galaxies, and he found the same general pattern in every case. There was always some sort of god or gods who represented a higher power that controlled fate. In every case, there was no way to prove that such a supreme being existed, and yet creatures lived their lives in order to appease him or her or them or it.

Schmydler also observed that most religions seemed to be rooted in the fear of death. It was as though these beings needed a way to deal with the unknown, so they had simply invented stories of a life after death. A common theme he saw in many religions was "If you please such and such a god, then you shall live in such and such a paradise in the afterlife." It was quite brilliant, really, and so imaginative, he thought.

Young Schmydler saw religion as an extremely effective means of manipulation and he was struck with an idea, which started out as an experiment. A joke, really. He knew that most ydleans had never even heard of religion and, as a species, had just accepted the fact that when they died, they would be gone forever. Schmydler thought up the idea of the almighty Oodle while he was drunk from ydlean beer one night, and thought the idea was so ridiculous that it just might work. He changed his name to Schmoodler and founded Oodlism in the following weeks. He was shocked at how easy it was to instill the fear of death and convert the ydleans into oodleans. He savoured his new-found power. With it came an ever-growing ego that bloomed into full-fledged narcissism. It wasn't long before Schmoodler was fully convinced that he, himself, was a supreme being. Schmoodler revelled in the knowledge of his influence over the entire planet every time he finished delivering one of his incomprehensible sermons, which were now broadcast planet-wide.

Why was Schmoodler so successful in acquiring his followership? Perhaps it was his power of conviction. Perhaps it was the infamous gullibility of the oodlean species. Or perhaps it was the fact that his family owned the highest grossing business in the universe and were therefore extremely influential in all sorts of political ongoings. The Intergalactic Trade Corporation, ITCo, held the monopoly on all interplanetary and intergalactic trade in the universe. The company owned every single astrobarge in circulation. When Schmoodler's great, great, great grandfather founded the company, its sole focus was the transport of ASG-based weight loss products, such as AntiPro™. ITCo's astrobarges made it possible to transport large quantities of treep from the ornian farms to the remote factory planets where labour was cheap and then distribute the finished product throughout the universe. Once these products became available universally, the industry exploded, allowing ITCo to expand their services. The more goods they were able to transport, the more money they made, and the more they could continue to expand. Eventually, they had bought out every last trade company and astrobarge in existence and became the largest employer in the entire universe. Reverend Groodle Schmoodler had taken over the family business when his father, Tyg Schmydler, retired. Although it was impossible to calculate his entire net worth, Schmoodler was rumoured to be history's first googolaire.

After delivering his sermon, the reverend snapped out of his self-congratulatory state, remembering that he had work to do. He made his way back to his office at ITCo headquarters to work on a proposal that, if approved, would improve the efficiency of intergalactic trade and increase his profits monumentally.

# CHAPTER 5

## The Cochleans

*Molassia cochlean*
Empire: *Acarbonata*
Domain: *Siliconia*
Kingdom: *Phonotrophia*

Near the edge of the elliptical Nasus Galaxy, the Molasses Planet monotonously revolved around an unextraordinary star. Slightly less monotonous (but only slightly) was the training session that was taking place near the surface of the planet's gooey exterior. Two young larvaluxi were trying their best to stay awake as the elder cochlean described the rules of the listentower in excruciating detail. If one of them fell asleep, they knew the grumpy elder would have it out on them. But it was exceedingly difficult to stay awake when the adult's instructions were whispered so quietly. The elder cochlean had much more sensitive hearing than the younger larvaluxi and could not breach the surface of its planet for more than a few minutes at a time. In fact, adult cochleans had the most sensitive hearing of any sentient being in the universe. They received their common name due to their striking resemblance to the human cochlea, a small spiral-shaped organ located in the inner ear. In humans, this organ contains billions of tiny hair cells, which bend in response to vibrations in the air caused by sound waves. Subsequently, the hair cells transmit nerve impulses to the brain, which then interprets the impulses as sounds, and that, in a nutshell (or perhaps more accurately, a cockle shell), is how humans hear. The bodies of adult cochleans functioned in much the same way, only they were much larger, approximately three to six meters in diameter, and contained many more hair cells of varying shapes and sizes. This allowed them to not only hear extremely faint sounds, but also to detect an extremely large range of pitches and to locate their sources.

Such sensitive hearing was both a blessing and a curse for the elder. It was a blessing because she relied on sound waves to create her own nutrition through phonosynthesis in the same way that a plant relies on light for photosynthesis. That, and it was very easy to eavesdrop. Her curse was that her hearing was so sensitive that she had to spend most of her time submerged in the goo that comprised her planet—goo that had a similar consistency to the molasses after which it was named. The high viscosity of the goo was difficult for soundwaves to travel through, which made life bearable for her. Bearable, but not particularly enjoyable, which was why, like most other adult cochleans, she was almost always in a foul mood.

"Are you two even paying attention?" she snapped at the young larvaluxi. The softness of her voice was somehow more intimidating than a loud one would have been, and the two trainees snapped to attention.

"Yes, ma'am," they whispered.

"I'm not sure that you fully understand the importance of our work. The PUE is relying on us to combat universal de-tuning. Do you realize what could happen if tuning slips too far?"

"Chaos of epic proportions," one of the trainees recited automatically.

"Yes, and it will be your generation that faces the consequences, not mine, so listen carefully."

The young trainees waited for the elder to submerge under the molasses and then glanced at each other nervously with their large yellow eyes. They looked nothing like the adults of their species, as they had not yet undergone metamorphosis. In their larvalux form, they had long bodies and two pairs of translucent wings that allowed them to fly freely throughout the atmosphere. They had not yet developed their sensitive hair cells and could tolerate the much louder volumes outside of the thick molasses. After approximately three years, the larvaluxi would undergo their first pupation. During this stage, they would shed their wings and legs, and their bodies would begin to elongate and flatten. Hair cells would start to grow on their abdomens. During the second pupation, their bodies would fold in on themselves to become long, hollow tubes with the hair cells on the inside. During this stage, the hair cells would become extremely sensitized. During the third pupation, their tube-shaped bodies would curl up into perfect Fibonacci spirals, which would then harden into the adult cochlear shells. Once this is completed, they would be mature adult cochleans unable to survive outside of the molasses. The process from the first pupation to mature adult would only take about two weeks (see biological drawings from the field notebook of universe-renowned field biologist, Jean Allgood, on the following pages).

After ~3 years, pupation begins. Hair cells form on abdomen and limbs are shed.

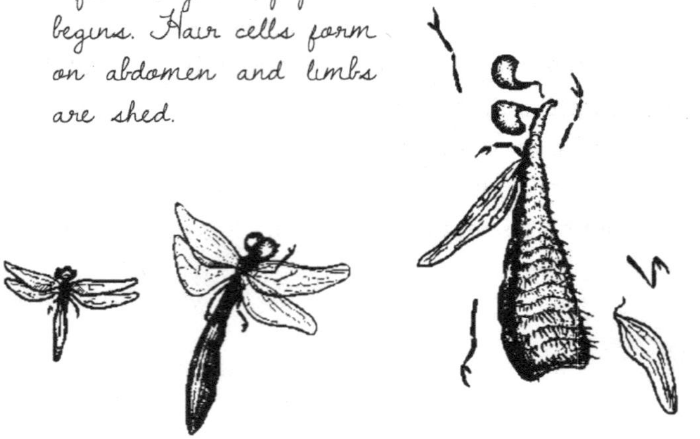

Once wings dry, larvaluxi fly out of the cochlear canal and can live outside molasses.

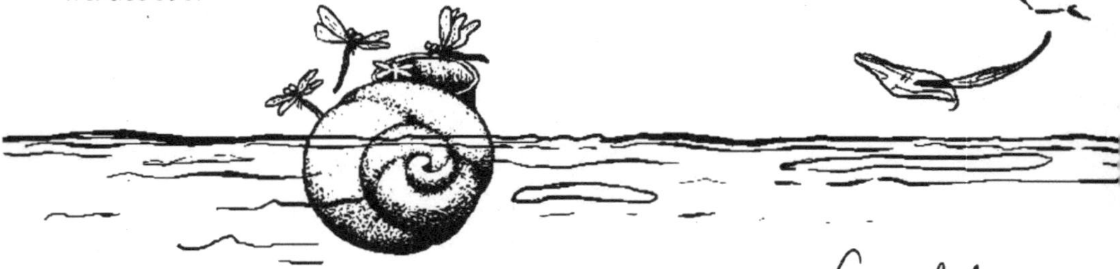

# Cochlean

Larvaluxi feed on goo to grow, releasing oxygen gas as a by-product. Mother floats to surface.

Embryonic goo fills cochlear canal as eggs develop into winged larvaluxi.

Abdomen flattens, elongates, and rolls into a tube-like structure with hair cells on inner surface.

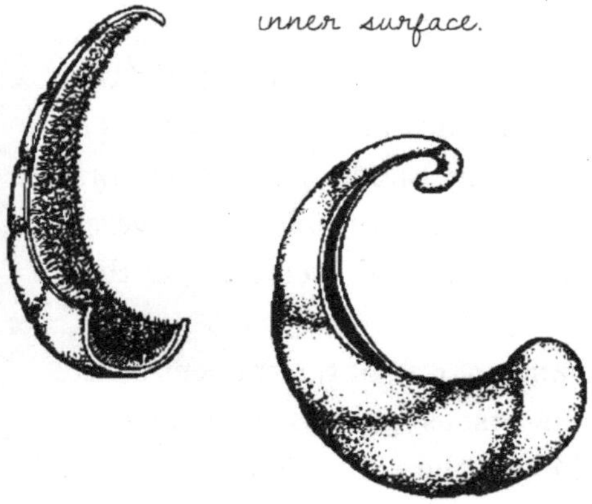

The tube-shaped body curves into a spiral and hardens into adult form.

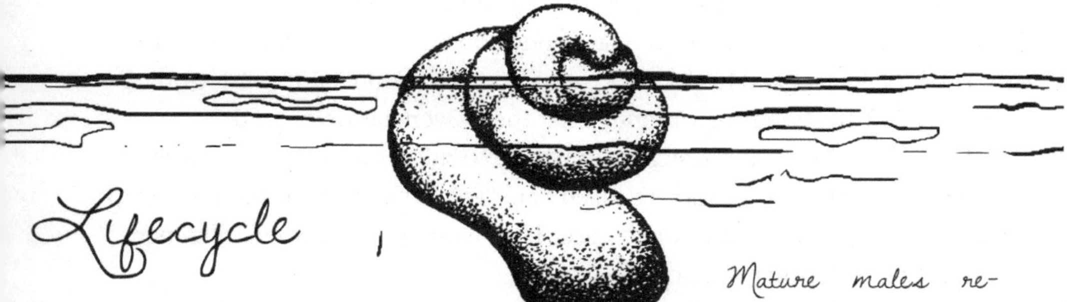

# Lifecycle

Mature males release gametes into molasses. Females ingest gametes from multiple males.

Six male gametes are needed to fertilize each egg inside the female's cochlear canal.

Fertilized eggs bind to inner surface of cochlear canal. Embryonic goo forms around them.

The cantankerous elder re-surfaced and continued with her lesson. "Now, who can tell me what 'PUE' stands for and what they do?"

"Protectors of the Universal Environment," the two larvaluxi said in unison.

"They're a government agency responsible for assessing and mitigating environmental risks in the universe as a whole," one of them finished.

"Good," the elder said. "When scientists like Dr. Snodgester Slayneli first proposed that large-scale intergalactic trade was responsible for universal de-tuning, corporations like ITCo were furious and did everything in their power to keep this from public knowledge."

"Why wouldn't they want the public to know?" one of the trainees asked. "They will be impacted by universal de-tuning just as much as everyone else."

The naivety of the young larvalux saddened the elder. She would have to be the one to break his poor, innocent mind. "Greed," she said. "These corporations only care about money. They don't care who or what gets hurt."

The larvalux cocked his head to the side in confusion. "But there won't be anything left to spend their money on if the universe is destroyed."

The elder winced in physical pain from extended surfacing, as well as the mental agony the corporations caused her. "That's what we've been trying to tell them for years, but they don't care. They won't be alive when it happens."

"But their offspring will be."

If the adult had shoulders, she would have shrugged. Instead, she dipped below the surface to temporarily relieve her burning hair cells and collect her thoughts. After a moment, she continued with her lesson, ignoring the trainee's last statement. "In response to the backlash from money-hungry corporations, the PUE began its mission to collect scientific data that supported the universal de-tuning hypothesis, and to spread public awareness of the issue. They built small devices called universal pitch transmitters, UPT for short. Each UPT was programmed to emit a single tone at a very specific pitch with a precision to the nearest 0.0001 hertz. Pitches were chosen based on a sample of planets scattered throughout the universe. For example, one UPT was programmed to match the consequent pitch of Earth, which, as you may recall from Dr. Slayneli's interview that we watched last session, was measured by a focusing sonoscope to be 392.0003 hertz."

Both larvaluxi hummed 392 hertz with perfect accuracy, but their auditory precision was not yet in the millionths of a hertz range.

"Close," the elder said, not bothering to correct them. "The pitch programmed into Earth's UPT was therefore exactly 392.0003 hertz. The purpose of the UPT was to serve as a baseline reading to compare with future measurements of Earth's consequent pitch. If the two readings did not match, then scientists could conclude that universal de-tuning had indeed occurred. A high powered focusing sonoscope was sent into orbit around Earth and would measure its consequent pitch once a day. This measurement was transmitted in the form of a single tone to us, here on the Molasses Planet, where an adult cochlean would compare it to the baseline tone played by the UPT and determine if there was a discrepancy."

"Is that what you're training us for?" one of the trainees asked.

"But we won't be able to do that until post-pupation!" the other said a little too loudly. He clapped his front tarsi over his mouth as he saw the elder flinch. "Sorry," he whispered.

"Take a look at the tower to your left," the elder said. The trainees glanced at the tall, narrow tower protruding from the molasses. "That's a listentower. There are several more like it dispersed around the planet."

"Listentower? I thought those were navigational markers."

"Yes, that's what you've been told. You see, we have to be very secretive about their true purpose. If ITCo finds out about it, they'll try to shut us down again."

"Again?"

The elder bobbed under the goo, leaving the two trainees in suspense. She returned after what seemed like an eternity and explained, "When ITCo found out about the PUE's pitch monitoring program, they were livid. They campaigned against the program and created propaganda to convince the taxpayers that universal de-tuning was a hoax and their money was being wasted. They even went so far as to plant double agents in the PUE who destroyed most of the UPTs. The final straw was a lawsuit in which ITCo sued the PUE for slander and won. The program was forced to shut down due to the financial blow."

The larvaluxi looked at each other in surprise. "They won? How?" one of them asked.

"Never underestimate the power of bribery," replied the elder.

"What do you mean?"

"It means ITCo paid off the judge," the other larvalux responded.

The elder rotated her shell slightly in her version of a nod and continued. "A handful of dedicated scientists vowed to continue their environmental mission. They salvaged the remaining UPTs and hid them throughout the universe to keep them out of the hands of ITCo. Each UPT was entrusted to a prominent supporter of the PUE who was responsible for keeping it safe and top secret in hopes that one day, we would be able to take more readings and prove that universal detuning was a real and imminent threat. The focusing sonoscopes were decommissioned but remain in orbit and are still functional. As far as public knowledge goes, the pitch monitoring program is on hold indefinitely."

The larvaluxi exchanged nervous glances. "Are we doing something illegal?"

"Illegal, no. Controversial, yes. Remember, you have both signed a very strict nondisclosure agreement." The larvaluxi nodded. "It is very important that you adhere to that agreement. ITCo has eyes and ears everywhere." They nodded again. "Back to what I was saying, the listentowers contain all of the equipment to receive signals from the sonoscopes and UPTs. Unfortunately, us adults cannot access the equipment, as it is located at the top of the tower. That's where you come in. You will each be stationed at a listentower. Your job will be to monitor incoming signals and report to your adult supervisor who will be positioned in the molasses below."

"That's it?" one of them asked. "We're like messengers?"

"'Communications Specialist' is your official title. And no, that's not it. Tomorrow, you will be shadowing a mature larvalux in this tower. He will show you how to operate the equipment and fill you in on all of the protocols." The larvaluxi gazed up at the tower solemnly. They were beginning to understand the importance of their position.

"Meet here at sunup tomorrow," the elder said. "Dismissed." Before either of the trainees could reply, the elder silently slid under the molasses and vanished.

# CHAPTER 6

## Groodle Schmoodler's Meeting with the PUE

Reverend Groodle Schmoodler, CEO of ITCo, had hated the PUE with a burning passion ever since they had accused his company of ruining the environment and skewed his reputation in the public eye, but he did not feel threatened by them. Even though they were a government agency, he knew his corporation was orders of magnitude more powerful than them. Still, they were a thorn in his side. They insisted on investigating every little detail of ITCo's business, which slowed down progress and meant they weren't making profits as quickly as he would like. Sure, he was the highest paid CEO of the highest earning corporation of all time despite the PUE's best efforts, but he could be making even more. Those nosy environmentalist hippies always sniffed out a way to delay things. They were constantly testing astrobarge emissions to ensure they weren't releasing more pollution than regulations allowed. One time, they even succeeded in temporarily decommissioning one of their older barges until its engine was replaced with a more efficient one. After that debacle, Schmoodler had found a way to cheat on the emissions tests by inserting special filters into the exhaust pipes, and then removing them afterwards. The PUE had also set up a mandate that forced the barges to be sterilized before entering the atmosphere of a new planet in order to remove any invasive species that may have hitched a ride. It was overkill and a complete waste of time, according to Schmoodler.

Schmoodler's secretary alerted him that the PUE representatives had arrived and were waiting for him in the conference room. It was Friday afternoon and enduring another interrogation by those imbeciles was the last thing he wanted to be doing. He spun as slowly as possible from his office, down the hall, to the conference room. Round stools, rather than chairs, encircled the long, imported mahogany table. This design was made for radially symmetrical oodleans, who did not use chairs with back rests, since they had no backs to rest on them. Schmoodler sluggishly made his way to his stool at the head of the table. Without acknowledging the visitors already seated there, he shouted at his assistant. "Doodlen! Why are there no snoodlecks?!"

Doodlen jumped to attention. "Oh my Oodle! Forgive me, sir, I will fetch some snoodlecks. Anything else, sir?"

"Yes, bring me some boodleoodler. I can't sit through another one of these meetings without a drink." He did not offer any refreshments to his guests. Doodlen nodded obligingly and spun off to retrieve the snacks and beverages. Schmoodler eyed the creatures of various origins sitting around the table. "Let's get this over with," he grumbled.

The president of the PUE was a tall, thin saganite by the name of Arec Ibo. Like all saganites, his monstrously large nose dominated most of his face, protruding out and then curving down like an eagle's beak. Continuing the bird-of-prey-analogy, one might compare the upper portion of his face to that of a horned owl. His eyes were so wide that they almost formed perfect circles, and his eyebrows were dark, thick, and unruly. When he turned sideways, the longest of the untamed hairs projected three inches from his face before curving back and rejoining the hedge. He spoke in an agonizingly nasal voice. "We received notice of your plans to build a" — he checked his notes — "a wormhole pipeline."

"Wormline," Schmoodler corrected, making a mental note to find whoever leaked the information to the PUE and fire them.

"A wormline, right. Could you explain what exactly that is?"

Schmoodler knew he couldn't tell Ibo the whole truth about his plan, or else the weasel would find a way to stop it from happening. He couldn't flat out lie, either, because he knew they would be watching his every move. So, he told them the truth, minus one or two minor details. "It's exactly what it sounds like," he said condescendingly. "A wormline is a flexible tube that runs through a wormhole, connecting two locations separated by vast distances of space and time," he explained, gesturing with three of his tentacle-like appendages. "The design is quite eloquent, I must say. It's a brilliant innovation of our chief engineer."

With an impressive effort from his forehead musculature, President Ibo raised an eyebrow. "What is the purpose of this wormline?" he asked.

Schmoodler grinned and replied, "To transport goods without the use of an astrobarge. We will be able to simply package up an order into a capsule and send it through the wormline. If it's successful, we won't even need astrobarges, which means our emissions will be reduced. It's good for the environment!"

Ibo considered this and then replied, "There's more to consider than just emissions."

"Like what?" Schmoodler snorted.

Ibo used his long but otherwise human-like fingers to list off the considerations: "For example, what is this tube made out of? Where will you harvest and manufacture the materials? What sort of power will be used to operate the wormline? Not to mention the potential increase in imports and exports."

The prying questions annoyed Schmoodler, and he struggled to keep his composure. "With all due respect, President Ibo, who said anything about increasing imports and exports? This is simply a new mode of transportation."

Ibo knew better than to fall for that. He knew that Schmoodler wouldn't spend time and money building this wormline unless it would increase his profits. "Like we've discussed in previous meetings, ITCo is already exceeding the maximum mass of intergalactically transported goods recommended by our scientists. Even at the current rate, you could be contributing to universal de-tuning. Perhaps you should focus your resources on a new business model."

Schmoodler rolled his eyes—all seven of them. "*Could be* contributing to universal de-tuning. You don't even know if this whole 'universal de-tuning' nonsense is real."

"Actually, our scientists unanimously agree—"

"Science! Ha! What about the economy?" Schmoodler interrupted.

President Ibo sighed. How many times would he have to have this argument? "There won't be an economy if there is no universe left for our future generations."

Schmoodler made a mocking gesture with a tentacle as he said, “Always talking about ‘future generation this’ and ‘future generation’ that. Your precious future generation will have nothing to live for if they have no income. They’ll be living in poverty. What kind of life is that? This wormline would create millions of jobs.”

Before Ibo could tell Schmoodler that no one would be living in poverty if he donated a fraction of his fortune to charity or paid his fair share of taxes, Doodlen returned with a large tray of live woodlerms and a jug of boodleoodler. Schmoodler poured half the jug of boodleoodler into the unnaturally large orifice on the top of his head, and then devoured six of the slimy, squiggling woodlerms, spitting out their severed heads right onto the table. The PUE representatives watched in disgust, trying not to stare, but morbid fascination rendered them unable to look away. Schmoodler used the break in conversation to figure out a way to get them to leave. “I’ll make you deal,” he finally said, spraying chunks of chewed up woodlerm guts into the air. “If you let me build my wormline, then I won’t sue you again.” He broke into a fit of laughter, which caused him to choke and cough out more partially chewed food.

“Not funny,” Ibo said firmly. “If you want us to even consider issuing a permit, you will need to fill out an application highlighting specific details of the project. We will need to see a comprehensive list of construction materials and your proposed location.”

Schmoodler schwallowed. “Why do you need the location?”

“So our team can conduct an environmental assessment of the area.”

“The site will be private property owned by ITCo,” Schmoodler said, and then took a swig of boodleoodler.

“Not until you have a permit,” Ibo shot back.

Schmoodler did not feel like arguing anymore. He just wanted them to leave so he could get drunk. “Sure, fine, whatever. I’ll have one of my employees send you the info.”

Ibo knew that Schmoodler was not taking this seriously. He chose one of Schmoodler’s eyes to focus on and shot daggers with his own in an attempt to convey the gravity of his words. “You are *not* to begin construction of any kind until your permit application has been approved, do you understand?”

"Yeah, yeah, I get it," Schmoodler brushed off the president dismissively. What he neglected to mention was that wormline construction was already well underway, and that he had no intention of taking any astrobarges out of circulation once it was finished. He would pay someone minimum wage to fill out the application to distract the PUE for now. Even if they rejected his application, he had support from hundreds of political parties whom his company had bribed. These meetings were just minor annoyances in the grand scheme of things.

President Ibo watched Schmoodler spit more guts with disgust and forced himself to swallow back the rising vomit. Doing so caused his voice to become even more nasally. "Very well then," he said. "I will have my secretary send you the application form."

"You do that," Schmoodler said and then dumped more boodleoodler down his gullet and belched loudly.

"Thank you for your time, Reverend Schmoodler," Ibo said, struggling to remain courteous. With that, the meeting was adjourned, and the PUE reps left. Schmoodler did not see them out. He stayed right where he was and ordered Doodlen to bring him another boodleoodler.

# CHAPTER 7

## Linda's Birthday

At noon on the day of her sixty-fifth birthday, Linda was bustling about tidying her house in preparation for her party. She enjoyed hosting, but on this particular occasion, she felt anxious. She was worried about the turnout. She estimated she had invited around fifty guests, but, since no one had replied to her numerous e-mails, she had no idea how many would actually show up. As an older woman who had never married or had children, and who had spent many years on another planet, socializing was a struggle. Add to that the fact that her only living relative resided in a senior's care home. Most of the time, special occasions only served as reminders of how lonely she was. Come to think of it, the only social events she ever attended these days were the ones she organized herself.

Linda pushed her self-pity aside and focused on the food. Since she didn't know how many guests she'd have, she didn't know how much food to make. When she had ordered groceries earlier that week, she had gone overboard, deciding that too much was better than not enough. Perhaps if she had an amazing spread, people would be more likely to attend her next party. She could throw a real shindig on . . . what was the next big holiday? Thanksgiving? Halloween? No. She checked the calendar app. Homecoming, that was it. Not to be confused with high school celebrations, Homecoming Day was a planet-wide holiday celebrated on August 21st, the day the great evacuation officially ended, and humans were allowed to return to Earth. Maybe she would decorate a cake with blue and green icing to look like Earth back before humans destroyed it. She could always smear some chocolate icing across the center to show the dead zone. She shook her head. As delicious as that might taste, it didn't seem very celebratory.

Linda reeled in her thoughts about a potential Homecoming party to focus on today's party. She thought about it some more and agreed with her earlier self that too much was better than not enough. She got to work preparing a wide selection of appetizers and desserts, including her own birthday cake. She agonized over what to write on the cake. "Happy Birthday Linda"? No, that seemed weird to write herself. "Happy Birthday Me"? That didn't seem right either. She finally came up with a phrase she thought was very clever and funny, albeit slightly morbid: "Sixty-five and Still Alive!" She was sure she'd get a laugh out of her guests. They would say to each other, "Oh that Linda, she sure is a hoot!"

The execution was not quite as brilliant as the idea. For some reason, she didn't think to write "65" numerically and instead spelt it out. Three-quarters of the way through the phrase, she realized her writing was much too large and she had to squeeze in the "Alive." In doing so, the "l" and the "i" smeared together and looked like a "u," and the exclamation mark looked like an "l." She looked at the finished product, which read:

**Sixty-five and Still Auvel**

Auvel? Good lord, she thought, that's a little too close to "awful," which is exactly how this cake looks. She hid the cake in the fridge where she wouldn't have to look at it. She turned and admired her table of appies. Overkill? Maybe. She had three plates of all the finest synthetic cheeses, crackers made from hydroponically grown grains, pickled asparagus wrapped in lab-grown bacon, smoked salmon (the expensive stuff from the fish farm, not the lab), several pounds of chicken wings (she wouldn't tell anyone they were the imitation kind made from grub protein), and trays of real vegetables grown in imported ornian soil. The dessert table boasted an assortment of locally grown Baffin Island tropical fruits, cookies made with termite flour, "I Can't Believe It's Not Butter!" tarts, and a fountain of melted artificial chocolate product. Her infamous peach punch was chilling in the fridge beside the embarrassment of a cake.

Linda was pretty sure she'd told people they could arrive at four. By five o'clock, no one was there. She changed her outfit three times, fixed her hair six times, and came very close to wiping all the icing off the cake and starting again. She had swept the floors, vacuumed the carpets, straightened the cushions, and dusted every single surface in her house. Now all she had to do was wait. At quarter after five, she decided it would be okay if she poured herself a glass of punch. She had to test it out, after all.

At five-thirty, the doorbell rang. Linda jumped up and sprinted to the door. She then realized she didn't want to seem too eager and counted to five before opening it. It was her Aunt Norma, hunched over and mumbling in her constant state of delirium. Linda saw the van from the retirement home drive away. "Hello Aunt Norma!" Linda yelled so that the nearly deaf old lady could hear her. "Thank you for coming!"

Norma didn't respond, not even a "happy birthday."

Linda helped her to the love seat and sat her down. "Would you like some tea?"

"Tea?" Norma said, disgusted. "You have to be careful about where you get your tea."

Linda thought that was an odd thing to say, but she didn't ask for clarification for fear her aunt would launch into one of her paranoid rants. She shrugged it off and asked, "What *would* you like?"

"Do you have anything stronger?" Norma croaked. Linda opened the fridge and Norma squinted at the contents and then pointed a wrinkled finger. "I'll take some of that there punch!"

Linda poured Norma a glass, then thought better of it. Instead, she mixed some peach juice with Sprite while Norma wasn't looking. God only knew what kinds of medications Norma was currently taking and how they would react with alcohol. It wasn't until she handed her aunt the drink that she noticed she had a gift bag hanging from her feeble wrist.

"What's this?" Linda asked. "You got me a present? Aw, you shouldn't have!"

"What?!" Norma shouted, then looked down, surprised to find the gift bag dangling there. After a moment of confusion, Norma's glassy eyes cleared and widened as she experienced a rare moment of lucidity. "Oh yes. This is for you. It is a family heirloom," she said in a very serious tone. Her eyes darted around the room, and then she whispered, "You must look after it and keep it safe."

Linda pried the gift bag from Norma's hand, which was now clutching it with surprising strength. Linda tossed aside some tissue paper and pulled out a small metallic disk with holes in the sides. It took her a second to recognize where she had seen a similar object before. Then she recalled that some of the women in her choir had them. It was a pitch pipe, which they blew into to find the starting note of an a cappella song. Norma wasn't joking when she said it was a family heirloom— this pitch pipe looked ancient. Linda wondered just how old it was. It was an odd birthday present, but then again, Norma was so old she probably didn't realize it. Linda tried her best to look appreciative as she thanked Norma for such a thoughtful gift. She put the pipe to her lips and blew into it. She tried a few different holes, but they all played the same pitch. *Great*, Linda thought. *A broken pitch pipe. Happy birthday to me*. Norma didn't seem to notice that the pitch pipe didn't work properly. Her eyes had glazed over, and she had regressed back to her mumbling, muttering state of confusion.

In addition to Aunt Norma, a total of twelve people showed up to the party: five ladies from choir with their husbands, Daisy from the diner, and old Mr. Thompson from next door, who spent most of the night attempting to flirt with Daisy and avoiding eye contact with Linda.

At seven o'clock, Linda was tipsy enough to forget how bad the cake looked and decided to whip it out. She half-jokingly requested that the Baffin Babes sing her happy birthday in harmony. "Look, I even have a pitch pipe!" Linda laughed and snorted as she retrieved her one and only birthday present and blew the pitch for the singers. They hesitantly obliged.

At the end of the evening, Linda sent everyone home with containers of food, but she still had too many leftovers. Norma was the last to leave, as the driver from the retirement home had forgotten about her. He apologized profusely as Linda helped him lift a snoring Norma off the couch and assist her into the van. "Wait here," Linda said and went inside. She returned with two large trays of goodies and told the driver to take it home or share it around with the folks at the retirement home. At least it wouldn't go to waste. When everyone was gone, Linda plopped down on the couch and stared at the pitch pipe. She gave it one last toot before passing out.

* * *

Several light years away, in a recently re-commissioned listentower on the Molasses Planet, a larvalux awoke to the sound of an incoming transmission. Sleepy at first, the larvalux was startled awake with the realization of what the signal meant. He flew down to the molasses below and called to his supervisor. He saw several thick bubbles break the surface, followed shortly by the adult cochlean.

"We've received a signal from a UPT," said the larvalux, who then played the recording from his handheld device.

In a whispery voice that would be inaudible to any other being, the adult asked, "Do you have any recent signals from the sonoscope?" The bright larvalux was pleased with himself. He had managed to hack into the decommissioned sonoscopes and had a backlog of transmissions.

"Yes, one from last week," he replied. He flew back up to the listentower and fetched the sound clip. He played the UPT transmission, then the sonoscope sound clip, and then the two together. To the undeveloped larvalux ear, the two sounded exactly the same. However, if the adult cochlean had had a face, it would have shown utter shock.

"There must be a mistake," she whispered. "The UPT must have malfunctioned. There's no way the pitch could be that far off."

"So, what should I do?" asked the larvalux.

"First, alert President Ibo. Tell him we have a pitch discrepancy of 0.5 hertz. Make sure to encrypt the message. Then, you must follow the protocol."

"The protocol?" The larvalux's eyes widened with the realization of what that meant. "But I have two trainees shadowing me tomorrow," he squeaked.

"We'll find another experienced Communications Specialist for them to shadow. Protocol always takes precedence."

The larvalux nodded solemnly. Since the pitch monitoring program had re-started in secret, no one had ever had to follow the protocol. He didn't think he would ever have to actually do it. He was nervous, but also excited. According to the protocol, he was required to find the UPT and bring it back to the Molasses Planet.

"Where was the signal sent from?" the adult asked.

The larvalux searched his device for a moment, and then responded, "Earth."

# CHAPTER 8

## Aunt Norma's Retirement Home

In the days following Linda's birthday, the nurses at the retirement home started noticing strange behaviours in Norma. She would tear apart her suite as though she were looking for something that she'd lost. She would empty out all her drawers and cupboards in a panic while the nurses watched in confusion. A friendly, plump nurse tried to help her one day. "Norma, dear," she said, "what is it you're trying to find? Let me help you." But Norma refused to tell her what the missing item was. She even accused several of the nurses, cleaning staff, and fellow residents of stealing it from her, but no one knew what "it" was. Every now and again, she would stop, as though she'd suddenly remembered something, and relax. The nurses reported this new behaviour to the on-site doctor, who, without speaking to Norma himself, increased her dosage of clozapine.

Exactly one week after Linda's birthday, on a stiflingly muggy evening, the two night shift nurses at the retirement home sat at the nursing station drinking coffee and gossiping. The younger one had only been there a week and the older one was filling her in on all the pertinent information about the residents. The younger nurse learned that Mr. Johnson in room 402 had a very attractive son who was around her age. The older nurse said he visited often and she was pretty sure he was single. The younger nurse laughed uncomfortably, quietly thinking how unprofessional it would be to date a patient's family member. She was saved from the conversation by a loud crash of thunder. They rushed over to the window and opened the curtains just in time to witness an impressive display of lightning. Seconds later, the sky opened up and released buckets of rain as the tropical storm intensified.

"It's not monsoon season for another month," the younger nurse said in surprise.

"Didn't see this one coming," the older nurse replied. "Weather forecast said nothing about a thunderstorm."

"Weird," the younger nurse shook her head.

The older nurse sighed. "I just hope the power doesn't go out again."

The storm lasted for nearly two hours. At around midnight, just as it was starting to die down, the phone rang. It was one of the residents, Mrs. Jones from 310, calling down to complain that her neighbour was having a very loud conversation. The two looked at each other, eyebrows raised.

"Who's her neighbour?" the younger nurse asked.

"Norma, room 308."

"Who could she possibly be talking to?"

The older nurse shrugged. "One of several of the voices in her head."

The younger nurse's eyebrows raised.

The older nurse simply smiled. "You haven't met Norma yet, have you?"

"No, I have not had the pleasure."

"We call her 'Revelations,'" the older nurse explained. "She's always mumbling about the destruction of the universe and the end of life as we know it."

The younger nurse frowned. "What kind of medication is she on?"

"The real question is, what kind of medication *isn't* she on?"

"That might be the problem," the younger nurse mumbled.

"Evidently, it's still not enough," the older nurse said. "I'll make a note for the doctor to up her meds again."

The younger nurse held up her hands. "No, not yet," she said. "I'll go talk to her." She was annoyed. She was new to this site, but she could already tell that the doctor couldn't be bothered to make a proper diagnosis. Most of the patients were severely over-medicated, many reduced to drooling vegetables. But she was "just a nurse," and it wasn't her place to comment on the doctor's decisions. She'd made that mistake once before and never heard the end of it from the pompous physician, which was why she had requested a transfer.

"Knock yourself out," the older nurse replied doubtfully.

The young nurse made her way up to the third floor and found room 308. She knocked on the door. "Norma? Are you there?" she called gently. There was no response. She used her master key to open the door and entered the room cautiously. She turned on the light and saw Norma, a tiny, shriveled woman with short, curly grey hair. She appeared to be fast asleep in her bed. The nurse scanned the room. There was obviously no one else in there. Some framed pictures on the wall caught her eye, particularly one very old photograph of a young woman in front of a crowd of people, all holding up signs that read "Environment Before Economy," "Universal Detuning is Real," and "ITCo Must Go!" It was one of the famous PUE protests she had read about. She took a closer look at the photo and realized that the young woman in the front must be Norma. *Wow*, the nurse thought. *Norma was an activist*. The discovery made her sad, knowing that she probably wouldn't be able to ask Norma what it was like. She was too far gone and apparently much too drugged up. She turned to look at Norma and nearly jumped out of her skin when she saw the ancient woman sitting up in her bed with big, bulging blue eyes.

"Hello, Norma. Sorry to intrude, but—"

"You won't find it here," Norma said smugly, a small grin lifting the corners of her creased lips.

The nurse tilted her head inquisitively. "Find what?" she asked.

"I know what you're looking for," Norma accused. "You're too late! I got rid of it."

The nurse had no idea what she was talking about. This must be what the older nurse had meant. She decided not to indulge the delusion and tried to speak rationally with Norma. "Mrs. Jones called and said you were speaking loudly. I just came up here to ask you to be quiet and go to sleep."

Norma's grin widened into a sickeningly sweet smile. "Of course, dear," she said. "He's gone now, so I can go back to sleep."

"Who's gone?" asked the nurse, peering around the room nervously.

"The larvalux," Norma said, matter-of-factly.

The nurse checked inside the closet and ensured the window was closed and locked.

Norma continued, "He came looking for it, too. But like I said, I don't have it." Norma leaned back onto her pillow and closed her eyes. As she was drifting off to sleep, she mumbled, "Isn't it wonderful, though?"

"What?" asked the perplexed nurse.

"This means they've restarted the program. There is hope for the universe after all." With that, Norma started to snore.

# CHAPTER 9

## The Larvalux

*Molassia cochlean*
Empire: *Acarbonata*
Domain: *Siliconia*
Kingdom: *Phonotrophia*

Eight days after her sixty-fifth birthday, Linda was sitting on her porch enjoying the fresh smell that followed the previous night's rainfall. She sipped her so-so cup of Earl Grey tea, wondering why she could never make it taste quite as good as senile old Daisy. Maybe that's what was missing—a dash of senility. "I'm well on my way," Linda said to herself, unaware that she had actually spoken aloud. "Just a few more years and I'll be joining Aunt Norma." She snickered. If anyone had been watching her, they would have assumed that she was indeed already there.

In the days following her birthday party, Linda had started to feel an overwhelming sense that something was lacking in her life, like she had failed to attain a higher purpose and needed to take immediate action before she was too old. But she didn't know what it was she wanted to do. She had no children and no husband, and both of those facts were very unlikely to change. That wasn't it. There was something else missing. At sixty-five, what could she possibly do to change the world, or at least fill the unwelcome void that was suddenly growing inside her?

She reflected back on her career as an English teacher, telling herself that she had already made a difference in the lives of many students. She had been extremely fortunate to travel to a foreign planet and teach students of another species. Barb from chorus had told her that it was perfectly normal to feel this way after retirement; that it took some time to get over the guilt we feel when we are no longer productive members of society. She called it a "three-quarter life crisis." The possibility that she had reached the three-quarter mark in her life did not make Linda feel better.

She decided a glass of wine would help ease her anxiety. She stood up slowly, knees creaking, and went inside to open a bottle of red. She poured herself a generous glass, then hobbled to the living room and settled onto the couch to re-watch a season or two of her favourite soap opera. She had just finished her second glass when she heard a soft thud. It sounded like a bird had flown into a window.

*Oh no, not again!*

Linda loved birds and she felt just awful when they hit her windows. She went to find the victim, mentally preparing herself to resuscitate if necessary. As she walked towards the sliding glass door that opened onto the veranda, she heard a second thud, and then a third.

*What in God's name?*

Linda raced to the door, hoping that she wouldn't find three dead birds on the other side. She opened the door and searched the floor of the deck. She didn't see anything. She hobbled down the stairs to check the back yard. Her neighbour, Mr. Thompson, watched as she got down on her hands and knees, rump in the air, and searched through the grass, which was in desperate need of a mow. She eventually gave up and headed back inside. She opened the door and there was a sudden *woosh* over her head. She watched as a huge bird flew into her living room, crashed into the wall, and then dropped onto her couch.

As she approached, she realized it was, in fact, not a bird at all. It had wings, but no feathers. It reminded Linda of a giant dragonfly. Its was about half a meter long and its wingspan was twice that. Its skin was smooth and shiny, and the light reflected off of it to create a rainbow pattern, just like an oil slick. It had four translucent wings, four arms and two legs. It had a human-like mouth, but no teeth, and large yellow eyes with long eyelashes. It was really quite cute. Linda realized at once that it was not native to Earth.

"Do you speak English?" she asked.

The creature nodded, still dazed from the collision.

"Are you okay? You hit that wall pretty hard!"

The creature took a few more breaths before it was able to speak. "Yes," it squeaked, sounding like it had inhaled a balloon full of helium. "I'll be fine."

"Alright, alright, just catch your breath. I'll be right back." Linda went into the kitchen and carefully read the label on the bottle of wine. No hallucinogens. She went back to the living room.

"Are you Linda Pumpernickel?" the creature asked, no longer panting.

"Why, yes, I am. How did you know?"

"Your Aunt Norma told me I'd find you here."

"Aunt Norma?! She was coherent enough to explain where I live?"

"Oh yes, of course! It was a dream come true to meet *the* Norma Pumpernickel."

Linda was surprised and confused. "How do you know Norma? And what on Earth are you doing . . . on Earth?"

The creature blinked at Linda, unintentionally batting its adorably long eyelashes. It was also confused, but soon came to realize that Norma had not even told her only surviving family member about her role in the PUE. It couldn't help but feel admiration for how seriously Norma took her job. "Norma is a very important supporter and former member of the PUE—the Protectors of the Universal Environment. She has led many rallies, fundraisers, and protests as part of an effort to educate the public and spread awareness of universal de-tuning."

Linda sat down, stunned. She had no idea about Norma's past. She barely knew her aunt until she was old and required Linda's help because the rest of their family had either moved away or passed away. She now realized that the reason she rarely saw her aunt when she was growing up was because she was busy trying to save the universe. "But universal detuning isn't proven, is it?" Linda asked. "I thought it was just a theory."

"Oh no, no, no!" The creature fluttered its wings in alarm. "It is very real, and its effects could be detrimental! The only reason we haven't published hard evidence is that the big corporations have shut down all of our research. But we've been carrying on in secret. In fact, Norma's UPT could be the key to saving the universe."

"UPT?" Linda wondered out loud.

"Universal pitch transmitter. Speaking of which, where is it?" the creature asked.

"Where's what?"

"The UPT."

Linda stared blankly at the creature.

"Norma said she gave it to you."

"I haven't the faintest clue what a UTP is," Linda said, shrugging.

"UPT," the creature corrected. "I must find it!" it said, its wings starting to vibrate.

"Now, now. Explain to me exactly what it is, and then perhaps I can help you."

The creature told Linda all about the PUE's Pitch Monitoring Program. It explained the UPTs and the sonoscopes and how ITCo had campaigned to cancel the program. Finally, it explained that after the PUE was infiltrated and many of the UPTs were destroyed, Norma was one of the people entrusted with the safekeeping of one of the remaining UPTs. "That must be why Norma didn't tell you anything. It was meant to be kept top secret," it explained.

Linda nodded, but she was still confused. "If she joined the PUE eighty years ago, then Norma would have only been nine years old," she said.

The creature thought for a minute, and then responded, "No, I believe she was thirty-one Earth years."

"But that would make her one hundred and eleven years old now."

"Oh yes, that's due to special relativity." The creature went on to explain that because Norma had travelled extensively at tachyon speed, her body had experienced eighty-nine years in the same time that the Earth had revolved around the sun one hundred and eleven times.

Linda was even more confused. "Well, I still don't know where that TUP thing is," she said.

"UPT," the creature corrected again. "Try to remember, has Norma given you *anything* recently?"

Linda thought about it, but she drew a blank. Her memory wasn't what it used to be. She was finding this whole ordeal rather odd and was fairly certain she was dreaming. "Would you like some wine?" she asked. "You look like you could use it. Wait—are you even old enough to drink?"

If it had eyebrows, the creature would have raised one. Clearly this earthling had no idea how dire the situation was. “No time for that. I must find the UPT.”

“Well, you feel free to take a look around. I’ll be in here watching my show. I think Edward is about to break up with Lily.” Linda refilled her wine glass and plopped herself down on the couch.

The creature fluttered its wings so that it was hovering like a hummingbird and started to search the house. It could not believe that this oblivious earthling was related to one of the most prominent environmentalists of their time.

Linda watched in anticipation as Edward entered Lily’s apartment. Was he really going to dump her? She had seen this season already, but it may as well have been the first time. She didn’t remember anything. Just as the plot was about to be revealed, her phone rang, and a holograph of Barb’s face popped into her living room. Linda tried, and failed, to hide her frustration.

“Hi Barb,” she answered, forcing herself to sound polite. “What can I do for you?”

“I can’t find my pitch pipe,” Barb said. “Can you bring yours to rehearsal this week?”

“I could, but it doesn’t work. It only plays one pitch,” Linda replied. She pulled the antique out of her pocket and blew into it several times to demonstrate.

“Oh drat!” Barb replied. “I guess I’ll have to call Sandra.” Barb squinted at Linda. “What the devil is that?!” she cried.

Linda looked to her right just in time to see the alien dart towards her and grab the pitch pipe out of her hand. “Sorry Barb,” Linda said. “I’ll have to call you back.” She ended the call and turned to the creature. “What are you doing?”

“This is it!” The creature said.

“I beg your pardon?”

“This is the UPT!”

“That piece of junk? It’s a broken old pitch pipe.” Linda took a large gulp of wine.

“No. This is Norma’s UPT.” The creature fiddled around with it, flipping it over in its four arms. “How do you send a transmission?” it asked.

Linda stared blankly.

"How did you make the sound?" it asked.

"You just blow into one of the holes on the side," Linda responded. She saw that the alien looked very upset. "What's wrong?"

"Norma must have removed the button and replaced it with breath-activated switch in order to disguise it as a pitch pipe."

"Ok, so what's the problem?" Linda asked.

"I don't have the same kind of lungs as you do."

"I see. That means you can't blow the pitch and compare it to the tone from the sodomy scope."

"Yes, exactly," the creature said, surprised that she had listened to its explanation carefully enough to *almost* remember the term "sonoscope."

Linda hiccupped. "Can you change it back to a button?"

"Do you know how to rewire a UPT?" it asked.

"Nope." She hiccupped again.

"Me neither."

They sat in an uncomfortable silence for what seemed like an eternity. Then finally, with a hint of reluctance, the creature spoke. "You will have to come with me."

Linda flinched, as though she were startled that she still had company. "Come with you where?" she asked.

"Back to the Molasses Planet."

"We don't have to go anywhere. I've got some molasses in the cupboard," Linda said, pointing towards the kitchen.

"No, the Molasses *Planet*, home of the cochlean species," the creature clarified. "I was sent here to retrieve this UPT, but it is no use to us if we cannot sound the pitch. The fate of the universe lies in your lung capacity."

"Am I having another choir stress dream?" Linda wondered aloud, and then sipped more wine.

"I promise this is not a dream," the creature said, and then poked her.

"Ow!" Linda said, glaring at the creature.

"See? Now come on, we have to go."

"Wait a minute! Slow down. I don't even know your name, and you want me to travel to another planet just so I can blow into a pitch pipe?!"

"I do not have a name. I am only a larvalux. I will not receive a name until I undergo all stages of pupation."

"Larvalux? That sounds like a brand of vacuum cleaner," Linda said, giggling until she hiccupped again. "How about I just call you Larv?"

"What's a vacuum cleaner?" Larv asked, puzzled.

"You don't know what a vacuum is?" Linda said, nearly spilling her wine. "How do you clean your carpets?"

"What's a carpet?"

Linda pointed to the floor.

Larv looked down. "Oh, we don't have carpets on the Molasses Planet."

"You want me to go to a planet with no vacuums and no carpets?" Linda sighed. "Why does it have to be me? You could ask any other human, and I'm sure several other species have the necessary lung capacity."

"Because this is a top-secret mission. We cannot tell anyone else about this. It is assumed that there are still double agents working for the PUE. No one can be trusted."

Linda narrowed her eyes and asked, "How do you know that I'm not a double agent?"

Larv just stared at her, knowing that there was no way this drunk Earth woman was intelligent enough to be a double agent. He kept that thought to himself and said, "Because Norma entrusted you with the UPT."

Linda's only rebuttal was another hiccup.

"Are you coming, or not?" Larv said, pleading with his big yellow eyes.

"I can't just pack up and leave," Linda stammered.

"Why not?"

Linda wracked her brain for a good answer. "It's not that simple," was all she came up with.

"Do you have something better to do?" the little alien asked.

"Well . . . " Linda struggled to think of a good reason not to go. "I have choir on Tuesday night."

"Does the fate of the universe depend on you going to choir?" the alien asked in complete seriousness.

"I . . . I suppose not."

Linda's first reaction had been an immediate no. Was she supposed to trust some strange alien she'd just met and follow it into outer space? The idea was absurd. Out of the question. But what was the alternative? Stay home and watch soap opera reruns and make mediocre needlepoints that no one else would see? Remain hidden behind tall Virginia at choir? Wait around until she inevitably shriveled up and died with no real friends or family to remember her? That didn't sound much better. She remembered the reason she had cracked open the bottle of red that afternoon: the feeling that something was missing, that she had a higher purpose. She didn't want to stay hidden. She didn't want to be forgotten. Maybe this was her chance. Maybe she wasn't dreaming after all. Maybe it was the wine talking when she asked, "When do we leave?"

# CHAPTER 10

## Arec Ibo

*Homo nasialus*
Empire: *Carbonata*
Domain: *Eukarya*
Kingdom: *Animalia*

After his frustrating meeting with Groodle Schmoodler, President Arec Ibo returned to PUE headquarters, which is what he called his living room. In order to pay the damages from the ITCo lawsuit, they had to give up their office space, among other things. Remembering the court case made him furious. It was obvious Schmoodler had bribed the judge when she happened to win free travel for life with Spacay Space Vacations, a subsidiary of ITCo, one month after the trial. Law enforcement turned a blind eye, chalking it up to a lucky coincidence. The truth was, they were afraid of what Schmoodler might do to them if they accused him of bribery. They certainly didn't want to be on the other end of the next lawsuit.

Ibo sat at his large office desk, which he had taken out of spite when they had moved out of the office, even though it looked ridiculous in his living room. It was pushed up against the wall that separated the living room from the bedroom. The desk was longer than the wall, and so the last five inches of it blocked the doorway. He had to turn sideways to enter his own bedroom. His wife hated it, but he refused to get rid of it out of principle. To him, it represented one small victory.

He opened his inbox and was surprised to find an e-mail from one of the listentowers on the Molasses Planet. He decrypted the message and nearly jumped out of his seat. "0.5 hertz?!" he shouted at his screen.

"What's that, dear?" his wife called from another room. Ibo was too stunned to answer. The datum was terrifying if it was accurate, but it was also exciting. He fantasized about shoving that number in Schmoodler's face and watching the collapse of his corporate stronghold. It would be the best "I told you so" moment of all time.

"Arec? What's the matter?" Ibo hadn't even noticed his wife enter the room. Ann Ibo was a tall, athletic human female with long, wavy brown hair and dark brown eyes. She was his third wife and much younger than him. They had met during a PUE protest before Ibo had divorced his second wife, about two years before he became president. She moved to Sagana with him, where interspecies marriage was legal. Since then, she spent most of her time writing online articles on controversial issues, such as interspecies marriage (she was lobbying to have it legalized on Earth), the dangers of ASG-based weight loss products, and, of course, universal de-tuning.

"Read this," was all he managed to say.

She stared at the screen. "0.5 hertz . . . is that a lot?"

"Imperceptible to our ears, but it's certainly a lot to a cochlean."

"So, what are you going to do?"

"I'm not sure yet. I have to consult with Nimbulus and Troodly." Ibo switched on his 3D telescreen and set up an urgent three-way call with his vice president and chief scientist. Within a few minutes, the two of them appeared holographically in the living room.

The PUE's Vice President, Nimbulus[4], was a mistoform, a species that belongs to the acarbonite empire. As the name suggests, his physical makeup was a cloud of gaseous particles, like mist. This made it quite difficult for carbonites like Arec Ibo to read his facial expressions or body language. It was usually safe to assume that he was in a bad mood.

Troodly, the chief scientist, was an oodlean, which caused some controversy among PUE members who thought she might be one of Groodle Schmoodler's double agents. But Ibo didn't believe that. Just because they were the same species didn't mean they had the same beliefs. Troodly was much more skeptical than most oodleans. She was a stone-cold atheist who believed only in facts and data acquired via the scientific method. When she was around other oodleans, she pretended to fall for all that Oodlism crap

4 *Nubes mistoformen:* Empire *Acarbonata,* Domain *Gasea,* Kingdom *Gaseona*

to keep up appearances and avoid suspicion. She didn't want Schmoodler's goons spying on her, or they might find her secret underground research facility, which was hidden below a woodlerm factory farm on planet Oodle. Ibo argued that it was advantageous to have an oodlean working for them so that she could keep an eye (or seven) on Schmoodler, rather than the other way around. Besides, her expertise in using computer simulations to predict outcomes in complex, multi-variable scenarios made her an ideal candidate for the job.

"What could possibly be so urgent?" asked Nimbulus. He was grumpy because it was the middle of the night in his space-time zone, and he had to reassemble his molecules for this unplanned meeting. Troodly remained silent, waiting for the president to speak. She wasn't one for small talk.

"Sorry to bother you," Ibo said, "but I've received some very exciting news. It's the first report from the Molasses Planet since the pitch monitoring program was restarted. The cochleans received a signal from a UPT on Earth and were able to hack into its sonoscope to obtain a reading. They found a 0.5 hertz pitch discrepancy."

Troodly, who most of the time exhibited an abnormally flat affect, was visibly alarmed. "0.5 hertz?! That's astronomical! Do you have any idea what that could mean for the planetary orbitals of Earth's solar system?" She was silent for a moment; Ibo could see in her eyes that she was making mental calculations. Little did he know, she was furiously scribbling notes with her fifth and sixth tentacle-like appendages, which were facing away from her camera.

"0.5 hertz doesn't sound very significant to me," Nimbulus chimed in. "Could it be possible that you're overreacting just a little bit?"

"Temperatures rising half a degree each year on Earth didn't seem significant at first, but look what happened. Over half the planet is now uninhabitable," Troodly stated flatly. She and Nimbulus had never gotten along.

"What Troodly means," Ibo interrupted, "is that seemingly small changes can set off catastrophic events."

Troodly nodded, then added, "According to my simulation, a pitch change of as little as 2 hertz could be enough to destabilize a star system, which means that the solar system is already a quarter of the way there."

Nimbulus was not convinced. "Before we start a panic, let's not forget that this is only one UPT, which has been inactive for decades. We can't be sure that it's even functioning properly."

"True," Ibo responded. "That's why the larvalux who received the signal is following protocol and is retrieving the UPT as we speak."

"Even so, I think it would be prudent to have more than one data point before we go public with this. Can we take readings from some of the other UPTs?"

"We can," Ibo replied, "but that's not the problem. It's getting the current measurements from the sonoscopes. We'll have to ask the larvalux how he hacked into the system."

Nimbulus added, "I think we also need physical proof that the change in pitch is actually affecting the planets. How do we know it's not the other way around? Which is the cause, and which is the effect?"

"According to my simulation—" Troodly began but was cut off by Nimbulus.

"I don't trust simulations. We need to take real, tangible measurements."

"Who would have thought a mistoform could be so dense?" Troodly muttered. She wouldn't stand for Nimbulus negating her life's work. He would never understand all of the variables that factored into her model.

"Enough with the bickering," Ibo said. "We have work to do. Troodly, I want you to assemble a team of scientists and look for any physical evidence of destabilization in the solar system."

"Evidence of destabilization? Are you saying you want me to measure the orbits to see if they've changed?"

Ibo nodded. "Yes, if that's what it takes."

"You realize they don't make tape measures for astronomical units."

Ibo nodded. "I'm sure you'll find a way," he said.

"What about the astrobarge emissions study?" Troodly asked.

"Put that on hold for now," Ibo said and turned to the other holograph in his office. "As for you, Nimbulus—"

Rather than awaiting instructions from the president, Nimbulus interrupted arrogantly. "I'll collect the remaining UPTs."

"Yes, that'll do," the president replied.

Troodly, who was a stickler for structure, didn't understand why the president had just allowed his inferior to choose his own assignment. It made her uncomfortable. She was debating whether or not it was socially acceptable to voice her concern when she saw someone else appear on the holograph. "Your wife," Troodly pointed.

Ibo turned around and was surprised to see Ann holding out a piece of paper for him. "What's this?" he asked.

"It's another report from the larvalux," Ann explained. "I took the liberty of printing it out for you."

Ibo read the transmission:

> UPT WAS LOCATED ON PLANET EARTH AT THE COORDINATES 70°33'55"N, 76°11'26"W. DEVICE WAS IN THE POSSESSION OF LINDA PUMPERNICKEL. MS. PUMPERNICKEL AND I ARE RETURNING TO THE MOLASSES PLANET.

Ibo's hedge-like eyebrows furrowed. "Linda? Who's Linda? What happened to Norma? And why is she going with him? Do we know anything about this woman?" Ibo asked.

"I've run a background check," Ann replied. "She's Norma's next of kin. She doesn't appear to be a threat. Retired English teacher, sings in choir, no husband, no kids, no other affiliations. As a matter of fact, she spent some time here on Sagana teaching English."

"That doesn't mean that she's not one of *them*," Nimbulus said accusingly.

"No, but I'd say the chances are highly unlikely," Ann said. "I don't think we need to worry." She waved her finger in the holographic display and pulled up a video clip from a satellite security camera. It showed a plump, old lady with orangey hair wandering down a suburban street, smelling flowers and apparently talking to herself.

"This still doesn't explain why she's accompanying the larvalux. How could she possibly be useful to him?" Troodly asked.

"That, I don't know," answered Ann.

"I'll deal with Linda and the larvalux," Ibo said, "You two have your assignments. Any questions?" He didn't wait for them to respond. "Good. We'd better get started then. Meeting adjourned."

# CHAPTER 11
## The Ellis Wormhole

Reverend Groodle Schmoodler was in a wonderful mood as he discussed plans for his wormline with his chief engineer, a brilliant, but fidgety oodlean by the name of Choodlen. They were in the viewing lounge of Schmoodler's extravagantly luxurious private space yacht, where they could see in every direction through a translucent dome. It was a magnificent sight to behold, especially for oodleans, whose radial symmetry allowed them to see in every direction at once. As Schmoodler gazed into the vastness of space, admiring the billions and billions of stars, he thought of all of the potential income that each star represented. This wormline would open so many doors for his already gargantuan business. His wealth was just like the cosmos, an immeasurable expanse full of an unquantifiable amount of beautiful, sparkling gems.

"Choodlen," Schmoodler rasped, "I'm going to make you a very wealthy oodlean."

"I appreciate that, sir," Choodlen replied, "but let's not get too ahead of ourselves. We still need all of the permits to go through."

"Don't you worry about that; that's my job. And I'm not worried at all."

"How can you be so certain?"

Schmoodler grinned. "Well, Choodlen, I've got friends in every corner of the universe. Most people don't know this about me because I don't like to gloat, but I'm a very generous oodlean. I know it's my Oodle-given responsibility to share the fortune that I've been blessed with. So, let's just say there are some very important people who owe me big favours."

"Sir, we're approaching the site," a sultry female voice said over the ship's intercom.

"Excellent!" Schmoodler said as he squinted through the window. A large metallic ring surrounded by an array of spacecraft came into view.

Choodlen also stared out the window at his creation. Years ago, he had suggested that Ellis would be an ideal starting point for the wormline, noting that it was the perfect location to commence construction away from prying eyes. ITCo had clandestinely purchased the space lot under a false name and kept the area heavily guarded. Now, it was finally all coming together, and it was a sight to behold. Choodlen eyed the huge metal ring that held the entrance to the wormhole open. "It looks bigger than the original plans," he said.

"Yes, we decided to stretch it out to maximize the volume of goods that can be transported," replied Schmoodler.

"What's the new diameter?" asked Choodlen, making a mental note to recalculate the dimensions.

"One hundred kilometers."

"We're going to need a *lot* of PVS," Choodlen noted. Polyvinyl styrozene, or "polystyrozene," was a material that Choodlen himself had engineered. It was extremely strong and flexible. The Ellis Wormline was to be constructed out of PVS so that it could bend and stretch throughout space-time within the wormhole. The end result would look sort of like a giant garden hose. Choodlen had also designed it so that it could not become kinked or decrease in diameter past a certain point. That way, exported goods travelling through the wormline would not get stuck and clog the line. It really was an elegant design. There were a few metaphorical kinks to work out still, such as figuring out how to control the exact endpoint of the wormline in space-time, but Choodlen decided not to bring that up at the present moment. Schmoodler was in a good mood, after all.

A buzzer sounded, alerting them that another craft was requesting permission to dock. The captain sealed off the docking bay and opened the hatch. A few moments later, the new foreman of ITCo's construction department entered the viewing lounge. The previous foreman had mysteriously disappeared, and Choodlen had yet to consult with the new one. Schmoodler introduced them, and Choodlen wasted no time pulling out the blueprints.

The foreman examined the blueprints for some time before asking, "How did you come up with this design?"

"Well actually, I took inspiration from Dr. William Sugarbaker's TRASH program, which transfers human waste and Earth rubbish into a black hole."

"Uck. Human waste, deplorable stuff!" the foreman exclaimed.

"Precisely," Choodlen agreed. "No one wants to go near the stuff, and that's why they only take the ships just close enough to the event horizon and then use large tubes to dump the waste from the ship into the black hole."

The foreman grimaced at the thought.

Choodlen continued, "It's really quite brilliant because the immense gravity of the black hole sucks the waste right out of the tube. No pumps required."

"Why doesn't the gravity pull in the entire ship?" asked the foreman.

"Ah, good question. The ship is too far away to be hugely impacted by the gravity. Basic stabilizing thrusters can hold it in place. The tube itself can expand and contract in length, like a worm. The tube is filled with waste while it is contracted and then as it extends towards the black hole, it eventually gets pulled in, along with the waste."

The foreman pondered this for a moment, and then asked, "Is all of the waste contained within one length of the tube?"

"No. The ships have enormous tanks, which are continuously drained by the tube."

"So, do they have to keep re-contracting then expanding the tube to get all of the waste from the tanks?" The foreman was envisioning the tube to function like an esophagus that essentially swallowed the wastes.

"Yes, for now, peristalsis will be required, but I'm working on finding a more passive way to transport materials. Constant peristaltic action uses a lot of power, which costs money."

"How would you make it more passive?" asked the foreman.

Choodlen smiled. "By adding water."

The foreman squinted in thought. "Water?"

"Yes. Water molecules are hydrophilic—they like to stick together—so once we get it started, it should keep itself flowing and carry the materials along with it."

The foreman closed his eyes, trying to envision what Choodlen described. "So, you're going to turn the wormline into a giant waterslide?"

"More like a giant siphon," Choodlen corrected.

"Where would the water come from?" asked the foreman.

"We would need to transport a huge volume of water out here initially, but I think we should be able to keep recycling it. As I said, I'm still working out the details."

Schmoodler became bored with the technical jargon, so he left them to it. He pressed the button that was implanted in his fifth appendage and pulled up his personal holographic profile. He saw that he had a new message, so he poked through the icon. All that appeared above his eyes was a list of names and coordinates—the locations of the UPTs that the PUE had hidden. A wide grin spread across his grotesquely large mouth, and, despite himself, he let out a deep, mucousy chuckle.

# CHAPTER 12

## Nilleby

Back on Earth, Linda and Larv waited for their shuttle to start boarding. It had been a long day of planning their trip to the Molasses Planet and they were both rather tired and frustrated, but they had a much longer journey ahead of them. The only route they were able to book at such short notice had five stops on different planets. Their first stop was a twelve-hour layover on a planet called Nilleby. According to Larv's holodex, Nilleby had no native species and no naturally occurring life-sustaining substances. It had an artificial atmosphere, and all of the food, water, and inhalable gases were imported. Therefore, it was home to a variety of colonists from various star systems who constantly fought over territory and engaged in illegal activities. It was strongly recommended that Linda and Larv did not venture beyond the spaceport. They sat in silence at the spaceport in Northern Canada until, finally, they heard the boarding announcement for their launch.

"Praise the Lord!" Linda exclaimed.

"Who's Thulord?" Larv asked.

"No one. It's just a figure of speech."

Larv didn't understand, but he didn't bother asking for an explanation. He was starting to accept the fact that humans were impossibly absurd, or at least this one was.

Linda shuffled onto the launch pad, Larv fluttering beside her. The spacecraft was one of the fancy, new models, which Linda had never flown in. The sleek, cylindrical vessel was enormous and could hold up to four thousand passengers. By the looks of it, this flight was completely booked up. The outer surface was covered in flashy advertisements. Most of them were for travel destinations and vacation packages, but the largest ad was for AntiPro™. The before-and-after photos of the model ran almost the entire length of the ship. Across the middle, a slogan read "Before you go, AntiPro!" convincing passengers that they should slim down before going on vacation. The letters were so large that the passengers could not read them as they boarded. They were meant to be read from much further away. Linda and Larv followed the signs to gate three of the ship and made their way up the ramp and through the door, which was located somewhere in the stomach flab of the poster girl's "before" picture.

They found their seats in the section designated for medium-sized species. This was a bit of stretch for Larv, who was on the smaller side. They lay back in their seats, which were reclined in the horizontal position for takeoff, and waited an eternity for the rest of the crowd to file in. Linda struggled to stay awake as an onscreen flight attendant guided them through all the safety checks and emergency procedures. Linda imagined the AntiPro™ poster girl pooping out the escape pods through the emergency exits and chuckled to herself. Larv focused intently as the flight attendant explained eight different ways to strap in safely for travel at tachyon speed. Different coloured straps corresponded to different body plans of the various species that might travel aboard the ship. Larv struggled to sufficiently tighten the red straps over his small frame, and Linda reached over to help him before securing her own blue straps. She then lay back and thought excitedly about how travelling faster than the speed of light would make her younger, like Aunt Norma. She didn't quite grasp the "relativity" part of Einstein's law.

All in all, it took well over an hour before they finally launched. As the thrusters boosted the craft vertically into the sky, Linda felt her stomach press into her spine. She tried to look over at Larv but found that the immense force glued her head in place. After they exited Earth's gravitational pull, she felt her stomach settle and was able to move normally. In fact, moving was easier than normal. She felt as light as a feather in the absence of gravity. This did not last long, though, as the captain announced that they would soon enter tachyon speed. The flight attendants floated down the aisles, pulling themselves along handrails, and checked that everyone still had their straps secured. Once they finished their safety checks, the captain counted down from ten and the ship lurched forward with magnificent force. Linda's eyes were forced closed, and she was now more firmly stuck in her seat than she had been for the initial launch. She imagined that the force on her face might smooth out her wrinkles. The thought made her smile on the inside, but she was currently unable to pry her lips into an actual smile. After a few minutes, her head started to pound, and she wondered how Larv's much smaller body was handling the pressure. Shortly thereafter, she passed out.

Three hours later, the ship slowed, and Linda came to. The engines died down as the ship was pulled into orbit around their destination. They remained in orbit until the ship was positioned above the correct location. Linda enjoyed the weightlessness of zero gravity and the ability to turn her head with ease. She looked out the window and saw the unseemly planet covered in brown smog that blew in swirls and hid the surface from view. Compared to this planet, Earth's dead zone looked like paradise. Mind you, from this distance, there was no saying what the actual surface looked like. Maybe it was lush and green under all the pollution.

As gravity pulled them through the atmosphere, Linda saw that this was not the case. The ship accelerated toward the dusty, brown surface so quickly it felt like they were free falling. Linda was certain that the engines must have failed. She wondered how she could possibly unbuckle herself and get to an escape pod while in a free fall. Luckily, she didn't need to attempt such a feat. There was a sudden jolt as the landing thrusters engaged and the ship stabilized in an upright position. Linda lay back in her horizontal seat and felt like she was floating on a cloud. Within a few minutes, they had landed safely on planet Nilleby.

Maybe "safely" isn't the right word. There was really nothing safe about Nilleby, as Linda and Larv would soon find out.

The flight attendants waited for the huge, domed ceiling of the spaceport to close above them. Then, they opened the doors and released the departure slides, which the passengers slid down onto the tarmac. Linda quite enjoyed the ride down the inflatable slide, but when she tried to stand up, she found it shockingly difficult and plopped back down. She felt heavy as her body readjusted to gravity, and she had only spent an hour or so without. She wondered what it must be like to spend several weeks in zero gravity. She also felt a wavy vertigo, like she had just returned to shore after sailing in high seas. She looked around to see if someone would help her up, but this was Nilleby and people here were not so considerate. Instead, she heard someone yell at her to move. She turned around just in time to see the next passenger sliding rapidly towards her. With great effort, she scrambled to her feet, then staggered forward, then back, then forward, then back again and fell right onto the passenger who had slid behind her. "Beg your pardon," she gasped as she struggled to stand up.

Without warning, the creature beneath her placed its feet on Linda's rear and heaved until she was upright. Linda started to say "thank you," but was startled into silence when she turned to face a hideous beast with one angry-looking eye partially covered by a bandana. It didn't make eye contact and pushed past her before she had a chance to say anything else.

"Rude," Linda mumbled under her breath. She wondered how sanitary it was to have a bandana covering half of one's eye as though it was replacing an eyelid. Then it occurred to her that maybe it *was* replacing an eyelid. The thought made her shudder.

Linda took a few shaky steps and looked around for Larv. She spotted him trying and failing to fly in a straight line toward her. Clearly, the tachyon speed travel was affecting his equilibrium, too. They eventually found each other and zigzagged their way to the terminal.

As she crossed the threshold into Nilleby Intergalactic Spaceport Terminal, Linda felt instantly overwhelmed. Compared to the shiny new shuttle they had just disembarked from, the spaceport looked like a slum. Under an enormous translucent dome, there were thousands upon thousands of small booths, poorly constructed out of some old, wood-like material (but not quite wood) that appeared to be rotting. The booths were not arranged in rows or any sort of orderly fashion but sprawled about all over the place, creating an overcrowded maze that was next to impossible to navigate. The booths were run by vendors who sold anything from food and drink to trinkets to substances that would be deemed illicit on any other planet. The merchandise spilled out into the narrow walkway, making some places very difficult to traverse.

As they made their way through, Larv kept flying ahead, unintentionally leaving Linda stuck behind one obstacle or another. Adding to her frustration were the relentless vendors who were almost violent in their assertiveness as they shoved merchandise at her, trying desperately to make a sale.

As she pushed her way past a souvenir booth, a particularly shady-looking alien grabbed at Linda with several sticky tentacles in an attempt to drag her into the store. In the process, one tentacle got stuck in her hair, nearly ripping it from her skull. She called to Larv, who immediately came to her rescue. It took him several minutes to untangle the gooey mess and set her free. Unbeknownst to Linda, he did not succeed in removing all of the slime, and the struggle had resulted in the left side of her bangs, which had been perfectly curled at the beginning of the day, pointing up like a solitary devil's horn.

They finally made it to an inner courtyard in the center of the maze, which contained a seating area. All the seats were taken, but at least they weren't being barraged by bloodthirsty salespeople anymore. When Linda caught up to Larv, she was tired and grumpy. "I can't believe we're stuck in this circus for the next twelve hours!" she exclaimed. "I would do anything for a cup of tea. Did you happen to see any in there?"

"I didn't notice," Larv replied.

"Oh well. I don't want to go back in there anyway."

"Good plan."

"I have a better idea."

Larv looked at Linda, wide-eyed, awaiting her idea. "Let's get out of this dump," she said.

"There's nowhere else to go," said Larv.

"Sure there is. Follow me."

Reluctantly, Larv followed Linda as she pushed her way to the other side of the terminal. He realized in horror that she was following the signs that led to the exit. "I really don't think we should leave the spaceport," he warned. "Remember what my holodex said? It's dangerous out there."

"Larv, nothing comes between an old woman and her tea. Don't worry, we won't go far."

"It's not safe!" Larv protested, but Linda was already out the door. She was on a mission. Larv sighed and realized he had no choice but to follow. He figured the best thing to do was to look up the nearest café on his holodex. That way, at least they wouldn't wander off any farther than they had to. He fluttered out the door and was nearly blown away by the intense wind. With surprisingly quick reflexes, Linda grabbed onto his leg to hold him down.

The outside world of planet Nilleby was exactly how it had appeared from outer space: brown, dusty, and barren. The wind was created as a result of artificial atmosphere production, which led to the rapid diffusion of inhalable gases throughout the planet. Despite the wind, it was stiflingly hot and muggy. It was so unpleasant that Linda was regretting her decision to leave the air-conditioned terminal, although she was too stubborn to admit it. They slowly made their way to the main road, which boasted an unusually wide variety of vehicles, ranging from the Super Deluxe Sagana Asteroid Sport with its star-powered quadruple engines and sleek exterior, to dusty, rusty, three-wheeled electric tricycles that were so wobbly they looked like they might fall apart at any moment. Linda couldn't remember the last time she'd seen such old electrically powered technology. Larv wondered how they managed to get so rusty on a planet that had no natural sources of water.

Despite the vast differences in makes and models, the vehicles all had one thing in common: none of them followed any sort of logical traffic pattern. Linda couldn't even figure out which side of the road cars were supposed to drive on. They were everywhere, weaving in and out, honking wildly. After waiting several minutes for a break in traffic, Linda and Larv carefully crossed the chaotic road and headed for the nearby community. The area surrounding the spaceport looked like a dirty, impoverished town, not unlike the slum inside the terminal. It went on as far as the eye could see. It consisted mainly of old, dilapidated low-rise buildings with small shops on the main floors and presumably living quarters above. The crooked rows of poorly made buildings and the abundance of shops paralleled the booths of the spaceport's indoor market. However, out here it was less crowded, and the shop owners were less aggressive than those in the terminal. Most of them stayed inside their shops. Linda figured this was probably due to the putrid weather conditions. She was grateful for the lack of heckling, but at the same time, she found these citizens to be creepier in general. She could feel them staring at her and Larv as they went by. Perhaps it was that obvious that they weren't from around these parts, or perhaps it was the fact that Linda's bangs were still standing straight up from the alien goo.

Using his holographic map, Larv managed to guide Linda in the right direction until they found Garrick's Teahouse. It was impossible to miss this oasis amid the slum. The exterior reminded Linda of Santa's Workshop. Her inner child was awed by the sight of it. The tea shop used an entire three-storey building, making it much larger than the surrounding businesses. The outer walls were painted so that it looked like it was made of logs, and there was a slanted roof that was obviously added on to give the building the look of a cottage or chalet. It was covered in bright, colourful lights. As they entered, Linda and Larv saw that there were even more lights on the inside than the outside. They came in many forms: antique lamps, string lights, and neon signs. The walls were covered in colourful abstract paintings and shelves that contained all sorts of strange trinkets that originated from several different planets.

*This Garrick fellow must be well-travelled,* Linda thought hopefully. *Perhaps well-travelled enough to have brought back tea from Earth.* She knew that was highly improbable, but the thought of a steaming cup of Earl Grey cheered her up. She bumbled her way to the vacant counter while Larv saved a table by the window, which was unnecessary since the place was completely empty. Linda looked around until she found a service bell. She rang it three times. She scanned the menu on the wall above the counter while she waited. None of it was in English, but at least there were pictures. The massive tea selection was mind-boggling. There were pictures of green and purple foam rising from the top of a mug, one that appeared to have eyeballs in it, and yet another that maybe had worms in the bottom. Linda told herself they were just bad pictures. She eventually found a normal-looking cup of clear orangey liquid. *That must be it!* She thought. *Even if it's not Earl Grey, it must be some sort of black tea.*

She heard loud footsteps clambering down the creaky stairs. As he turned the corner and made his way behind the counter, Linda was horrified to see that Garrick[5] was the monstrous, one-eyed humanoid with the bandana who she fell on when departing the space shuttle. She almost turned to leave, but then he spoke to her with a pleasant British accent.

"Welcome to Garrick's Teahouse. How may I help you?" His voice was as smooth as butter, which was unexpected, given his gruff exterior. Linda stared at him thinking that he must have a lovely singing voice.

"You. . . you speak English!" she stammered.

---

5 *Anthropomorphia cyclopsian:* Empire *Carbonata,* Domain *Eukarya,* Kingdom *Animalia*

"I do, indeed," he responded. "One of my three hundred alien tongues. What I lack in depth perception, I make up for in language acquisition," he joked.

Linda wasn't sure whether or not to laugh, so she just smiled awkwardly.

"What can I get for you?" Garrick asked.

"I would like a cup of this," she said, pointing to the picture on the menu.

"Of course. I just received a fresh shipment this morning. I think you will enjoy it very much."

"Lovely!" Linda exclaimed. "Could you point me towards the lady's room?"

"Of course, right this way," he pointed. "Take the stairs up to the second floor and turn left."

"Thank you." Linda hobbled up the stairs, still stiff from travel. When she reached the top, she saw that the second floor contained another seating area, but it was much darker and the black walls were covered in psychedelic neon paintings, which glowed under black lights. There were also private booths with curtains that could be closed to block out the rest of the world. She heard a snivelling sound to her right and looked over to see that one of the booths was occupied and the curtain was open, revealing two very thin humanoid creatures. Their cheek bones protruded from their faces in an unnatural way. Linda wasn't sure whether or not that was a normal feature of their species or if they were extremely malnourished. The one who had snivelled continued to whimper, and its eyes were bulging and darting around in paranoia. It looked like it was having a nervous breakdown.

The other one saw Linda staring and said, "Don't worry about him, he's had a little too much tea," and then closed the curtain. Puzzled, Linda shrugged, and continued to the lady's room for a much-needed tinkle.

When she returned and sat at the table with Larv, another group of strange, twitchy customers entered the teahouse and went straight upstairs. Linda was about to tell Larv what she had seen up there when Garrick arrived and served her tea on a tray with a small jar of honey and two creamers. "I was wondering why you looked so familiar, and I just realized that I saw you at the spaceport earlier," he said.

"Oh, really?" Linda pretended not to remember him.

"Something about you is different now though, but I can't put my finger on it. Maybe it's your hair? Anyway, I must apologize if I seemed rude. Sometimes those trips to pick up my, uh, merchandise . . . can be rather stressful."

"You have nothing to worry about. I don't remember anything rude at all," Linda lied.

Garrick smiled and went upstairs to tend to his new customers. Linda looked down at her steaming cup of tea. She bent over and breathed in the steam, smelling the sweet aroma. It wasn't quite Earl Grey or orange pekoe, but it was close enough. She watched the tea leaves slowly dye the water, the orange tendrils curling out from the tea bag before settling on the bottom of the cup. She watched for a while, hypnotized, and then added the honey and both of the creamers. She stirred for nearly a minute straight, which was rather annoying for Larv, who had much more sensitive hearing and cringed every time the spoon clinked against the side of the cup. Finally, she tapped the spoon on the edge of the cup and placed it face down on the saucer. She picked up the mug, cupping its warm girth in both hands, and smelled it again. Finally, she took a cautious sip, making sure not to burn her tongue. As the sweet pleasure invaded her mouth, she immediately became light-headed. "Larv, you don't know what you're missing."

Larv, who had observed the whole ritual with curiosity, figured that she was right. He had never experienced pleasure from food or drink, as his species only absorbed microscopic particles or phonosynthesized to obtain energy. He didn't have taste buds, so he couldn't even fathom the concept of enjoying a cup of tea. By the look of it, he was, indeed, missing out. However, it wasn't long before Larv realized that something was not quite right. Linda's behaviour seemed even more peculiar than usual. By the time she had finished half the tea, she had a big smile plastered across her face and her eyes were as wide as saucers.

"Isn't this place just fantastic?" she exclaimed, "so many pretty colours." Larv didn't respond, but Linda continued talking at him. "What colour would you call that painting?" she said, pointing. "I think it's purplish-green." She took a long sip of tea. "Oh my, that lamp over there has a mouth! It's talking."

"Uh—" Larv began.

"Shhh! Listen. It's trying to say something. Greenish-purple ponies dance with purplish-green unicorns. But what's the difference between greenish-purple and purplish-green? How can you tell which is the pony and which is the unicorn? But their horns are so dull! It must be in the hooves! Ohhh, they shimmer in the star light! Don't eat that mushroom! The toad will disappear if it eats the mushroom. Beware the fungus with the spiky orange top. It's a puff ball of Sagana that will poof and fluff . . . it could choke you!" She burst into a fit of laughter.

Larv slowly pulled the teacup from her grasp. She didn't seem to notice, as she was too busy babbling and giggling nonsensically. He pulled out the tea bag and looked closely at the tea leaves. They were moving! Now, Larv was no tea expert, but he knew that these were definitely not leaves of any sort. They were some sort of insect. He took the spoon and poked at one of the insects, which then squirted an orange liquid into the air. The "tea," which had dyed the water orange, was actually an excretion released from the insects when they were stressed. In this case, Larv's prodding caused the stress, but in the teacup, it was the boiling water that induced the defense mechanism. Whatever this insect excretion was, it must have contained some sort of psychotropic chemical. In essence, Linda was as high as a kite. Higher, in fact.

Larv took the cup and flew over to the sink behind the counter and poured out the last few sips of tea. When he turned back to the table, Linda was no longer there. A wave of panic washed over him, and he frantically began searching for his intoxicated companion. He found her having a staring contest with one of the abstract paintings on the wall. She was standing with her face about two inches from the painting, not blinking.

"There's something behind this painting!" she declared after some time. She kinked her neck to look around the painting, which was when she caught her own reflection in the window. Startled, she jumped back. "See!" she pointed at her reflection. "There's a monster hiding behind this painting! It has one horn! The other must have been cut off in the battle with the Knights of Wangerhoover." The so-called horn was the left half of her bangs that the alien in the spaceport had grabbed. The tentacle slime had dried and hardened so that her hair was now as solid as an actual horn.

Larv tried to talk some sense into her. "That's you! It's your own reflection."

Linda looked at him, and he could see that her pupils were so dilated that she had no iris left. "Me?" she said, disbelieving. She turned back to the window and brought her hand up to the horn-like protrusion of hair. "My goodness! I'm turning into a varicose demon! It must have been that fungus. Oh, I knew I shouldn't have inhaled the spores! What should I do? Help!"

Larv didn't know what to do or say. He had already made the situation worse by pointing out her pointy reflection. His sensitive auditory receptors picked up the sound of the creaking stairs as Garrick made his way back down. "Help!" Larv pleaded, flying towards the cyclops. "She's gone mad!"

Garrick immediately assessed the situation and knew exactly what was going on. He slowly approached Linda and said in a calm voice, "There, there, now, how about you take a seat over here?"

Linda eyes him suspiciously. "I will not fall for your cyclops trickery!" she exclaimed.

Garrick took a step towards her.

"Stay back!" Linda shouted. "I have a horn and I'm not afraid to use it!"

Garrick took another step forward. Linda bent her head down, pointed her horn at him and pawed the ground with her right foot, like a bull about to charge. Slowly, without breaking eye contact, Garrick pulled a tablecloth from the table beside him. He took another step towards Linda.

"I warned you!" she shouted and then brayed like a drunken horse and charged. At the last second, Garrick stepped aside and held out the tablecloth like a matador's cape. Linda, who was expecting to hit Garrick with considerable force, went right through the tablecloth instead, and her forward momentum caused her to fall face-first onto the floor. Garrick quickly covered her head with the tablecloth.

"We need to inhibit external stimuli," he explained to Larv. "They will only feed into her tea fantasy."

"Tea fantasy?" Larv asked.

"Yes, the high from the tea causes hallucinations. They're quite famous. Surely that's why you sought out my shop?" Larv looked puzzled. "I'll explain in a minute," Garrick said, "but now, we best get your friend up to the second floor where she can come down in a sensory deprivation booth."

Larv did his best to help guide Linda up the stairs, but in the end, Garrick more or less had to carry her. He slid her into a booth and closed the black curtain. Then, he cautiously removed the tablecloth from Linda's head. Her eyes were still wide, and her pupils were still invading her irises. Her horn, however, had been bent down so that it was now dangling in front of her left eye. It was no longer a horn, but a flop of crispy hair with dried slime flaking off. Her eyes went crossed trying to focus on it.

"I'll be right back," Garrick said.

"Don't leave me with her," Larv squeaked, but the one-eyed humanoid rushed downstairs. Larv watched Linda awkwardly, hoping she wouldn't try to get up and wander around again. Her eyelids were now drooping, and she had begun to drool. Garrick returned with a steaming mug.

"Oh no, not more tea!" Larv protested.

"It's just hot water. Here, let's dip her hair in there and wash off that mess."

At this point, Linda had forgotten her brief stint as a demonic bull and was refreshingly complacent, although she continued to mutter under her breath, just like her Aunt Norma.

"Ok, let me explain everything," Garrick said. "On Nilleby, teahouses are different than those on other planets. We serve tea laced with various types of psychotropics—mind-altering drugs. It's actually quite a successful industry that draws tourists from all over the galaxy; from places where most of these substances aren't legal. I'm sorry, I just assumed you two knew what you were getting into."

Larv's big innocent eyes just stared at him. "But they're legal here?" he asked.

"On Nilleby, everything's legal," Garrick said with a grin. "So, how did you end up here then?"

"We're just passing through," Larv answered. We have a twelve-hour layover between flights. I told Linda we shouldn't leave the spaceport, but she wouldn't listen."

"You were right. You shouldn't have left." Garrick said. Larv looked like he was about to cry, if only cochleans had tear ducts. "Now, now," Garrick consoled. "She'll be fine. What species is she?"

"Human, from planet Earth."

"Earth? Never heard of it."

Larv shrugged. "You're not missing much."

Garrick examined Linda. "I think she should be okay. Most mid-sized species with decent metabolic rates come down within an hour or two without any side effects.

"But there *could* be side effects?" Larv said, worried.

"Just keep her in here for a while, away from any sort of sensory stimulation. She should be fine."

To Larv, Garrick seemed unsure, like he didn't quite believe his own words.

"Anyway, I must go tend to my other customers." Garrick started to walk away, and then turned back to Larv. "Oh, and whatever you do, don't let her go up to the third floor." With that, he vanished and closed the curtain behind him, leaving Larv alone with Linda the Lunatic in the sensory deprivation booth.

# CHAPTER 13

## The Mabitu

Empire: *Acarbonata*
Domain: *Unknown*
Kingdom: *The Mabitu*

Several hours after drinking the drugged tea, Linda Pumpernickel was still zonked. Larv was beginning to worry that they would miss their connecting flight. Even if they made it to the spaceport on time, would Linda make it past security? He gazed over at the muttering pile of pink flesh sprawled out on the bench across from him and was quite convinced that she would not. On the bright side, the sensory deprivation booth seemed to keep her from having further violent episodes. Instead, her head slumped forward as though the weight of it were too much for her neck to bear, and she drooled continuously. All Larv needed was for her to lose consciousness. How would he get her to the spaceport then? Maybe Garrick could help carry her. It was the least he could do after drugging her. Larv looked at Linda, and after a brief inner debate, decided it was safe to leave her. She would be fine alone, just for a minute, while he found Garrick.

Larv flew downstairs to the front counter, but Garrick was not there. He did a quick lap of the first floor and didn't see a single soul. He flew back up to the second floor and checked every single booth. No one. Even the tweakers had left. There was only one place left to look: the third floor. He flew cautiously up the dark, narrow stairway and paused in front of the thick, steel door. He touched the handle and could feel the rhythmic vibrations of a heavy bass beat. It took all his strength to pull the door open, and when he did, he immediately regretted it.

It turned out that the reason the door was so thick was to block the sound. As soon as it was opened, agonizingly loud electronic dance music assaulted Larv's sensory cells. He had a strong urge to slam the door shut and get out of Dodge, but he had to find Garrick. He forced himself to enter the large room and circle the dance floor. The only light came from multiple strobe lights that weren't quite in sync with each other. With each flash, Larv caught glimpses of sweaty aliens, pressing up against each other, pulsing to the beat. An array of arms, wings, tentacles, antennae, flagella, and other unrecognizable limbs waved in the air. He flew higher to get a better view, and that's when he spotted Garrick. The monoptic monsieur was surrounded by a circle of patrons who cheered him on as he danced up a storm. Larv was impressed that his large body could move so fluidly. He was not impressed that his host had obviously indulged in the psychotropic tea. He would be of no help.

Larv left the club, carefully closing the door behind him, and went to check on Linda. Her head rested on the table in a puddle of drool, and she continued to mumble. The hopelessness of his situation made Larv very anxious. He was so busy worrying that he didn't notice the rumbling sound coming from somewhere outside until his sensory cells started waving like wacky inflatable tube men in the wind. He buzzed over to the window that overlooked the street below. He saw a large dust cloud rising up about two blocks away. His initial thought was that some sort of windstorm was coming their way, and he felt a jolt of panic at the idea of being blown away whilst trying to escort Linda the Bull back to the spaceport. He looked up to the sky for any clues about the weather. It was then that his peripheral vision caught a flash of something run past on the street below. His big eyes darted downwards, but he wasn't able to get a good look. All he saw was a single bubble that floated up to his window, popped, and released a shower of glitter that slowly fell back down to the road below.

Seconds later, a full-blown stampede came barreling around the corner, filling the street with hundreds of crazed creatures of all shapes and sizes. They appeared to be in some sort of wild, trance-like state and it was as though they were running away from something . . . or perhaps chasing after something. Larv thought they must have all had a cup of Linda's tea, which would explain why they seemed to be acting out the running of the bulls. He watched with horrified fascination as they charged through the intersection at an alarming rate, shoving each other and trampling the fallen. Where were they going in such a hurry? What were they after?

After a couple of minutes, the mob of marauding minotaurs was out of sight, minus a few of the unfortunate ones who had been trampled beyond mobility. The dust began to dissipate in the wind, and Larv made his way back to the booth. He pulled back the curtain and what he saw startled him so intensely that it set off a reflex response to his wing musculature. The jolt thrust his small body upwards with such force so as to enthusiastically acquaint his head with the ceiling. The unforgiving nature of gravity then promptly sent him back downwards, and the dazed alien found himself crumpled on the floor. He slowly got up, shook himself off, and then stared, bewildered, at the thing sitting in the booth across from Linda. Linda was completely oblivious to the intruder, or even Larv, for that matter.

The thing was unlike anything Larv had ever seen before. Mind you, he hadn't seen much during his short life, which, until recently, was confined to the dismal solitude of a listentower located on the Molasses Planet. He couldn't tell whether it was solid, liquid, or gas, or all of the above. Its body appeared either moist or just really shiny, and it was emitting a soft, white glow. And were those . . . ? Yes, they were. Bubbles. The creature was so extraordinarily out of the ordinary that Larv did not possess the vocabulary to describe it further. But there was one thing he knew for certain: it was beautiful. So beautiful, in fact, that it made his insides flutter and sputter and his mind turn to mush. All he could do was stare in awe and admiration.

* * *

There is a particularly fascinating creature that is known throughout the universe as the Mabitu. This creature is so elusive that it has been deemed mythical by most; a universal unicorn, so to speak. Others believe that it once existed but perished long ago. Others, still, believe that it is real and very much alive. According to this minority, the Mabitu avoids contact with other beings—and for good reason. They say its body constantly releases a type of airborne organic compound (we'll call it a pheromone for all intents and purposes) which, when sensed by another being, evokes an uncontrollable courtship response. Pheromones are very common throughout the universe, so this idea is nothing new. It is, however, unique in its cross-species effect. Individuals of every intelligent species in the known universe, regardless of gender or sexual identity, are irresistibly drawn to the Mabitu's allure; hence the name "Mabitu," which stands for "Most Attractive Being in the Universe." Because of this, it is very dangerous for the Mabitu to be around most creatures. It is constantly at risk of being mobbed like Paul McCartney in the throes of Beatlemania. Furthermore, individuals within the mob would react with violence and aggression towards their own friends and family members in a desperate attempt to win the Mabitu's affection. This, according to some, has led to great riots and even started a war that led to the destruction of a small planet in the center of the Seachelle Galaxy.

To most, this is simply an urban legend, like Big Foot or Nessie. They enjoy the stories, but disregard any evidence of the Mabitu's existence, calling it an elaborate hoax. Some believers argue that the Mabitu, overridden with fear for its own life, as well as insufferable guilt for the conflicts it has unintentionally caused, banished itself to an uninhabited planet in a distant corner of the universe.

*Or did it?*

* * *

Larv realized he was staring awkwardly at the effervescent entity sitting across from Linda in the sensory deprivation booth and looked away. That was when he noticed that Linda was completely unconscious. "Oh no, no, no, no, no!" he shouted. "Wake up! Linda? Can you hear me?"

"No!" shouted the glowing invader in not one, but three voices that rang together in a perfect triad. "Don't wake it up."

Larv stopped what he was doing and, once again, stared at the thing. He was taken aback by its voices, which, like its appearance, were beautifully androgynous. "I must wake her up," he finally managed. "We have a space flight to ca—"

"Shhhh!" the thing begged, staring deeply into Larv's big yellow eyes. "I'm in great danger," it whispered. "That mob is after me."

Larv was confused, but he obeyed. They sat there in silence, aside from Linda's snoring, for several minutes. "I don't hear anything," whispered Larv. "And I'm a cochlean, so I think it's safe to say you lost them."

"You're a cochlean?" asked the thing, surprised.

"Yes, you've heard of us?" Larv asked.

"Yeah, but I thought cochleans looked . . . different."

"Oh, right," replied Larv. "Yes, adult cochleans are spiral-shaped. I am a third instar larvalux, so I haven't pupated yet."

"Does that mean you haven't reached sexual maturity?" it asked.

Larv thought that was a rather odd question to ask a new acquaintance, but the thing looked very serious, so he answered, "That's correct."

The thing glanced warily at Linda. "What about that? What *is* it?" It appeared mildly disgusted by the pile of pink flesh snoring on the table.

"That's Linda. She's a human, but she's a bit out of it at the moment."

"Has she reached sexual maturity?" it asked as one of its bubbles floated over to Linda. It watched in horror as the bubble landed on her nose, sat there for a brief moment, and then popped. A cloud of glitter rained down from where the bubble had been, and some of it entered Linda's nostrils as she inhaled. The creature prepared to run. Linda wrinkled her nose but did not wake up.

"I think she's surpassed it," Larv replied.

"Surpassed what?"

"Sexual maturity."

"What do you mean?" The creature seemed horrified by this idea.

Larv explained, "In the final stage of their life cycle, human females undergo a phase called menopause, after which they are no longer reproductively viable." The thing let out a huge sigh of relief. Larv was even more confused by the oddly personal nature of the conversation. It made him suspicious. "Why are you so interested in our ability to reproduce?" he asked.

The thing glanced around nervously, and then whispered, "Ever heard of the Mabitu?"

Larv shook his head.

"The Ma-bi-tu," it overenunciated. "You know, the most fabulous creature in existence?"

"Ohhh, yes I think my broodmate told me those stories. Why?"

"Stories? What do you mean, *stories*?"

"Stories about the Mabitu. The mythical creature—"

"Mythical?! Jesus, I need to get out more."

"What's Jesus?" Larv asked.

"Just some slang word I picked up on my travels."

Larv just stared.

"Anyway, that's not important. The point is, the Mabitu isn't just some story, it's real!"

The thing seemed disappointed that jumping for joy was not Larv's immediate reaction. The young cochlean was more interested in the bubble that was drifting across the table.

"Hello?" the thing snapped at Larv to get his attention. "Don't you get it?"

"What is there to get?" Larv asked, still tracking the bubble with his eyes.

"It's *me*. I'm the Mabitu!"

Up until recently, when he met Linda, Larv's life had been very serious. He had not spent much time joking around, but he was familiar with the idea of it. He presumed that this is what he was currently experiencing and forced a fake laugh. "Good one," he said.

"I'm not joking," said the thing. "Why do you think that mob was chasing me?"

Larv figured that it had stolen something from them. That seemed to be the most logical explanation, especially on this lawless planet. But he did not want to make such an accusation to a stranger who could very well be mentally unstable or hallucinating from Garrick's tea. "You tell me," was all he managed to say.

"These bubbles that you can't keep your eyes off of . . . watch." The thing pointed to its own glowing body as a stream of bubble appeared from within. "They're coming from me."

Larv watched, transfixed, as the bubbles floated towards him.

"They contain the most potent, cross-species pheromones in the universe," the thing explained.

Larv reached out and popped one, watching with fascination as the glitter slowly rained down.

"Stop that!" The creature who claimed to be the Mabitu snapped. "If other beings get a whiff of that, they won't be able to resist falling madly in love with me." It mimed a motion that seemed to indicate that it was tossing non-existent hair over its shoulder.

"What about me?" Larv asked skeptically. "Why aren't I uncontrollably mobbing you?"

"Luckily, you and your friend seem to be immune because neither of you are in the reproductive stage of your respective life cycles."

Larv eyed the creature suspiciously. It *was* extremely beautiful. Could the stories be true? "If you're the Mabitu, then why did you come to Nilleby?"

"As your friend found out the hard way," the thing gestured towards Linda, "this planet doesn't enforce any sort of ban on substances. So, chemists and pharmacologists come here to experiment. They have easy access to all sorts of chemicals that are illicit or tightly regulated on most planets. I came here in search of a drug that can tame my pheromones. I admit, it was an act of desperation, but it was a last resort. You have no idea how hard it is to look this good." The invisible hair was once again tossed.

"I can't imagine," Larv mumbled.

"So anyway, I contacted a chemist who agreed to help me. She said she'd concocted an antidote that was ready for testing, so I came to Nilleby to try it out. I had to acquire a private ship, since I can't use public transit, for obvious reasons.

"That must have been expensive." Said Larv. "How did you get enough currency units?"

"You don't want to know." Before Larv had time to speculate, the Mabitu continued. "Anyway, when I got to her lab, she lost control. She was a huge creature, and she couldn't resist me. She started to come at me, so I panicked and ran down the street. As I ran, more and more ugly things joined the chase." It shuddered at the thought of ugly things. "As I came around the corner, I ducked into this café, and that's how I ended up here."

Larv thought the story was so far-fetched, it might actually be true. "So, you didn't get a chance to try out the antidote?" he asked.

"Unfortunately, no, but I know where it is."

"You can't go back out there without getting mobbed again," said Larv. "What are you going to do?"

"I don't know. I haven't exactly had a chance to figure it all out." The Mabitu thought for a moment, then said, "I guess the only option would be to send someone else to pick it up for me." It looked directly at Larv and raised an immaculately shaped glitter eyebrow. Larv understood what the Mabitu was suggesting.

"I'm really sorry, but I have to figure out how to get Linda to the spaceport on time. We have a space flight to catch in—" Larv looked down at his holodex. "Oh no! An hour! I have to wake her up and get moving!" Larv's wings started to vibrate.

"Shut up, I have an idea," declared the Mabitu. "You can fly, *and* you're small enough to fit through most windows. If you help me get the antidote, I'll give you a ride to wherever you and your weird friend are going. I have a private ship, remember?"

Larv was hesitant. He didn't know anything about this creature. Everything it said could have been a lie. And what about this beast of a chemist?

As though it had read his mind, the Mabitu reassured Larv that the chemist wouldn't be back in the lab any time soon. She had been caught up in the stampede and had probably been trampled. It let out another exaggerated shudder at the thought of the hideous creatures outside. "The sooner you get in there, the sooner you can get out and be on your way," it insisted.

Larv looked back at Linda, who was still out cold and nearly drowning in the growing puddle of drool. He realized that the private ship might be the only option. There was no way that he would be able to get Linda to the spaceport in her condition.

"You would be willing to take us all the way to the Molasses Planet?" he asked.

"Anywhere you want," promised the Mabitu.

Larv swallowed back the lump of uncertainty that had risen up inside his thoracic cavity. "Okay, I'll do it."

# CHAPTER 14

## Troodly's Lab

Troodly, chief scientist of the Protectors of the Universal Environment, had been awake for two straight oodlean days and nights. She spent most of the first day wondering why Ibo had actually agreed with Nimbulus and had sent her off to measure planetary orbits when she was so close to finishing her emissions simulation and nailing Schmoodler for his gas-guzzling astrobarges. Perhaps she could work on both assignments simultaneously. As much as she preferred working alone, she would need help. After much deliberation, she decided to delegate the emissions study to someone else. It was mostly just data entry left to do anyway. She contacted another PUE scientist and told them to hire an intern to do the job.

On the second day, she began brainstorming how to measure the planetary orbits quickly and accurately. Every idea she came up with required expensive equipment that the PUE did not have funding for. She was growing tired and frustrated when an idea came to her by accident. Some time during the second night, Troodly started to nod off. As she did, her sixth tentacle-like appendage went limp, slid across the lab bench, and knocked over a mirror, shattering it on the floor and waking her up abruptly. When she opened all seven of her eyes, she was blinded by bright light coming from every direction. She squinted and realized the shattered mirror was reflecting the ceiling lights all over the room, lighting up the laboratory like a Griswoldian Christmas light display. As she observed the beams of light bouncing from one reflective surface to the next, she was struck with a brilliant idea and spent the rest of the night devising a plan.

Her plan was much too complicated for the average non-scientist to understand, but the general idea was as follows: huge mirrors would be placed in orbit around each planet. A giant lens would focus sunlight into a condensed beam, just like how a magnifying glass can be used to start a fire, only on a much larger scale. When the planets lined up just right, the beam would be reflected from mirror to mirror. Troodly would measure the time it took for the light beam to travel between the mirrors, and then use the speed of light constant to calculate the distances.

The tricky part would be coordinating the mirrors so that the light beam would reflect at the correct angles, and, most importantly, avoid hitting any of the planets. If this were to happen, the condensed sun beam could burn the inhabitants of the planet like ants under a magnifying glass. She would need to be extremely careful with her initial calculations.

Unfortunately, forty-eight sleepless oodlean hours had fogged Troodly's normally razor-sharp mind. Her state of exhaustion may have been what caused her to mistake a one for a seven, and to carry this error down through several calculations.

# CHAPTER 15

## Ryp Comet

*Homo sapien*
Empire: *Carbonata*
Domain: *Eukarya*
Kingdom: *Animalia*

Linda was standing in the corner alone, trying desperately to drink her joobai faster so that she would loosen up, but the stuff tasted foul. She was always a little awkward at parties until she'd had a few drinkies, and this time was especially difficult because she didn't know anybody—that and the fact that she was wearing a fluffy, pink bunny suit. She had just arrived a month earlier and was the newest English teacher at the Sagana Intergalactic Language Institute. She was told by the other teachers that this was a Halloween party, since it was, indeed, Halloween back on Earth and they had spent the last week teaching their students about it. The saganites were fascinated with the concept of Halloween and other weird and wonderful Earthly rituals. It was Linda's favourite day. She loved dressing up in elaborate costumes and pretending to be someone else for a little while. But tonight, she seemed to be the only one in costume and hiding behind it was the last thing she could do.

As she stood there by herself, working up a buzz, she looked around the room. She could see that some of her colleagues had already far surpassed her level of intoxication. Indeed, one was already passed out on the couch. Most of them, however, were standing in clumps, engaged in excited chitter chatter. She looked over towards the door just in time to see a new guest arrive. Lo and behold, he was wearing a costume! Linda was excited and relieved all at once. She wasn't exactly sure what his costume was supposed to be, but she was pretty sure it wasn't how he dressed normally. Perhaps he was some sort of superhero? He was wearing big black boots, a silver jumpsuit with the letter "M" on the chest, and a black cape. As her eyes scanned the caped newcomer, she became aware of his smoldering good looks. She drank in his tight*ish* body and his *somewhat* chiseled jawline. His dark eyes burned with passion and his superhero stance exuded confidence. His confidence must have been contagious, as Linda decided right then and there that she was going to pursue this fine specimen, bunny costume or not. She tossed back the rest of her drink. Target located. Locked and loaded.

Without skipping a beat, Linda strutted over to the sexy, silver-clad stud and pulled a line she'd been holding onto for quite some time, waiting for the right moment to use.

"I'm not here to put boots on a caterpillar." There was a slight possibility that Linda didn't fully understand what she had just said.

"Pardon me?" he asked. Luckily, he did not understand what she had just said either.

Somehow, Linda didn't let this awkward miscommunication fluster her. Instead, she smiled flirtatiously and said, "What's your name?"

"I'm Ryp," he said, a crooked grin appearing on his formidable face. "And you must be the new teacher."

"Linda. Linda Pumpernickel." She twirled one of her bunny ears with her finger.

His grin grew as he eyed her bunny costume. "I heard about what happened with Earth and the evacuation," he said. "It must be hard for you."

Linda shrugged. "It needed to be done. That poor planet took quite a beating." Linda thought she saw a twinkle in Ryp's eye when she said this and lost her train of thought for just a second. "Anyway," she continued, "it's nice to get out and experience new cultures."

"Right," Ryp nodded. He took a sip of his drink. "Well, Linda, it must be hot in that bunny costume."

He spoke with an accent that Linda did not recognize, but she found it extremely attractive. They ended up talking and laughing and drinking joobai and trying to mimic each other's accents for hours. He told her of all the weird and wonderful places he'd travelled to. Apparently, as a boy, his father's job required them to move around a lot. His family originated from a planet called Thera, which is considered Earth's sister planet. The two are very similar and contain very similar species; however, it is located on the other side of the universe. Despite this impossible distance, Linda couldn't shake the feeling that he seemed familiar—like she'd met him before. He felt the same way. Neither of them could think of a time or place where they may have crossed paths before. In all his travels, he had never visited Earth, and Linda had never left it until recently. They shrugged it off and figured they must have met each other's doppelgangers at some point.

As the night was wearing on and the joobai started to make them sleepy, Ryp Comet asked Linda if she would like to step outside for some fresh air. Smitten, she agreed, and they went up to the rooftop, where they could see three of Sagana's five moons beaming in the clear, night sky. The moon in the center was full and the two on either side of it were crescent-shaped, creating the pagan symbol of the goddess. That was how Linda felt—like a goddess. A fluffy pink bunny goddess. Ryp was also relatively new to Sagana, and neither of them had ever seen anything like it (the moons, not the bunny costume).

"It's beautiful, isn't it?" Linda said.

"It surely is," Ryp replied, but then his tone darkened. "It's too bad there are monsters out there trying to destroy it."

"What ever do you mean?" Linda asked.

"Surely you must know about universal de-tuning and the greedy corporations responsible?"

"Oh, yes, of course," Linda lied, making a mental note to look into it later.

They continued to gaze up in silence. Linda felt Ryp take her hand and, ever so slowly, pull her closer to him. She could feel that he was cold in his thin, silver suit, so she covered his arm with her fur-clad one. At that point, Linda was overcome with an irresistible urge to kiss him, not with her bunny nose, but with her real, human lips. She turned towards him, placed her hand on the back of his head, closed her eyes, and pulled his face towards hers.

As their lips met, Linda was surprised at how damp his were. In fact, she wasn't sure that what she was feeling were lips at all. It was as though his face had completely liquefied. She tried to pull him closer, but felt her face submerge into a pool of lukewarm liquid.

* * *

Startled, Linda opened her eyes and found herself lying face-down in a puddle of her own drool. She had a sore neck and a pounding headache. Slowly, she pushed herself up off the table and sat up. She looked around, bleary-eyed, and saw that she was in a restaurant booth surrounded by thick, black curtains. She had no idea how she had gotten there. As her eyes began to focus, she realized that she wasn't alone.

"Ryp?" She asked, weakly. "It's really not very gentlemanly of you to take advantage of a lady who's had one too many cocktails."

Larv and the Mabitu looked at each other. They didn't know what to say. Was this round two of Linda the Bull? Had the drugs still not cleared her system? Linda squinted as her eyes adjusted to the soft glow of the Mabitu.

"Where's Ryp?" she asked.

"Who's Ryp?" asked Larv.

"But he was just here . . ."

"No one named Ryp was here, Linda. You were dreaming."

Linda was rather confused indeed. "Where am I? Who are you?"

Larv introduced Linda to the Mabitu, who was quite relieved that she seemed unaffected by its pheromones and slightly less disgusted with the pink lump of flesh once she wiped away the drool. Linda stuck out her finger and popped a bubble. The glitter dust that rained down caused her to sneeze but didn't seem to affect her otherwise. As Linda sobered up and started acting like her normal self again, Larv explained everything that had happened.

"I did *what*?" Linda tried to imagine herself charging like a bull. "That explains why my hip is so sore," she chortled, and then reached out to pop another bubble.

"You shouldn't do that," the Mabitu warned. "It could attract unwanted company."

"My apologies." Linda crossed her arms over her large bosom. "I'm about done with this planet, Larv. Is it time to head back to the spaceport?"

By this time, they'd already missed their connecting flight. They were stranded on Nilleby until they could find the Mabitu's antidote. Larv explained the arrangement they'd made while she was unconscious. "Well, what are we waiting for?" she asked. "Where's the lab?"

* * *

Groodle Schmoodler chuckled his mucousy, hacking cackle as he watched the holographic footage of a crazed Earthling charging like an angry bull through the Nilleby café. Schmoodler had eyes everywhere—not just his seven actual eyes that encircled the top of his head and the cavern of phlegm that he called a mouth, but he also had access to security cameras all over the universe. He laughed so hard that he started to choke on his own thick saliva, igniting a coughing fit that spewed grotesque gobs of goo in a disgusting, yet impressive, trajectory. His faithful assistant, Doodlen, had the misfortune of standing within said trajectory and was the helpless victim of one particularly sizeable projectile. He was gobsmacked. After several minutes of geysering, the good reverend regained control of his bodily functions and was able to speak.

"I forgot how ridiculous Earthlings were!" He gurgled and sputtered again.

Doodlen ducked just in time to avoid the spray.

Schmoodler continued, "They're ugly buggers, aren't they? So . . . *dry*. And that tuft of hair! What do you think its purpose is?"

Doodlen was unable to speak, as he was currently suppressing a gag, but he managed a shrug.

"Anyway, I don't think we have anything to worry about here," Schmoodler said. "That should be an easy UPT extraction. Contact one of our gwishank friends and have them track it down." Doodlen dutifully nodded, although he dared not open his mouth, lest a glop of Schmoodler schaliva schlipped in.

# CHAPTER 16

## The Gwishank

*Gwishank tenuis*
Empire: *Acarbonata*
Domain: *Siliconia*
Kingdom: *Mineralphagia*

Imagine a camera tripod, but instead of a camera on top, there is a bald, human-like head. The head has a face composed of two vertical slots for eyes and a small square-ish mouth. Indeed, this face resembles a typical North American power outlet. Now imagine this camera tripod has two long, thin arms, and at the end these arms, there are hands, and at the end of each hand are four of the longest fingers you've ever seen. There is no discernible thumb; rather, all four of the fingers are opposable. What you are imagining is the basic form of a gwishank.

Schmoodler had several gwishank agents who either lived on, or frequently visited, Nilleby, so it worked in his favour that one of the UPTs had ended up there. The gwishank species originated on a planet not too far from Nilleby. They had used the previously barren planet to test out their artificial atmosphere and terraforming technologies. They are said to be some of the most technologically advanced beings in the universe. This is partly due to the fact that they lack the part of the brain responsible for empathy. They have no ethics committees to prevent them from any sort of experimentation. In addition, the greed centers of the gwishank brain are greatly exaggerated, which means they will do almost anything for money. It is without question that the gwishanks were mainly responsible for the perfunctory and lawless nature of Nilleby. These traits also made gwishanks ideal agents to carry out Schmoodler's dirty work.

Presently, the holodex fastened to the skinny wrist of one of Schmoodler's gwishank agents was beeping. Its owner, however, was unconscious. He had been seriously injured after being trampled in the streets of Nilleby a few hours earlier. He had found himself amid a stampede of crazed creatures, chasing after some unknown entity that they were helpless to resist. His wiry body did not stand a chance in the mob, and he had been thoroughly crushed. Once they had passed, the discombobulated gwishank had somehow been able to drag himself into a building. A much larger being had then carried him into a booth and given him a steaming mug of tea that made all his pain disappear. Shortly thereafter, his concussion got the better of him and he had lost consciousness.

When he came to, he had no idea how much time had passed. He whipped open the black curtains and winced as the bright light poured into the booth, causing his slot-like eyes to squint vertically into mere slits. He immediately turned his head away from the light, and this was when he noticed a small reflective object under the table. He reached down, nearly passed out from the head rush, and grabbed the glimmering gadget. Once it was out of the sunlight, it looked like a dull, disc-shaped, metallic piece of junk. He noticed holes along the outside edge. As a gwishank, he was naturally curious about this unknown piece of technology and began fiddling with it. He stuck his long, slender fingers into the holes, but nothing happened. He held it up to his eyes and tried looking through the holes, but he could not see anything. He pressed his mouth against one of the holes and took a deep breath when he was distracted by the beep of an incoming holographic transmission from the office of Reverend Groodle Schmoodler, CEO of ITCo.

He was surprised to see the exact object he was holding projected in the holograph, with instructions to confiscate it and take it to planet Oodle immediately. The agent sighed heavily. In his current state, space travel was the last thing he felt like doing. However, when the holograph highlighted the huge sum of money offered for the successful return of this "UPT," the greed center of his gwishank brain lit up like a Roman candle. The holograph also showed 3D images of a small alien with large yellow eyes and wings, and an ugly pinkish-coloured alien with a lumpy body and an abnormal tuft of hair located on the top of its head. The message explained that these two aliens were in possession of the metallic disc, and he was to take it from them by any means necessary.

He stuck his head out of the booth and looked around the teahouse. He did not see the dynamic duo from the holograph anywhere. Perhaps they had left it behind for someone else to pick up. If that were the case, they might arrive any minute. The gwishank slipped out of the teahouse as inconspicuously as possible (which isn't that difficult when one is as thin as a microphone stand) and made his way to the astrobarge docking station at the far end of the spaceport.

# CHAPTER 17
## The Chemist

*Tyranno rana*
Empire: *Carbonata*
Domain: *Eukarya*
Kingdom: *Animalia*

Despite all evidence to the contrary, Linda could be quite clever. Not clever in a traditional sense, however. She wasn't particularly good at mathematics. She didn't have a great memory—a fact her choir choreographer was painfully aware of. She certainly wasn't what one would call "street smart." Linda's particular type of intelligence was unique. It was more creative in nature. She had a vivid imagination and could picture things clearly in her mind; things that didn't exist in the real world. When she was younger, she had found this skill to be extremely useful for coming up with fun lesson plans for her English students. Her students thought she was completely loony, but they found her endearing. She was that eccentric teacher who kept things interesting because they never knew what to expect.

Contrary to most people, as Linda got older, her imagination only grew stronger. However, after retirement, she no longer had a productive outlet for it. She had no students to share her inner world with, so instead, her inner world became even more inner. Sometimes, Linda would find herself sitting in her chair in front of the TV realizing three episodes of her favourite soap had gone by and she had absolutely no memory of them. She had been completely zoned out, lost in her own mind, deep inside Linda Land.

Recently, she had been spending more and more time in Linda Land. She was vaguely aware of the outside world—she dedicated approximately one third of her frontal cortical energy to it—but Linda Land was much more interesting. This magical fantasy world preoccupied the remaining two thirds of her frontal cortex, nearly her entire auditory and visual cortices, and the majority of her limbic system, give or take. Perhaps it was her way of blissfully ignoring all of the problems that would otherwise overwhelm her. Unlike her Aunt Norma, the great adventurer who did everything she possibly could to fight the powers that be, Linda sought shelter in her imagination, where she could exist in peaceful denial of all of the problems in the universe. This defense mechanism had worked very well for Linda, up until the point when the problems of the outside world literally came crashing into her living room in the form of an eagle-sized, dragonfly-like alien.

Only forty-eight Earth hours had passed since then, and in those forty-eight hours, everything had changed. Linda now found herself on a foreign planet with two odd but charming new alien friends, and she was still shaking off the cobwebs from an extraterrestrial drug-induced delirium—not to mention the tachyon-speed intergalactic travel. On top of all that, she had just agreed to help one of these aliens, whom she had just met, to steal an illicit substance from a crazed chemist, and then escape on a stolen spaceship. All in two days' work.

Presently, she found herself climbing up a rusty, old drainpipe on the side of an industrial, shabby (but definitely not chic) building. The fact that the pipe was rusty was rather peculiar, since Nilleby's artificial atmosphere was painfully dry, and it never rained. This would lead one to wonder, why was there a drainpipe there to begin with? Perhaps it had something to do with the fact that it was attached to the side of a building that housed a plethora of illicit laboratories with questionable practices for the safe disposal of liquid wastes. Of course, none of these thoughts crossed Linda's mind, as she was too busy focusing on her mission and trying her best not to drift off into Linda Land and drop the rope that was tied around Larv's foot to prevent him from blowing away in the strong wind. Unfortunately, they couldn't find a very long rope, so she had to climb up the drainpipe while poor Larv flapped about in the wind like a kite, occasionally crashing into the side of the building.

By the time Linda had climbed high enough for Larv to crawl through the second storey window, he was struggling to stay conscious, and his lassoed leg had stretched about four inches longer than the rest. He plopped onto the lab bench inside the window and spent a moment waiting for his head to stop spinning before he untied the rope from his numb tarsus. He looked around the lab and thought, disheartened, *This is going to take a while.*

The room was long and narrow, with a large laboratory bench running lengthwise down the middle. The bench was covered in beakers, volumetric flasks, graduated cylinders, and various other glassware of all shapes and sizes that looked like it had never been properly cleaned. It was also riddled with rusty ring stands with clamps clasping flasks precariously above Bunsen burners. It was obvious that whatever liquid had been inside the flasks had been neglected until it had boiled off, leaving a layer of residue baked into the glass. Underneath the bench was an assortment of overburdened drawers and shelves for storing all sorts of lab equipment in questionable condition—microscopes, lamps, analytical balances. The left side of the room boasted a series of fume hoods and storage cabinets for acids and bases. On the right side, there was a room labeled "Chemical Storage" and a wash up area, which Larv presumed had never been used before. The size of the room and the extent of the clutter was overwhelming for the pre-pubescent cochlean. He scanned the room with his large yellow eyes and decided to start searching the bench for the small vial of green liquid that the Mabitu had described to him.

He hovered over the bench and slowly made his way along its length, carefully scouring the surface. He heard a loud crash behind him. Startled, he turned and realized the wind created by his wings had knocked one of the scuzzy flasks off the bench. He realized he could no longer fly and proceeded to crawl along the top of the bench, taking great care not to knock over anything else. He was glad to rest his wings, which felt unusually tired. He figured the fatigue was probably due to the space travel and the adjustment to the new atmosphere. Repeatedly smashing into the side of the building hadn't helped either.

He looked under the messy data sheets covered in an indecipherable scrawl. He opened every single drawer and sifted through piles of instruments. Nothing. At the far end of the bench, he came across a shelf that held glass tubes of varying sizes, each containing a different type of specimen suspended in solution. He smelled the putrid odour of formaldehyde. *Creepy.*

Suddenly, he saw something move out of the corner of his large yellow eye and jumped almost higher than when he had first encountered the Mabitu. However, he was robbed of a record-breaking height when his head made contact with an air duct hanging from the ceiling. A loud clang sounded as he dented the galvanized steel. His vector was promptly reversed, sending him dizzily back down to the bench. Today was not his day. He shook his head and realized the movement that had startled him was his own reflection in a stainless-steel dish of sorts. He took a closer look at his own image and was surprised to see a small reddish bump on the front of his thorax. A rush of panic undulated through his entire body, but he quickly suppressed it. *It's probably just a bruise from smacking into the side of the building,* he told himself. But a tiny voice in the back corner of his brain whispered that the blemish and his tired wings were signs of something much more disastrous.

Meanwhile, Linda was finding that clinging to the drainpipe was becoming quite, well, draining. She managed to rest her feet on a couple of bolts protruding from the pipe, so at least she wasn't holding herself up by her arms. Although, she thought, she could probably use the upper body conditioning. She noticed that her arms had become rather flabby lately, like chicken wings. She imagined herself turning into a plump, featherless chicken. She chuckled at the thought, which was simultaneously amusing and disturbing. She then pictured the chicken version of herself in a factory farm, with a giant person in a lab coat shoving a feeding tube down her throat.

Unbeknownst to Linda, this was a strangely prophetic thought, since, on the other side of the window, a giant brute in a lab coat was quickly approaching the lab. Larv heard the loud footsteps approaching from the corridor and dove into an empty glass tube on the specimen shelf. He immediately regretted his decision, partly because it was quite cramped in there, but mostly because it was clear glass and he was in plain sight of the chemist, but it was too late to find a new hiding spot. Luckily, he blended in amazingly well with the other specimens. He watched as the beast, who looked like an unfortunate cross between a tyrannosaurus and a toad, burst into the room and started throwing things off the bench in a rage. Broken glass shattered across the floor and mystery liquids sprayed farther than Schmoodler's most impressive mucous projectile. If Larv had been religious, he would have prayed that she didn't get a hold of his tube. Instead, he just hoped.

After several minutes of smashing and crashing, cussing and hissing, and some more smashing and crashing, the tyrano-toad seemed to regain control of her temper and collapsed onto a stool, which was instantly engulfed by her ponderous posterior. Watching wide-eyed from his hiding spot, Larv was suddenly and disturbingly reminded of the homonym for "stool." As he was desperately trying to force this image out of his head, he saw the chemist reach into the pocket of her white lab coat and pull out a green vial.

*The antidote!*

She motioned to smash the vial but stopped herself. She put it back into her pocket, sighed loudly, and began cleaning up the mess she had made. After picking up the broken glass with her thick, clawed fingers, she grabbed an industrial vacuum cleaner and started sucking up the puddles that were scattered about the dirty floor. The vacuum's canister gurgled and belched as various chemical solutions mixed together. When it could no longer handle the indigestion, a yellowish vapour started spewing out of the vacuum head. The chemist grumbled and removed the canister from the vacuum, walked dangerously close to the window that Linda was precariously balanced below, and dumped the concoction down a funnel that was protruding from the wall.

By this point, Linda was firmly and securely rooted in Linda Land, where her poultry alter-ego had made its way into a kitchen and was in the process of being breaded. She noticed the kitchen was getting warmer and warmer. Then, she noticed the pot of boiling oil sitting on the stove. She was about to be deep fried. The chef grabbed her and tried to toss her, kicking and squawking, into the pot, but Linda the Chicken resisted vehemently. She could feel intense heat on her wings and feet, which were clinging to the side of the pot, holding the rest of her plump, breaded body out.

The heat became so intense that she was knocked out of Linda Land and back into reality, where her hands and feet were indeed very hot. The chemicals that the chemist had carelessly dumped down the funnel had reacted violently and exothermically and were now burning through the drainpipe to which Linda was clinging.

She now had two options: she could let go and fall down two stories, or she could climb through the window. She chose option B. She managed to squeeze herself through the small window and plopped onto the now dry, but still dirty, laboratory floor. She landed directly in the immense shadow of the looming tyrano-toad, who was staring at her, puzzled. The chemist had heard her squawk a few seconds earlier and had witnessed the entire scene.

Linda looked up. "Oh, er, why hello there," she stammered.

The chemist continued to stare.

"I'm, uh, looking for, er . . . are you the manager of this lab?" Linda sputtered.

The chemist, who was accustomed to addicts trying to steal drugs from her lab, eyed Linda suspiciously. "Who are you and what do you want?" she growled.

Linda flinched at the intensity of the chemist's deep voice and began to ramble. "My name's Linda. I'm from a little planet called Earth. It's really quite a lovely little planet really. It's in the Milky Way galaxy. Have you heard of it?"

Larv realized that, whether intentionally or not, Linda was providing the distraction he needed. He slowly and awkwardly pulled himself up out of the glass tube. As quietly as he could, he buzzed right behind the chemist and positioned himself to reach inside the gaping pocket of her lab coat.

"I was recently at this teahouse, you see," Linda continued. "And, well, you know, I had this really excellent tea. I thought it was just plain black tea, like an English breakfast. You know, normal tea. But oh my, it certainly wasn't English breakfast, or Earl Grey, or even camomile, for that matter."

Larv's thin arm reached into the pocket.

"And then I thought maybe it was black currant, but that wasn't quite right either."

He felt the smooth glass of the vial and tugged.

"Anyway, my point is, it was none of those normal teas. I mean, not normal where I'm from. It had quite the kick if you know what I mean."

He gently slid the vial all the way out of the pocket.

"You're another one of Garrick's junkies," the chemist accused.

Larv slowly backed away.

"Oh, yes, Garrick! That was the lovely gentleman at the teahouse," Linda said, now intentionally stalling the chemist.

"How many times do I have to tell him not to tell his customers where my lab is!" The chemist said, visibly frustrated.

"So, you are the genius behind that blend?" Linda stammered. "I'd like to purchase, uh, whatever it was called. A bulk order to bring back to my planet."

Tyrano-toad's tongue shot out of her mouth and licked each of her bulging eyeballs before she spoke again. "I absolutely do not do business with rogue junkies," she snarled.

"Oh, but listen to this," Linda said, pointing a finger. "I can . . . uh . . . offer you a generous . . . uh . . . honorarium."

The chemist stopped to consider this. "What kind of honorarium are we talking about?"

Just as Linda was piquing the chemist's interest, one of Larv's wings gave out and he crashed into the bench, knocking over a beaker. The chemist turned towards the sound and saw Larv clutching the green vial. She turned back to Linda, her anger causing her face to scrunch up in a shockingly accurate impression of a constipated pug. "What's that thing doing with my anti-pheromone solution?" she growled.

Somehow, instinct took over and Linda's body reacted. With surprising speed, she darted past the chemist, grabbed Larv under her arm and sprinted out the door like a wide receiver making a run for the end zone. The only problem was that she wasn't quite certain where the end zone was. Luckily for her (and for the Mabitu earlier that day), the chemist was not a natural born sprinter. Linda managed to tap into her inner bull, which Garrick's tea had revealed earlier, and charged down the stairs at an impressive rate for a woman of sixty-five. She made a hard right and ran all the way down the corridor on the main floor, only to realize the exit was on the other side, to the left of the stairway. She turned around and sprinted back. As she passed the bottom of the stairs, the chemist nearly collided with her, but Linda ducked at the last moment, tripping the brute and sending her crashing into the adjacent wall. Linda, surprised at her own agility, flung open the door and darted out into the street. By an extraordinarily fortunate turn of luck, it was at this very moment that the Mabitu pulled up in its private spaceship.

"What are you waiting for? Get in!" it yelled as the hatch opened. Linda dove into the ship just as the chemist came crashing through the door in a fury. As they sped away, the Mabitu left behind a trail of bubbles that would soon burst and rain their aphrodisiacal glitter upon the dusty planet for the last time.

# CHAPTER 18

## Troodly's Disaster

Troodly wasn't the type of oodlean to doodle or to doddle. In fact, her biggest pet peeve was when oodleans (or any other species, for that matter), spent all of their time talking and discussing and having meetings, and meetings about meetings, and meetings to arrange meetings about meetings, and follow up meetings, and never actually doing what it was they meant to do. Troodly was a go-getter. She walked the walk—well, she twirled the twirl, to be more accurate. She was a radially symmetrical being with seven tentacle-like appendages, after all. As soon as she had finished designing her mechanism for measuring planetary orbits, she had gone straight to work assembling it.

In less than fifty-two oodlean hours, Troodly had finished installing the last super-gigantor mirror on the Lysithean moon of Jupiter. Of course, she hadn't achieved such a feat single-handedly. Having seven tentacles, nothing she did was single-handed, but in this particular instance, she had assembled a crew of engineers and an intern to help her strategically place the mirrors throughout the solar system. They had used a fleet of specialized oodlean spacecraft, each containing seven robotic tentacles, to install and adjust the position of each mirror within a micrometer of accuracy. You may be wondering how she got the funding for such heavy-duty machinery because it certainly did not come from the PUE's meager fund. Troodly had to get crafty. You may recall that most oodleans tend to be quite gullible, as was the case when Schmoodler so easily converted them to Oodlism. Troodly was able to loan the equipment from ITCo under the guise that she was working on a marketing campaign for AntiPro™. The giant mirrors, she had explained, would allow space travellers to see the ads on the sides of their ships as they flew by. No one questioned her or the fact that the writing on the ads would appear backwards through the mirrors.

Once all of the mirrors were in place, Troodly towed the mega magnifying glass somewhere between Mercury and the sun and made sure it was positioned at precisely the right angle, which, in fact, was not a right angle at all.

"Positioning magnifying glass," a voice said over the intercom.

"Adjust two degrees northwest of two O'clock," Troodly's voice responded.

"Adjusting . . . adjustment complete."

"Magnifying glass in position."

All that was left to do was open its cover at the exact moment that the mirrors lined up in the correct configuration. It was a planetary ballet and Troodly was the conductor. She tapped her holodex and opened her space-time application that contained the countdown clock. Ten minutes later, she initiated countdown procedures. "One minute to laser beam activation. Everyone in position and ready to take your measurements. We only have one shot at this."

The engineers sat upright and alert at her command. They were ready.

Troodly began the countdown. "Five . . . four . . . three . . . two . . . one. Opening cover." She pushed the large red button, which retracted the cover and unveiled the magnifying glass. The lens fervently gathered every photon in range and unified them into one extremely hot, bright beam of radiation that shot out the other end to find its target. It pained Troodly that she was unable to witness her magnificent invention with her own eyes, as doing so would most certainly blind her. Because of this, all of the windows to the ship's exterior were covered by total black-out blinds. She waited three minutes, and then said into the intercom, "Mirror 1, did you get a measurement?" There was no response. "Mirror 1, Mercury, report your data."

A tentative voice responded, "The beam hasn't reached Mercury yet."

"Impossible," Troodly said. Light traveled fast. Very, very fast. The beam should have hit the first mirror by now. There must have been a delay in the recording equipment. "Mirror 2, do you have a reading?"

"Negative."

Troodly knew the beam would take approximately eight minutes to reach the Mirror 3 in its orbit around Earth, and so she continued to wait. After ten minutes, she asked for an update. She received none. There was nothing they could do but wait the four hours until the beam reached Neptune, and hope there was simply a delay in the data transmission from the light sensors on the mirrors. If worse came to worse, they would have to retrieve the data manually from each mirror. It would be a pain, but they could do it.

Worse did not come to worse. Worse came to much, much worse. As the oblivious crew sat in their windowless ship, the beam of ultra-intense radiation found its way to Mercury—not the mirror that was orbiting Mercury, but the planet itself. Photon after photon bombarded the surface, penetrating deep into the core. The small planet heated to such extreme temperatures that its rocky exterior melted, and within minutes, the entire planet vaporized. The beam continued its course and headed straight for its next victim, Venus. It, too, was obliterated, clearing a path that led directly to Earth. Somewhere in the tropical zone formerly known as Siberia, a priest *almost* realized that after all his years of Armageddon fear mongering, the end was finally here. Before his retinas could translate the blinding bright light into electrochemical signals and send them through his optic nerve to his brain for interpretation, the beam had already vaporized Earth, and then moved on to Mars. It met its match when it reached Jupiter. The gas giant proved too large for the radiation to destroy, at least not before Troodly realized something was wrong.

"That's odd," she said pointing to the radar screen. "The first four planets have disappeared." The engineer stationed next to her shrugged. "The beam must be interfering with the radar."

"I don't think so. We still haven't received any data from the mirrors either. Something's not right. I'm covering it back up." She pressed a button and the steel cover slid over the lens. She stared at the radar screen for several minutes, but the planets did not re-appear.

"That's not good," the engineer said.

"Time to investigate," Troodly said.

"How will we know where to find the planets if they don't appear on radar?"

"We'll have to make our best guess using our own eyes."

Troodly opened the blinds, pointed the ship in the opposite direction of the sun, and tried her best to fly in a straight line. She would soon come to realize that despite her best efforts, she would not be able to find the missing planets.

# CHAPTER 19

## The UPT

Luckily for Linda, Larv, and the Mabitu, Nilleby was several lightyears away from Earth's solar system in an altogether different galaxy. As they flew through Nilleby's artificial atmosphere, Linda realized she was still clutching Larv under her arm and released her grip on the battered cochlean. Larv was not expecting the sudden release and tumbled straight to the back of the ship, which, at their current angle of elevation, was also the bottom of the ship.

"Oh deary me! I'm so sorry, Larv. Are you okay?" Linda asked.

Larv winced and clutched the red bump on his thorax. "Fine," was all he managed to squeak. It took his tired wings three attempts to get him moving. Linda didn't notice his struggle, and the Mabitu was too busy flying the ship to pay them any attention. With great effort, Larv lugged himself into the safety of a chair with a one-seat buffer between himself and Linda, and strapped himself in. Once they were far enough away from the gravitational pull of Nilleby, the Mabitu put the ship into neutral and turned to face the others.

"What now?" it asked with all three of its voices in perfect harmony.

Linda and Larv were both exhausted from recent events.

"I suppose the plan is to get this thingy to the Marmalade planet," Linda said sleepily.

"Molasses Planet," Larv corrected.

"What's a thingy?" asked the Mabitu.

Larv tried to hush Linda. Their mission was supposed to be top secret. Linda seemed to have forgotten this very important detail. "The pitch pipe thingy," she tried to explain. "Here, I'll show you." Linda began to fumble around in her pockets.

"It's a . . . uh . . . an antique," Larv lied. "We're antique collectors and we have a buyer on the Molasses Planet who is very interested in pitch pipes."

"Riiight," replied the Mabitu, skeptically. A stream of bubbles appeared from its effervescence and floated gleefully away, free at last, until they made contact with the walls of the spaceship and burst. Larv momentarily forgot about the pitch pipe as he stared in a trance-like state at the sparkles that exploded from the bubbles, fell, and then flickered out like miniature fireworks.

Linda continued to fumble around. "It's in here somewhere," she mumbled. She checked all of her pockets again, including the secret pocket in her pendulous bosom. Finally, she shrugged and admitted, "I can't find it."

Like a race car driver ejecting from his car after hitting a brick wall at 100 miles per hour, Larv was ejected from his blissful trance. "What did you just say?!" he demanded.

"I can't find the pitch pipe," Linda repeated.

"What do you mean, you can't find it?"

"I mean it's not here. Gone. Vanished."

The normally calm, cool, and collected cochlean was reaching his wit's end. "Keep looking!" His voice was even higher pitched than usual.

"This 'antique' must be worth a lot," the Mabitu muttered.

"It is!" Larv shouted, now in a state of panic. Larv had unstrapped himself and was ransacking Linda's pockets.

"Hey . . . ah! That tickles! Stop it!" Linda squealed.

"We have to find it!" Larv shrieked. He then made the mistake of reaching towards Linda's secret bosom pocket.

*FWAP!*

Linda had Larv in a choke hold so fast, he didn't know what hit him. The Mabitu leaned back, amused, and began to munch invisible popcorn.

"*Hands off!*" Linda said in a voice so stern and so deep that she surprised herself. "I already checked there."

Larv stopped struggling immediately and Linda released her grip. He panted for a while, wondering what had set off Linda's bout of rage. *Humans are peculiar creatures*, he thought. His mind snapped back to the pitch pipe crisis, and he managed to calm himself down enough to speak reasonably. "I need you to think hard. Where did you last see the UPT?"

Linda thought for a moment, and then said, "I remember feeling it in my pocket right after we landed on Nilleby. I checked to make sure it was still there after crashing on the slide."

"And that's the last time you checked for it?"

Linda thought long and hard. She tried to re-trace her steps through the spaceport, to Garrick's Teahouse. She couldn't remember another time that she had checked on the UPT. Anything could have happened while she was under the influence of the tea.

"We have to go back," said Larv. He turned to the Mabitu, "Turn this ship around. We need to go back to Nilleby, now!"

"For a rusty old antique?" asked the Mabitu, puzzled. "No way. I am not going back to that dump. I barely made it out alive the first time."

"Turn this ship around right now, or I'll . . . I'll . . ."

"Or you'll what? Flutter me to death? And even if you did, can *you* drive this thing? Because I'm pretty sure *she* can't," the Mabitu said, looking at Linda. "You two should find a new hobby." It looked them both up and down judgementally. "Might I suggest cosmetics?"

It took a moment to sink in, but then Linda huffed at the insult. Before she could think of a suitable comeback, Larv blurted, "The future of the universe depends on it!"

The Mabitu eyed its passengers suspiciously. "You seriously want me to believe that the future of the universe depends on your antique dealing? If you want me to take you on a wild goose chase, then you'd better start telling me the truth."

"We had a deal," Larv said. "We got you your antidote, now you take us back to Nilleby."

"Yes, and our deal was for me to take you straight to the Molasses Planet. None of this back-and-forth faffing about."

"We need to get that UPT!" Larv pleaded.

"Then tell me what it really is. I'm not getting involved in any sketchy business."

Larv looked at Linda, who shrugged. He could not think of a plausible lie on the spot. "Fine, I'll tell you, but you have to promise not to tell a soul."

"Who would I tell?" said the Mabitu. "I can't even get within a kilometer of most sentient beings. I'm so deprived of social contact that most of the population thinks I'm a myth!"

"That's a good point," Linda said, then turned to Larv. "Just tell him . . . er, her? Them?" Linda looked at the Mabitu for clarification.

"Don't hurt yourself, hun," the Mabitu chuckled. "Just say 'it.'"

"Say what?" Linda asked.

"It."

"What?"

"It!"

Larv realized what was going on an interjected: "Use the pronoun 'it' when referring to the Mabitu."

"Ohhh! My apologies," Linda said to the Mabitu, and then turned back to Larv. "Just tell it about the pitch pipe thingy."

Larv sighed in defeat. "Fine," he said. "Are you familiar with universal de-tuning?"

"Yeah, sure," said the Mabitu.

"Are you aware of its threat to the universal climate? The cataclysmic consequences that will take place if universal de-tuning continues at its current rate?"

"Not really," admitted the Mabitu. "And I am pretty well-read, so it can't be that bad."

"Wrong," said Larv. "It's bad. It's really bad, but it's not well publicized because greedy capitalists like Groodle Schmoodler have smothered any scientific studies from being published. They want to keep the public in the dark so they can continue profiting from intergalactic trade, which is the leading cause of de-tuning."

"Keeping that sort of info from the public is totally illegal," said the Mabitu.

"It doesn't matter how illegal or immoral it is," said Larv. "Schmoodler is the wealthiest being in the universe. He can just pay off anyone who disagrees with him. Or pay someone to threaten anyone who gets in his way."

"A corrupt rich dude. Why am I not surprised?" said the Mabitu, rolling its eyes.

"He sued the PUE for slander," Larv continued. "He said we gave ITCo a bad image by claiming they contributed to universal de-tuning."

"We?" asked the Mabitu. It pointed at Linda and Larv. "You two work for the PUE?"

"Yes." Larv explained their mission to use the universal pitch transmitters and sonoscopes to collect data and show the public the imminent risk they faced. "We have to work in secret because Schmoodler has spies and double agents everywhere."

The Mabitu understood and appreciated the importance of their mission more than most sentient beings. It had such a long lifespan that the effects of universal de-tuning were a direct threat to itself, not its children or grandchildren. It was in its best interest to help them. It reluctantly agreed to go back to Nilleby to find the missing UPT.

* * *

Schmoodler's gwishank agent from Nilleby was perched on his three tripod legs in a shipping container full of AntiPro™ in the cramped cargo hold of an astrobarge that was headed to planet Oodle. He was once again fiddling with the metallic disc that was apparently called a "UPT." Schmoodler's holographic transmission had failed to mention what it was or what the initials stood for. He wondered why it was so important that he had been offered such an unfathomable sum of money for this mission. He shook it. He listened to it. He tried pushing on it. And then, he blew into it.

The disc made a rather plain noise of bleak timbre. He tried blowing into all twelve holes, and they all sounded the same. The monotonous nature of the sound led him to believe that it was not any sort of alien musical instrument. Besides, why would Schmoodler pay so much for a musical instrument? Perhaps it was a torture device. Maybe if the same pitch were played over and over again, it could wreak havoc on one's psyche, like Gwishankian water torture. But that still wouldn't explain the exorbitant price tag. The curiosity was maddening to the technophile, and he had to suppress his impulse to take the mystery disc apart to examine its innards. He forced himself to put it away and distracted himself by fantasizing about what he would do with all those currency units.

* * *

As the Mabitu took the ship out of neutral and oriented it back towards Nilleby, the red bump on Larv's thorax started to vibrate ever so slightly. The developing hair cell was picking up a very distant soundwave, converting it into electrochemical energy, and sending it through Larv's sensory neurons into his brain for interpretation.

Could it be . . . Yes, it was. The tone was precisely 392.0003 Herz, or G4 on the musical scale. And it wasn't coming from Nilleby.

"Stop!" He shouted.

The Mabitu turned. "What now?"

"We're not going back to Nilleby," said Larv.

"What do you mean, we're not going back to Nilleby? After all that? You people need to make up your minds!"

Linda looked at Larv, just as puzzled as the Mabitu. "Yeah Larv. Did we not just decide to go back and get the UTP?"

"It's called a *UPT*," corrected Larv. "And it's not on Nilleby anymore."

"How could you possibly know that?" asked Linda.

"Because I can hear it. Someone else has it, and they've blown into it twelve times now. It's not coming from the direction of Nilleby."

"Impossible!" exclaimed the Mabitu. "You're a larvalux. I thought only fully pupated adult cochleans had hearing that sensitive."

Larv moved his hand to reveal the red bump on his thorax. It was protruding even further than a few hours ago. "My first cilia," he choked. "It's beginning."

"FML," the Mabitu sighed. "We have to get you back to the Molasses Planet."

"No! Not without the UPT," argued Larv.

Linda was perplexed. "Can someone please explain to me what's going on?" She pointed to Larv's thorax. "What is that red thing? Are you sick?"

"He's not sick," explained the Mabitu, "but he will be in serious trouble if we don't get him back to the Molasses Planet before he pupates."

"Pupates?" asked Linda.

"His body is changing into its adult form. Adult cochleans can't live outside of their home planet. It would be like a squyrex in starlight."

"A what?" asked Linda

"A mistoform in steam," said the Mabitu.

"Huh?" Linda had no idea what the Mabitu was referring to.

"A dunklebop out of sulfuric acid."

"A dunkle what?"

"Don't you know anything about the universe beyond your home planet?!" lectured the Mabitu.

Before Linda could answer, Larv chimed in: "Like a fish out of water."

Now that was an idiom Linda could understand, but how it applied to Larv's situation was not immediately apparent. She squinted as though she were trying to see a far away object. The Mabitu turned around to see what she was looking at.

"Pupate," she mumbled. "Out of water . . ."

The Mabitu turned to Larv. "Is she okay?"

"Shhh, just give her a minute," Larv whispered.

Finally, she squinted hard enough that her optic nerve pushed down on a cog with enough pressure to get the gears turning in her brain. Slowly, realization dawned on Linda's face and her eyes widened. "You mean, after he goes through puberty, he won't be able to breathe anymore?"

"Something like that," said the Mabitu

"Well, it's more like I won't be able to tolerate soundwaves in a gaseous medium," Larv mumbled.

"You what?" Linda asked, once again confused.

"Just stick with the fish out of water analogy," interrupted the Mabitu. "The point is, he won't be able to survive outside of his home planet."

Linda turned to the cochlean. "Oh Larv! That's awful! We must get you back to the Marmalade Planet!"

"It's *Molasses*," said Larv with obvious frustration. "And no. Our priority is to retrieve the UPT. So, we'd better get on it. Mabitu, fire up the engines and head that way," Larv ordered, pointing in the direction of an astrobarge full of AntiPro™ that was heading towards planet Oodle.

# CHAPTER 20
## Choodlen's Surprise

Aboard his luxury space yacht, Reverend Groodle Schmoodler was sucking back squirming woodlerms and guzzling oodlean beer by the gallon. He was still chuckling to himself about the video footage he had seen of the ridiculous-looking earthling and the cute little larvalux fumbling their way through one of the most dangerous planets this side of Ursa Major. He had sent out a notice to his gwishank agents on Nilleby offering an unreasonably high bounty for the confiscation of the UPT. He was confident the confiscation would be carried out quickly and without much of a fight from the dynamic duo. For now, all he could do was wait. He passed the time by gorging himself on oodlean hors d'oeuvres and getting decidedly drunk whilst admiring the view through his 360-degree window.

It took three rings of his holographic communication device to arouse Schmoodler from his stupor. It took him four tries to tap "answer" on the touch screen, as his tentacle-eye coordination was severely impaired. Finally, a hologram of his chief engineer, Choodlen, appeared in front of him.

"What d'ya want?" Schmoodler slurred, his voice raspier than ever.

"Requesting permission to board, sir."

Schmoodler rolled all seven of his eyes and sighed deeply. "Is that really necessary? Kind of busy here."

"Yes sir, I do believe it is necessary," Choodlen said, avoiding direct eye contact. "I have important news regarding the progress of the wormline construction."

"Fiiine. But it better be good news. Don't you kill my mood, Choodlen." Schmoodler tried to point a floppy tentacle at the hologram, but his aim was slightly off to the left.

"Thank you, sir," Choodlen said, and then vanished. If Schmoodler hadn't been so inebriated, he might have sensed the unease in Choodlen's voice or noticed how his eyes were even shiftier than usual.

Choodlen's ship docked with Schmoodler's luxury space yacht and the edgy engineer twirled through the airlock. Schmoodler tried to twirl towards his liquor cabinet to get another drink, but the spinning motion amplified the dizziness brought on by intoxication. "Can I offer you a boodleoodler?" Schmoodler asked as he bumped into a stool. "Or how about a roodlem?"

Choodlen darted towards a small side table that was holding a half-empty bottle of boodleoodler and grabbed it just in time, milliseconds before Schmoodler crashed into the table and knocked it over. "No thank you, sir. I don't like to drink on the job."

"Nonsense!" Schmoodler exclaimed. "As your boss, I insist!"

"Sir, I really shouldn't . . . "

"I'm not telling you; I'm *asking* you," Schmoodler sputtered. "I mean, I'm asking you, not telling you . . . er . . . you know what I mean. Tell me what you drink, or I'll choose myself."

"Uh . . . I guess I'll have a . . . er . . . a roodlem and coodlekoodle."

"Atta boy!" Schmoodler said, patting Choodlen with a floppy tentacle. He fumbled through the cabinet to find a glass. "Ya know, Choodlen, we never get to just sit and talk about normal stuff. It's always business this and wormline that." He gestured with the same two tentacles that were holding the alcohol and the mix, spilling them all over. "How's the family?" Schmoodler poured the drink, managing to get some of the liquid into the glass. Choodlen watched in horror as Schmoodler filled the tumbler with mostly alcohol and very little mix. "How's the wife? The kids?" Schmoodler slurred, passing Choodlen the drink. Choodlen nearly dropped the glass as Schmoodler shoved it at him.

"Well sir, I, uh, don't have a wife or kid," he stammered. "You strictly forbade it when I was hired." Choodlen took a sip of the impossibly potent potable and barely suppressed a gag.

"And *that's* why you're the best!" Schmoodler asserted, pointing a floppy tentacle at him. "No distractions."

"None whatsoever," Choodlen muttered under his breath.

"Families are overrated," Schmoodler assured him. "You gotta look out for number one . . . *me*!"

Schmoodler chuckled at his own joke. The chuckle turned into a laugh. The laugh turned into a cackle. And then Schmoodler lost all control. He bellowed and flailed his tentacles around, knocking empty bottles (and some full bottles) off tables and shelves. Then, he started choking on his thick mucus. He hacked and he coughed, and just as he was starting to turn blue, he spat up the largest loogie Choodlen had ever seen. It was the size of a baseball, and it launched all the way up to the twelve-foot ceiling of the luxury space yacht and stuck there. Schmoodler didn't seem to notice, but Choodlen kept one of his seven eyes on that mucus ball for the next several minutes as Schmoodler attempted small talk. Every now and again, a droplet would form on the end of the loogie and drip down towards Schmoodler. Choodlen was fairly certain he saw several drops land in Schmoodler's drink, and at least one land directly in the gaping crevice of a mouth from whence it came.

Choodlen laboriously sipped on his mind-numbingly strong beverage. The more he sipped, the lesser his urge to gag, and the more his mind was distracted from the loogie . . . and the bad news he would sooner or later have to relay.

* * *

Half an hour and three drinks later, Choodlen was feeling more relaxed than he had in recent memory. He hadn't felt this relaxed since before he began working for Schmoodler five years ago. He had always felt intimidated by his powerful employer, even a bit fearful, he was ashamed to admit. Now, he had no idea why. The two of them were getting along famously and laughing up a storm. In fact, they had been laughing so hard that the ball of phlegm on the ceiling had multiplied. Choodlen could not quite remember what had been so funny. Did Schmoodler just tell him that he invented Oodlism as a social experiment, just to see if people would fall for it? What a funny joke! This guy, his new pal, was hilarious. Why had Choodlen never seen this side of him before? He burst into another fit of laughter.

To look at the two oodleans, one would think they were the best of friends. Sadly, this was actually the closest thing to friendship that Choodlen had experienced in years. Most of his adult life had been dedicated to serving Schmoodler, and he constantly worried about what might happen if he made a mistake. There was a rumour that previous employees who screwed up had mysteriously disappeared. Therefore, he had taken Schmoodler's advice (direct order, more like it) to heart and avoided close friendships or relationships of any kind. Now, Choodlen could see that Schmoodler had probably been joking all those years ago and he had taken him way too literally. He felt silly, but relieved.

"So, what was it you came here to tell me?" Schmoodler finally asked.

"Huh?" Choodlen was caught off guard.

"What was the reason you boarded my ship? It must be important if you felt the need to disturb my alone time."

Choodlen chortled. Schmoodler did not. He had gone from laughing and joking around to dead serious in seconds.

"Oooh, right, about that," Choodlen snorted. "It's actually quite funny, really. I was so nervous to tell you about it earlier."

"Nervous?" asked Schmoodler suspiciously. Choodlen would only be nervous if it was bad news. He felt the rage that perpetually flickered inside his abdomen like a pilot light ignite into a fire that swiftly raised into his throat. Before it could explode out of his mouth, Schmoodler suppressed his anger, and instead, used the most pleasant tone of voice he could muster (which, with his saliva-overproduction issue, wasn't all that pleasant). "Now Choodlen, my most trusted employee, you know you can tell me anything. Transparency is our motto here at ITCo."

"I thought the company motto was 'profit takes priority.'"

"Now, now Choodlen, let's not get tangled up in the fine print." Schmoodler felt the heat rising up his esophagus again and swallowed it back down, along with a congealed wad of phlegm. "Go on and get whatever it is off your mind. You'll feel better once you do, I promise."

"Well, now that we're good pals, I feel like I can tell you anything."

Schmoodler winced at being called "pal," but he pushed it aside for the time being. "Of course you can. Now spit it out."

Choodlen suppressed another laughing fit at the irony of Schmoodler, master of mucus, telling him to "spit it out," but he could not stop the stupid smile from spreading across his face. "Wormline construction has been delayed," he said.

The smile made it extra challenging for Schmoodler to contain his anger. How could this dingus deliver such terrible news with a smile? "Delayed?" Schmoodler demanded. "What you mean, *delayed*?"

"We received a transmission from the Safety Board. They won't allow us to continue construction until the wormline passes safety regulations."

"The Safety Board? How did they even find out about the wormline?" Schmoodler's anger was becoming more and more apparent. "I'll bet that meddling miscreant Arec Ibo had something to do with it. He couldn't shut us down for environmental reasons, so he went to the Safety Board. Why can't he keep his gigantic nose out of my business?!"

"I . . . uh . . . don't know, sir." Even in his state, Choodlen could see the switch flip somewhere inside Schmoodler, and it immediately sobered him up. Would Schmoodler blame him for the delay? Even though it was clearly not his fault, he was the bearer of bad news, and there was no one else around to punish. What would his punishment be? Choodlen shuddered to think about it.

"Well, mister smarty-pants engineer, how do you propose we remedy this situation? You *do* have a way to test out the wormline, don't you?"

"Uh, well, we've sent tracking devices through the wormline, and, uh . . . well, we've only lost the signal. It turns out that space-time travel interferes with the universal positioning technology. The Safety Board seems mainly concerned about how to ensure the safety of workers who have to go near the wormline. They want to know what will happen if someone . . . uh . . . f-falls in."

"How close does a worker have to be to the wormline to get sucked in?" Schmoodler asked, staring out the window at the giant ring structure in the distance.

"Not very close. The gravity is pretty strong."

"How close?"

"The point of no return, when the pull would be too strong for a crew to save them in time, would be approximately eighty kilometers."

If Schmoodler had a front side and a back side, he would have turned around to press a button on the console behind him. As it were, he did not need to turn in any direction, and he simply used his two eyes and one tentacle-like appendage facing the console (on the side of him facing away from Choodlen) to find and press the button. A screen turned on that appeared to be showing the cockpit of the ship. A voluptuous female oodlean in a captain's uniform appeared.

"Reverend Schmoodler, what can I do for you?"

"Captain Joodlenwoodle, could you take us closer to the wormline? I need to get within eighty kilometers of it. We're performing an . . . inspection."

"Sir," Choodlen interrupted, "are you sure that's a good idea?"

"Choodlen, I've never been more sure of anything in my life."

"Well, sir, I'm not sure we'll be able to see much from the outside."

"Don't you worry about a thing, Choodlen. I just want to take a look for myself."

"If you say so."

Choodlen could not see that Schmoodler was typing something into the touch screen on the console with two of his tentacle-like appendages. As he pressed "send," Captain Joodlenwoodle, who was still visible on the screen, looked down, gave Schmoodler a look as if to say, "Are you sure?" and then a discreet nod of understanding.

A moment later, all of the interior lights of the luxury spacecraft went out.

"What happened?" Choodlen choked.

"It appears the lights are malfunctioning again. This happened last week. Don't worry it's an easy fix. We just need to flip the breaker. Choodlen, it would be a huge help if you could do it for me. You are an engineer, after all, and I'm afraid I've had too much to drink."

Choodlen, who was once again feeling fearful of his boss, was willing to do almost anything to stay on Schmoodler's good side. "Of course, not a problem. Where is it?"

"It's on the exterior circuit board on the port side of the ship."

"Sorry, sir, did you say exterior?"

"Ah, yes. A bit of a pain. You'll have to suit up. These darn luxury space yachts are designed to maximize comfort on the inside, so they put the circuit boards on the exterior. Poor design, if you ask me. Here, suits are this way."

Schmoodler led Choodlen to a cloakroom containing four different sizes of spacesuit designed to fit most oodleans. It took several minutes for Choodlen to find all seven tentacle sleeves in his suit because of the dim lighting provided only by the exterior lights shining in through the windows—and because he wasn't *completely* sober.

When he was finally ready, Schmoodler led him to the airlock, nudged him inside, and then closed the safety door. He pressed the intercom button. "Alright Choodlen, opening the exterior hatch now."

"Wait! Where's the tether?" Choodlen shouted.

Schmoodler ignored him and opened the hatch. Choodlen shot out, untethered, into the vacuum of space. Schmoodler cracked open another boodleoodler and watched through the large window of his lounge room as Choodlen disappeared into the Ellis Wormline.

"There's your safety test," he muttered, then broke into a fit of mucous-filled maniacal laughter.

# CHAPTER 21
## The Intern

*Thud, thud, thud.*
*Thud, thud, thud.*
*Thud, thud, thud.*

The sound of the intern's severely swollen tentacle slapping against Troodly's temporary office door aboard the borrowed ITCo spacecraft grew fainter and fainter. What started off as the sound of a large wet snake slapping the door had dimmed to the volume of a spaghetti noodle being thrown against a wall. The oodlean intern had worn out all seven of his tentacle-like appendages knocking on Troodly's door. He had been given the inglorious task (that one would only give to an intern) of trying to coax Troodly out of her office in which she had locked herself immediately following the destruction of the inner planets of the solar system, which she would henceforth only refer to as "The Disaster."

With one last thud, the intern gave up and limped his way down the corridor, tears of pain leaking into his cavernous mouth hole on the top of his head from the seven eyes that encircled it. It was a salty and slimy affair. The intern felt bad for failing at the only task he'd been given other than retrieving caffeinated beverages for the higher ups. He'd been promised actual work entering data for an emissions study, but so far, he hadn't yet been deemed worthy. He was determined to prove his capability as a scientist and follow in the tentacle steps of his idol, Troodly. However, she was making this rather difficult by ignoring him. She must be feeling really terrible after what happened with those planets. He pictured her sitting there in her office, staring blankly at the wall. Perhaps she was in a state of denial. Perhaps she was feeling intense guilt thinking about all of the beings she had just destroyed. He didn't blame her for needing some alone time, or for disabling her communication system, but the second-in-command insisted she come out. Apparently, she had an important incoming video call or something. The intern wondered why the second-in-command couldn't take the call for her. Now, he would have to report back that she was completely unresponsive. He stopped. *No. I won't do it. I can't fail at this.* If he had a front side, he would have turned around and walked with newfound determination back to Troodly's office. Instead, he simply reversed his clockwise twirl into a counterclockwise twirl.

Troodly was neither staring blankly at the wall in denial nor feeling intense guilt. She wasn't feeling much of anything, really. She was too busy for the frivolity of emotions. As soon as The Disaster had occurred, she went straight to work figuring out how to fix it. She decided she could simply travel back in time and prevent it from happening.

The issue wasn't so much *how* to travel back in time. Troodly had figured this out, at least, in theory, ages ago as a graduate student. The issue back then was that her research grant applications to actually build her proposed model were all rejected due to "ethical considerations surrounding the temporal paradox." Her funding was cut, and she was forced to abandon the project. Since then, Troodly had developed a deep, burning hatred towards ethics committees. The whole topic of ethics bored her greatly. She hated the circular arguments that ethical debates inevitably led to. She viewed them as an obstacle to discovery. On the other tentacle, she understood why they were necessary. A professor once told her to imagine what could happen if the technology fell into the tentacles of the wrong oodlean. "What would Groodle Schmoodler do with it?" he used to say. It was a legitimate concern, especially regarding time travel. He would surely use time travel for profit, regardless of what damage it would potentially cause. Knowing this did not quelch her frustrations, but it did shift her anger from ethics committees to the corrupt beings who would surely use this technology irresponsibly.

Needless to say, Troodly was forced to abandon her plan of creating an actual time travelling device. Instead, she had switched her focus to complex digital simulations with the idea that she would be able to predict what would happen if someone travelled back in time and altered history. The results were not good. Without showing anyone, she had quietly tucked this work away and switched her focus again, this time to predicting the effects of universal de-tuning. It was this study that had landed her a job with the

PUE. It had also landed her several threats from Groodle Schmoodler. It was dangerous for anyone to be an outspoken environmentalist these days, and even more dangerous if you were an oodlean. To smooth things over with Schmoodler, Troodly had followed the old adage, "Keep your friends close and your enemies closer." She had assured him that her study was a ruse to get hired by the PUE and agreed to be one of Schmoodler's informants. She had even gone so far as to show her face at his intolerable sermons. Due to her current predicament, Troodly had temporarily forgotten her professor's warning. She hadn't completely forgotten it, but she was choosing to ignore it. Surely, she could slip into the past, warn herself to double check her calculations, and then come right back. No harm, no foul. She frantically searched through her old hard drives until she found the one labelled *Grad School – Time Travel Study*. "Ah-ha!" she exclaimed excitedly. She now had all the science, but she still faced one major obstacle: funding.

*Thud, thud, thud.*

*Is someone throwing noodles at my door?* Troodly wondered. The sound had been so faint. *It must've been my imagination*, she thought. *When was the last time I ate?* Troodly had a bad habit of getting so engrossed in her work that she sometimes forgot to eat for days. As much as she didn't feel like encountering others, she decided she'd better take a twirl to the canteen. Maybe if she was stealthy enough, she could go unnoticed and avoid awkward conversations. She opened the door and was greeted with a tentacle to the face.

"What the—?"

"OH MY OODLE! I am sooo sorry Ms. Troodly!" It was the intern.

"What did you do that for?" Troodly demanded.

"I didn't mean to, I swear! Please forgive me! Are you okay? Can I get you some ice for your face?"

"I'm fine. You really didn't hit me that hard. It was just unexpected." Troodly looked at the young oodlean and realized she'd never seen another of her own species working for the PUE. Most of them were Schmoodler supporters who questioned nothing that spewed from his disgusting mouth. She was suspicious that he might be one of Schmoodler's spies.

"Who are you?" she asked.

"Steve," he said with a lisp. "My name's Steve. I must say Ms. Troodly, it is such a great honour to finally get to talk to you. I'm a huge admirer of your work!"

"Steve?!" Troodly gasped. "Does Schmoodler know you call yourself that?"

"Oh crap! I meant Stoodlevoodle."

"Don't worry about it, Steve. I won't tell. Word of advice, though: don't let anyone on planet Oodle hear you say that. There's a reason I go by Troodly, even when I'm here. It's so I don't get used to my non-oodlized name."

"What's your non-oodlized name?"

"Don't worry about that, Steve." From their brief interaction, Troodly was beginning to think Steve was harmless, but she didn't want to take any chances. "What happened to you?" she asked, looking down at Steve's puffy, purple tentacles.

"Oh, ummm . . ." Steve didn't want to admit to Troodly that he had been knocking on her door for the past hour. "I, uhhh . . . was in a fight." It was the only thing he could think of on the spot.

"Huh. You don't seem like the fighting type to me." Troodly shrugged it off and starting twirling down the corridor towards the ship's canteen.

"Where are you going?" Steve said as he twirled after her.

"What's it to you?"

"Well actually, Ms. Troodly, I came to get you. You have an urgent video call."

"Oh for Oodle's sake," Troodly sighed. "Can't someone else take it?"

"They said they'll only talk to you," Steve replied.

"Who is it?" Troodly asked, although she was pretty sure she already knew.

"I'm afraid I'm not privy to that information."

"Fine, I'll take the call," Troodly sighed. "Do me a favour, Steve."

"Anything for you ma'am." Steve straightened up, excited at the possibility of completing a real task for his idol.

"Get me a ration from the canteen. My blood glucose level is not optimal."

"Yes, ma'am!"

"And not that powdered crap. I want the good stuff. I'm craving . . ." she thought for a moment, and then said decidedly, "noodles."

"One order of noodles, coming right up!" Steve said enthusiastically as he hurried towards the canteen. Hurried, that is, until he remembered how much pain his tattered tentacles were in. As soon as he turned the corner and was out of Troodly's sight, he slowed to a hobble. Despite the pain, he was excited to have finally spoken to the genius herself and that she had asked him a favour. Sure, it wasn't the most scientific request, but it was a start.

Troodly holed herself back inside her office and switched on the communication system. The alert for the incoming call popped up on her touch screen. She hesitated. *It's probably Arec Ibo calling to fire me,* she thought. *Or the Intergalactic Enforcement Agency calling to arrest me.* She took a deep breath and touched the icon. To her surprise, it was neither of the above. Instead, she saw the image of a well-fed oodlean wearing a black robe with a clergy collar, specially tailored to fit the oodlean form.

"Reverend Schmoodler?" She was not expecting *this*. She composed herself. "To what do I owe the pleasure?"

"Troodly, my child! It's been far too long. I can't remember the last time I saw you in the congregation."

*Oh, here he goes,* Troodly thought. *He's being all priestly*. She knew that he put on his reverend act as a tool for manipulation. It actually worked on most oodleans. What better way to manipulate someone than to make them feel small by calling them "child"? Or make yourself out to be God's messenger? Troodly could see right through it, but she also knew what he wanted to hear.

"I apologize for that, Reverend. My work has taken me off the planet a lot lately. I have been chanting the Oodle every night before bed though."

"That's good to hear," Schmoodler responded with a fake smile. "Speaking of your work, I heard about your little . . . incident."

"News travels fast," replied Troodly. At first, she was surprised that he already knew about The Disaster, but she quickly remembered that he had minions everywhere.

"I must say, I had my doubts about where your loyalties lie, but you're back in my good books. Well done."

Troodly couldn't believe what she was hearing. Was Schmoodler *congratulating* her for committing genocide? She forced herself to play cool. "Thank you, Father," she responded.

"You sure put an end to that PUE project. Did they really think they were going to find any evidence for that universal de-tuning fairy tale of theirs?"

"I imagine so," Troodly lied. "Idiots," she added.

"I mean, you *really* put them in their place. Do you think you may have gone a little too far? Is Ibo going to trust you after that?"

"Time will tell," Troodly said flatly.

"You haven't spoken to him yet?"

"I've been avoiding it," she admitted. This time, she was being completely honest.

"Well, I wanted you to know that you did the right thing, but maybe next time, try not to completely destroy billions of ITCo consumers."

Troodly couldn't hide her anger at that. "Don't you mean billions of innocent lives?" she retorted.

"I understand how you might feel guilty about that, my child. I want to remind you that the Oodle is all forgiving if you can chant its name indefinitely."

*Too bad that's impossible*, Troodly wanted to say. Instead, she said, "Thank you father. I hope I can find peace in the Oodle during this difficult time." It took all her will power to sound genuine.

"That's not the only reason I called," Schmoodler rasped. "I wanted to let you know that there's a job opening at ITCo, since I'm sure you will lose your current one after this."

"You think so?" asked Troodly, doing her best to hide her sarcasm.

"Let's not fool ourselves, my child. Do you really think you'll receive funding ever again after blowing up four planets?"

Troodly paused. He was right. She hadn't figured out how to fund her plan to travel back in time to prevent The Disaster, let alone the rest of her career. Then, like the breaking of day, an idea dawned on her. Schmoodler had endless amounts of money. Endless resources. And he most certainly did not enforce any sort of ethical protocols. Perhaps if she were to do him a favour, he might provide her with the funding she needed.

"What's the job at ITCo?" she asked.

"I'm glad you're interested! I need a new chief engineer for a very important construction project."

"New?" she inquired. "What happened to the previous chief engineer?"

"He was . . . in an accident," Schmoodler said. "Not to worry, it wasn't work related."

Troodly knew he was lying, but she pretended to believe him. "What's the project?" she asked.

"It's highly confidential," Schmoodler said. "You will be required to sign an NDA before I reveal any details."

"How am I supposed to accept a job offer if I don't know what the job is?"

Schmoodler looked around as if someone might be listening in on their conversation. "Is there anyone else in the room with you?" he asked.

"No." Troodly was unaware that at that very moment, an exasperated Steve had arrived outside her door with her noodles and was trying desperately to knock loud enough for her to hear his damaged appendage through the thick steel.

"Swear on the Oodle that you will not tell a soul about this," Schmoodler demanded.

Troodly obediently raised her third and sixth appendages and made the sign of the Oodle. "I swoodleoodler," she swore, in the most serious tone she could muster.

This seemed to convince Schmoodler. He looked around the room one more time, and then whispered, "I'm building a wormline."

"A *what*?" Troodly leaned closer to the screen.

"ITCo has innovated a new way to maximize the efficiency of the transport of goods," Schmoodler explained excitedly.

Troodly already knew about Schmoodler's wormline project. Arec Ibo had ranted about it enough. But she had to act oblivious. She grew more and more angry as Schmoodler droned on about ITCo and the Ellis Wormline. She knew that the PUE hadn't approved its construction, and yet it was already well underway. Why was she surprised? She should have seen this coming from the entitled megalomaniac.

Her anger quickly turned to glee as Troodly realized this was exactly the opportunity she needed. She could use the wormline to travel back in time and save the incinerated planets! She waited for Schmoodler to finish explaining how much money the company would save and how much he would pay her. As a raging narcissist, he assumed that everyone else was exactly like him and only cared about money. When he finally finished his spiel, she said, "I'm in."

"Praise the Oodle!" Schmoodler exclaimed, raising three of his tentacles into the air and looking up. "Great to have you on board, Troodly."

*Pleasure's all mine*, thought Troodly.

"Our foreman is on site as we speak," said Schmoodler. "You can meet him there, and he'll catch you up on all the technical details of the project."

"What about you?" asked Troodly.

"As much as I'd love to meet you there myself and give you a proper ITCo welcome, I've got to head back to Oodle for Sunday Mass."

Troodly couldn't believe her luck. She would be able to scope out the wormline without Schmoodler's prying eyes.

The video call came to an end and Troodly scrambled to gather her things together. As she scrambled, she came up with a plan to hijack an escape pod and fly towards the Ellis Wormhole without the rest of her crew noticing. In order to do this, she had to move fast, while they all thought she was still moping in her office. Furthermore, their ship had to be close enough to the wormhole that it was in range of the escape pod. It would be a close call, but Troodly figured she could do it if she left within the next fifteen minutes. She grabbed her bag, flung open the office door, and twirled as quickly as she could toward the escape pod bay. She moved with such haste that she didn't notice Steve waiting for her with her bowl of noodles.

Steve stood there shocked as Troodly twirled out of sight faster than the Tasmanian Devil. He was still trying to digest the information he had just overheard through the door. What had just happened? Had the brilliant scientist he'd worshipped his entire life actually just agreed to go work with Schmoodler? What was she thinking? *This can't be happening, this can't be happening*, he thought over and over in a state of sheer panic. He was so panicked, in fact, that he could hear a beeping sound inside his head. The beeping grew louder and louder. Steve suddenly realized the sound wasn't in his head. It was coming from Troodly's office. She had another incoming video call. He snapped back to his senses and barely managed to catch the office door before it latched shut. He spun stealthily into the office. He couldn't believe what he was doing, but if his greatest fear was true, then it was up to him to save the PUE. He motioned to answer the video call, then hesitated. What if it was Schmoodler calling back? What would he say? Then, he imagined all the praise he would receive if he were to save the PUE. He could see the headline already: *Intern Saves PUE, Promoted to Chief Scientist.* Before he could stop himself again, Steve slapped the screen with his sore tentacle and answered the call.

A nasally voice shouted into the speaker: "Troodly, what the hell happened out there?! You were supposed to measure the planetary orbits, not blow them up!"

On the screen, Steve saw only nose.

"Troodly, say something!" the nose demanded.

When Steve didn't respond, the nose turned down and to the side, revealing a wide, perfectly circular eye that pierced through the video monitor and shot daggers of intensity directly at him. "You're not Troodly. Who are you? And where's Troodly?"

Steve was distracted by the wide, glowing eye and the caterpillar-like eyebrow that rested above it.

"Hello?"

Steve couldn't look directly into that eye, but he knew it looked familiar. He knew it was someone important, but who was this strange looking being whose nose covered most of his face? Then it struck him. "You . . . you're Arec Ibo!" he shouted at the screen, lisping worse than normal in his excitement.

"Yes, and who the hell are you?" Ibo demanded.

"I'm Steve—the intern."

"Intern?"

"Listen, Mr. Ibo. Troodly's a traitor!"

"Huh?"

"You have to do something, quick!" Steve started panicking again. "She stole . . . escape pod! She's . . . Schmoodler!" He was out of breath and was having trouble translating his thoughts into words.

"She's Schmoodler?" Ibo asked. "Troodly is Schmoodler? Schmoodler is Troodly?" Ibo's eyes widened. "I should have known!"

"No!" Steve huffed and puffed and then continued. "She's going to work for Schmoodler! I just overheard their conversation. I wasn't trying to eavesdrop, I swear! I just went to get Troodly a bowl of noodles, and when I came back, I heard them talking and I—"

"Whoa, slow down there, son," Arec Ibo replied in a much calmer, albeit just as nasally, tone than before. He was starting to put the pieces together.

This poor intern had been through some trauma since the whole exploding planet incident. Now, what was he trying to tell him about Troodly? Had she gone off her rocker, too? “Take a deep breath and tell me everything you know.”

Steve did as he was told and explained everything to the president of the PUE. When he was done, Arec Ibo thanked him for the information and assured him that he’d done the right thing. Steve was pleased with himself, but also in a bit of shock. He couldn’t believe Troodly would do such a thing. He didn’t know what to feel. He sat at Troodly’s desk and slurped down the bowl of noodles he’d so eagerly fetched for the traitor moments earlier.

Arec Ibo leaned back on his armchair in the PUE headquarters in his living room on planet Sagana. Could it be true? Had Nimbulus been right all along? Putting his trust in an oodlean had been a risk, but Ibo really thought she was different from the rest. Maybe he had been wrong.

# CHAPTER 22

## The Other End of the Wormline

Choodlen didn't remember much from the actual wormline. Either traveling through space-time was instantaneous and there was nothing to remember, or he had lost consciousness somewhere along the way. Either way, when he popped out the other end and came to, he found himself falling through the orange sky of an unknown planet. He was surprisingly calm about falling to his death. Panicking wouldn't do him any good, after all. He looked down and spotted a small dot. He watched as the dot grew larger and larger. Eventually, he was able to see a metallic sheen coming from the dot, which was no longer a dot, but looked more like a mountain. He soon realized that he was looking at a massive heap of metallic waste from the construction of the wormline.

Of course, it made sense that bits of metal that had been accidentally dropped would end up going through the wormhole, and it made sense that by being tossed into the wormhole like a piece of garbage himself, that he would end up in the same place. He recalled a few months back when one of the construction workers had been fired for losing an expensive piece of machinery that was used for attaching polystyrozene to the opening of the wormline. *Betcha I know where to find it now*, he thought to himself, grinning. As the metallic mountain rapidly approached, he took comfort in the fact that his death would be immediate. Details of the metal scraps began to immerge as his body fell helplessly closer and closer to the ground. When he was about three seconds away from oblivion, he spotted the lost machine near the top of the trash heap, then closed his eyes and prepared for impact.

The impact came, but not in the way Choodlen had expected. Could it be that the transition from life to death was so seamless? He didn't feel any different. He had felt a thud, but no pain. In fact, the thud was rather soft, as though he'd landed on a giant pillow. And he felt like he was still moving. The wind whipping past his helmet told him that he was no longer falling, but he was moving laterally across the sky. He took a deep breath (more evidence that he was, indeed, still alive) and opened his eyes.

The pillow he'd landed on was covered in brilliant orangey-yellow feathers that rippled in the sunlight. He soon realized that the rippling effect was caused by the movement of the feathers as gigantic wings flapped on either side of him. He was lying on the back of a huge bird that was flying through the sky. Had the bird saved him from becoming but a splatter on the surface of this foreign planet? Did the bird even know he was there? It was so big that Choodlen surmised that it might have not even felt the weight of his comparatively tiny body.

He used the artificial suckers on his spacesuit's tentacles to grip tufts of feathers as the bird made a hard left. The sharp turn allowed Choodlen to see over the side of the large body to the ground. They weren't very high up. Choodlen waited until the bird made another sharp turn, and then let go. He tucked and rolled onto the ground, knocking the wind from his lungs, but otherwise causing no damage to himself or his spacesuit. The movement caught the eye of the enormous avian, which circled back and landed a few feet from a gasping Choodlen. It looked at him and cocked its head to the side in curiosity.

If Choodlen had ever seen Sesame Street, he would have noticed a similarity between this creature and Big Bird. Only this creature was much larger and did not possess the heavy eye lids of someone who had been smoking suspicious substances. Perhaps it looked more like a giant orange emu but with larger wings, like an albatross, that allowed it to soar long distances without flapping. It definitely had the longer neck and relatively small head of an emu, but it was fluffier and had a tuft of feathers on the top of its head like a Polish hen.

Once Choodlen caught his breath, he lay as still as possible, waiting to see what the bird would do. It was big enough that if it so desired, it could easily swallow him down in one gulp, spacesuit and all. After a few minutes of pecking around at the ground, the bird seemed to forget that Choodlen was there. It let out a squawk and then flew off. Choodlen started to get up, but the slight movement attracted the bird's attention again. It landed near him, cocked its head, pecked around for a while, and then flew off again.

This song and dance happened several more times. Each time Choodlen thought the coast was clear and tried to get up, the bird would come back. He didn't know what to do. As the wormline was still under construction, they hadn't calculated its current drop point. He didn't know where he was, he didn't know *when* he was, and he couldn't walk anywhere to find out. All he could do was lay there motionless and brood. He thought about Groodle Schmoodler lulling him into a false sense security, luring him into the exit hatch and ejecting him, untethered, into the vacuum of space. Five years of loyal service and this is how he's treated? Ridiculous. He wished the fall had killed him. It would have been better than being eaten alive by a giant bird. He contemplated whether or not to remove his helmet. He didn't know if this planet's atmosphere could support oodlean lungs. He didn't know if he cared. A tickle on his face made it awfully tempting.

# CHAPTER 23
## Planet Oodle

Linda, Larv, and the Mabitu had been following the sound of the UPT for several hours when the astrobarge came into view.

"There it is," said Larv. "It's in that ship somewhere." Linda squinted through the window. She could barely see the small dot far off in the distance. It was at that moment she realized she'd lost her glasses. They were probably on Nilleby somewhere. Or perhaps on that astrobarge along with the pitch pipe.

"That little speck is a ship?" she asked.

"Just you wait," the Mabitu replied.

Linda watched in amazement and horror as the ship got bigger and bigger, like a scuba diver watching a whale slowly come into view. But this was no whale. Linda estimated this ship could hold ten thousand whales, all in separate, very spacious tanks. The enormity of the ship was overwhelming. "It's the size of a small planet!"

"Maybe a moon," corrected the Mabitu, in all seriousness.

Soon, they were close enough to see the advertisements for AntiPro™ covering the exterior surface of the astrobarge. One featured an image of a gwishank model strategically posed beside a microphone stand for perspective. The two were similarly proportioned. Scrawled across the bottom of the photo was the phrase "You, too, can be as thin as a gwishank." Another ad showed a smiling saganite holding what looked like a giant bottle of nose spray and the phrase, "Now available as an inhalant!" Yet another showed a human child playing video games captioned, "Proven to cure childhood obesity."

"What nonsense!" Linda gasped. She turned away from the window. "I can't look at any more of that propaganda!"

"The universe is messed up," agreed the Mabitu. After a moment of silence, Linda and the Mabitu both looked over to Larv, wondering why he hadn't commented on the despicable display in front of them, only to find that he was no longer beside them. They found him keeled over in pain at the back of the ship, clutching at the red bump on his abdomen.

"Oh dear, Larv! Let me take a look." Linda rushed over to his aid. "Move your hand."

"No!" Larv squeaked.

"Just move it, I need to see!" Linda grabbed his hand and moved it away, revealing a thick, dark hair protruding from the red bump. "Oh my," she whispered. "Not all that different from human puberty, is it now?"

At the sound of her voice, Larv winced and covered the hair again.

"Psst!" The Mabitu motioned for Linda to come over.

"What?" she asked as she made her way back to the front of the ship.

"Shhh." The Mabitu leaned over and whispered in Linda's ear, "Larv has sprouted a cilium. It's extremely sensitive to sound, especially when it's out in the air and not submerged in molasses. That's why he needs to get back to his planet."

"I can hear you!" Larv squeaked. "And I'm not going back without that UPT!"

Linda thought for a moment. "Maybe we can cover it with something else in the meantime."

"What do you mean?" The Mabitu asked.

"We just need to find something with a consistency similar to that of molasses."

"That won't work!" insisted The Mabitu. "You know it's not *actually* molasses on his planet. Besides, I highly doubt this ship has anything like that."

"Now, now, Mab. You just stay there and focus on driving this tin can. I'll take a look around and see what I can find."

"What did you call me?" The Mabitu gasped in an effort to sound offended, but it secretly liked its new nickname. It then flipped its imaginary hair and turned back towards the ship's control panel.

Linda set off to find some sort of relief for her poor pupating pal. She rummaged through cupboards and overhead storage bins and emptied out first aid kits. She searched under seats but saw only heaps of a canvas-like material. She dug through the drawers at the back and found spare ship parts, all sorts of tubing, and tools. Nothing remotely similar to molasses. When she found the emergency food supply, she got distracted and fixed herself a snack. Then, she continued to rummage and ransack and pillage and plunder, all the while mumbling to herself under her breath, despite the pain it was causing Larv. But Linda didn't notice his grimaces. She was on a mission—and it was quite possible that her mission was taking place, at least partially, in Linda Land.

As Linda was busy scouring the ship, her tongue was busy exploring her back molars, desperately trying to remove the peanut butter that was stuck there from her snack. The thing with peanut butter was that although it was delicious, it was annoyingly sticky and difficult to eat. It didn't seem to matter how much water she drank, the peanut butter prevailed. With agonizing effort, a light bulb slowly started to flicker inside Linda's brain. On and off, and then on again. It repeated this pattern several times until, finally, the filament heated up just enough to emit a soft glow. "Aha!" she exclaimed victoriously.

Larv was very worried. The Mabitu was too busy flying the ship to pay attention to was what happening behind it. If it had turned around, it would have seen Linda furiously spooning peanut butter out of the jar and into a backpack. Four large jars of peanut butter later and the backpack was half-full.

"That should do it," she said, admiring her work. "Alright Larv, hop in!"

"You cannot be serious," he responded.

"Come now, it's not a fashion show," Linda said, clapping for him to hurry up. "Sheesh, teenagers these days."

Larv didn't move. Linda carried the backpack over to him. "There you go, now be a good lad and climb in."

When Larv continued to refuse, Linda took a deep breath, and sang the loudest, highest soprano note she could.

"Ahhhh! Stop!" Larv squealed, writhing in pain.

Linda continued to sing. "Geh-eh-et ih-ih-in the baaaaag," she sang to the tune of the "Queen of the Night aria."

"No!" Larv Protested.

To the tune of "O mio babbino caro," she sang, "Yooouu will feeeel much better if you get in thhhheeeeee baaaag!"

Suddenly there was silence. The Mabitu wondered what was going on behind it. Slowly, it turned around and saw the most ridiculous sight. There sat a defeated, but reluctantly relieved, Larv poking out the top of a backpack that Linda was now wearing, peanut butter running down the sides.

"What the—" started the Mabitu. Then, it looked past Linda and Larv and saw the mess Linda had made in her search. "Bish, what did you do to my ship?!"

Before Linda could answer, they were interrupted by the beeping sound of Larv's holodex. "I need to answer this," he squeaked. "It could be President Ibo." The only problem was that the holodex was on his forelimb, which was currently submerged in peanut butter. "Help!"

Linda set down the backpack and pulled Larv's arm out of the peanut butter. It made a smacking sound as his arm was freed from the suction. Linda found a paper towel and wiped off the peanut butter as best as she could. Larv answered the call and a splotchy hologram of Arec Ibo appeared.

"Hello? Are you there?" Ibo asked. He couldn't see Larv because the camera was still covered in peanut butter. Linda wiped more if it away.

"I'm here, President Ibo," Larv replied.

"What's wrong with your camera? You look blurry."

"It's a long story," Larv sighed.

"Well, we haven't got the time for that. I have important news. Are you in a secure location?"

"Yes, sir."

"It turns out that our chief scientist has gone off to work for Schmoodler," Ibo announced. "Do no contact her. If she tries to contact you, do not respond!"

Larv was shocked. He didn't know Troodly personally, but he had heard great things about her. "Understood, sir," he responded.

Ibo continued, "Unfortunately, she sabotaged a mission to measure planetary orbitals. All inner planets of the solar system have been destroyed."

Larv didn't know what to say. He looked over at Linda sympathetically.

"You mean . . . Earth is gone?" she asked.

"That's correct," Ibo replied. "I'm sorry for your loss."

Linda was stunned into silence as her brain hesitantly tried to absorb this information.

"Thankfully," Ibo continued, "you have the UPT."

Larv cringed, and then tried to say something, but Ibo cut him off.

"It's the only piece of evidence we have left to prove our case for universal de-tuning. It's imperative that you get it to the Molasses Planet as soon as possible."

"Right, about that—" Larv began, but this time, it was Linda who cut him off.

"Yes, Mr. President. We're on our way there now," she lied.

"Wonderful," replied Ibo. "That's the only good news I've heard all day. I appreciate your continued dedication to the PUE. I must go now and deal with this Troodly situation. I'm glad I can count on you two. Thank you."

Before Linda or Larv could reply, Ibo's image disappeared back into Larv's sticky device.

"What was that all about?!" Larv asked. "You just lied to the president of the Protectors of the Universal Environment!"

"I did not lie." Linda protested. "We'll get that UPT back."

"How can you be so sure?" Larv fretted. "What if it falls into the wrong hands? It probably already is in the wrong hands. How else did it magically board that astrobarge?!"

"You know what, Larv? I just lost my planet. My home, my supply of tea, Daisy's Diner, Aunt Norma, my choir. All gone. Poof. Nothing left," Linda lamented. "I have literally nothing to lose. I will do everything in my power to get that darn UPT back, if it's the last thing I do!"

Larv was doubtful. "So, what? Are you going to jump onto that astrobarge and hijack it? Huh? Even if you were able to get in somehow, what are the chances you would be able to find the UPT?"

"Hey! Would both of you SHUT UP?!" The Mabitu shouted with its three voices forming a scary-sounding diminished chord.

Linda and Larv stopped and stared at the Mabitu.

"We're definitely not going to get that UPT back if you two keep bickering like an old married couple!" it scolded. "The barge is heading towards planet

Oodle. That's only an hour away. We can follow it there and then get the UPT. It'll be easier than trying to board."

"How do you know it's going there?" asked Larv.

"Take a look," the Mabitu said, pointing out the window.

Larv and Linda both saw the LED sign on the side of the ship, located just above the third breast of an alien model in another horrifically inappropriate AntiPro™ advertisement. The following message scrolled across the sign:

*** * * RTE 379 – NLBY TO OODLE * * ***

"Do either of you know what day it is on Oodle?" Asked the Mabitu.

Larv checked his holodex. "It's Sunday, why?"

"Oodleans are very routine creatures. They have certain rituals for each day of the week. If we know what they're doing today, then it'll be easier for us to blend in. And it just so happens that Sundays are oodlean Mass days."

"What does that mean?" Linda asked.

"It means that Schmoodler will be there, doing his whole reverend bit," the Mabitu explained. "All the oodleans will be crowded together listening to him and chanting. It's like a weird cult thing. This should make it easier for us to slip in and out unnoticed though."

"Wait a minute," Linda said. "How are you supposed to go unnoticed? Won't they sense your pheromones and get all hot and bothered, like what happened on Nilleby?"

"No time like the present to test this out," the Mabitu said, holding up the bottle of antidote they'd stolen from the chemist.

"Oh, Mab, I don't know if that's a good idea . . . what if it doesn't work?"

"Then I'll provide a distraction while you two find the UPT."

"What if you take too much?" Linda worried. "Can you overdose on that stuff?"

The Mabitu inspected the bottle, searching for dosage instructions, but none were to be found. *That's what you get for custom ordering illegal drugs from a sketchy chemist on Nilleby*, it thought. "I'll start with just a tiny drop, and we can bring the bottle with us if I need to take more. We can put it in the backpack with Larv."

"I guess that'll have to do," said Linda.

"Wait a minute," Larv chimed in. "How are we going to blend in with oodleans?!"

Once again, the light bulb in Linda's brain flickered on and a thoughtful grin spread across her thin lips. "I have an idea."

* * *

"This was a terrible idea," Larv squeaked from underneath the cloak Linda had fashioned from the canvas-like material she'd found in the spaceship. All her practice sewing costumes for choir had come in handy after all.

"Remember," said the Mabitu, "you can't walk in a straight line. You have to twirl like an oodlean. I hope you've been practicing your runway walk."

"Piece of cake," Linda said. "I do choreography all the time in my show choir. Linda paused. "I used to, that is, before they were all blown to smithereens. Well then, I guess that makes me the best dancer alive."

"Best *human* dancer," the Mabitu corrected.

Linda managed to twirl three times before tripping over her tentacles that she'd made from the tubing she'd found in the ship. She staggered to her left, and then to her right, and then fell on her rotund rump, nearly ejecting Larv from the backpack. The suction of the peanut butter was the only thing that saved him.

"We're all going to die," mumbled Larv, whose mood had taken a turn for a worse since sprouting the painful hair cell. He was also feeling frustrated that he was stuck in the backpack and no longer in control of his own fate. He suspected that even if he was not in the backpack, his wings were more or less useless now. The fact that he would spend the rest of his life—assuming they made it off Oodle alive—confined to a gooey prison was utterly depressing. The pupation hormones were not helping his mood either.

The Mabitu had its own anxieties about the mission, namely finding out if the antidote worked. It was, however, trying to hold it together and appear confident for Linda and Larv. It had managed to land their spaceship in a small clearing in an oodlean forest that provided them just enough cover to go unnoticed, but was also close enough to Schmoodler's megachurch that they could walk there (and run all the way back to the ship, if need be). Luckily, all of the oodleans would be wearing their ceremonial cloaks, which blocked their 360-degree vision. This was a very good thing indeed, the Mabitu realized as it watched Linda fall to the ground. It helped Linda back to her feet.

"Try spotting. It'll help with the dizziness," the Mabitu advised.

Linda stared blankly ahead as though she hadn't heard a thing.

"It's when you try to keep your eyes focused on one spot as you twirl—"

"I know what spotting is," said Linda. "No need to Mab-splain."

The Mabitu laughed, making a strange sound that Linda had never heard before. She started to laugh at the sound of its laugh. Even grumpy Larv joined in, and his high-pitched squeal made Linda laugh even harder. Soon, they were all in hysterics, but no one knew if they were laughing at Linda's terrible joke, the sound of each other's laughs, or if they were all so anxious about their mission that they had completely lost it. Mostly likely, it was combination of all three.

When they finally managed to pull it together, the Mabitu pulled the purple vial out from somewhere within its effervescent aura. "I'd better take some of this now, before the oodleans catch a whiff of me." It nodded towards the bubbles that were slowly floating in the direction of the megachurch.

"Oh Mab, do be careful!" Linda pleaded. "You didn't see the ghastly state of that lab!"

With some effort, the Mabitu pulled the cork out of the vial and then gagged immediately. The potency of the odour coming from such a tiny container was as impressive as it was sickening. The scent soon wafted over to Linda and Larv, who had similar reactions.

"I knew it would have to be strong to cover up my pheromones," said the Mabitu, "but I never imagined anything this bad!"

"Good Lord, of all the horrible smells on Earth, nothing even remotely compares," said Linda.

"I'm glad it's my hearing that's extra sensitive and not my sense of smell," said Larv.

The Mabitu reached into the vial, pulled out a dropper, and then squeezed one tiny drop onto its outstretched tongue. As beautiful as the Mabitu was, the face it made in reaction to the taste was worse than someone taking a shot of Buckley's and chasing it with a lemon wedge. It certainly tasted awful, but would it work? "We'd better go now," it said. "I'm not sure how long the effects will last. I have a pretty fast metabolism, obviously." It flipped its imaginary hair.

"No need to brag about it," said Linda.

"Look," Larv said. "The bubbles!"

The stream of bubbles floating out of the Mabitu thinned. Linda watched as the last bubble floated away and vanished in the oodlean sky. She stared at the Mabitu for a while longer, waiting to see what would happen. No more bubbles appeared.

"I guess that means it's working," said the Mabitu's three voices as it handed the vial to Larv for safekeeping. "Let's go."

Larv cringed as he took the vial. Even though the cork was back in, the foul stench lingered. He shoved it deep into the peanut butter to block out the scent. Then, he was nearly flung from the backpack again as Linda followed the Mabitu into the forest with an unsteady twirl.

The trees of planet Oodle, if you could call them that, bore a strange resemblance to the oodleans themselves. They had long, thin trunks, like palm trees, with wavy, tentacle-like leaves where the fronds would be. Linda observed one such tree and thought it looked like a long skewer with an octopus on top. Was it her imagination, or were the leaves moving? It wasn't windy down on the forest floor, but maybe there was a slight breeze blowing through the treetops. The strangest thing about the leaves was that they glistened, as though they were coated in slime. It wasn't until Linda stepped on a freshly fallen leaf that she realized they really *were* coated in slime. Where did all the slime come from? As though in response to Linda's thoughts, something dropped to the ground with a soft thud to her left. She turned, startled, but didn't see what had made the noise. She heard another thud, this time to her right, and then another directly in front of her. Finally, she spotted the source of the noise. It looked like a wriggling sea cucumber falling to the ground. She looked up and saw hundreds of them precariously dangling from the treetops on long strings of slime that stretched thin and threatened to break. The top of her head instinctively started to tingle in anticipation of one of them dropping on her. "What *are* those?" she asked, covering her head.

"Woodlerms," the Mabitu responded. "Don't worry, they're harmless."

"Woodlerms? Why are they dropping out of the trees?" Linda asked.

"Why does a bird fly in the sky? What does a fish swim in the sea? It's just their natural habitat." The Mabitu was proud of itself for making a reference that the earthling would understand.

"They're disgusting!" Linda complained.

"The oodleans don't think so. Ever wonder why their mouths evolved to be on the tops of their heads?"

Linda thought about it for a moment. "Oh god! They eat those things?"

"By the dozen."

"Yuck!" Right on cue, an especially juicy woodlerm landed on Linda's head with a plop. She screamed and wildly swatted at the creepy crawly. The Mabitu chuckled and sped on ahead. Linda had to run to catch up, ducking and dodging the disgusting danglers. She was no longer twirling. There were no oodleans around to see her anyway.

As they trudged deeper into the thicket, the ground was covered in wriggling woodlerms and slimy leaves. Linda cringed. To ease her mind, she imagined she was walking on giant spaghetti noodles instead. She had always wondered, after all, what it would be like to swim in a pool full of spaghetti. What if she were to try twirling again? Would she be like a giant fork and gather up all the noodles? For the first time in a long time, the practical side of Linda's brain won the battle with the fantasy side, and she fought the temptation to try it out. This did not stop her, however, from *imagining* herself spinning around in the noodly leaves and becoming hopelessly tangled up until she fell over, unable to move. She giggled at the thought.

"What's so funny?" asked Larv.

Linda nearly had a heart attack at the sound of his voice. She had forgotten that he was still strapped to her back. "Oh nothing," she responded. "Just this whole situation, I suppose."

Larv didn't understand what could possibly be funny about their situation.

Linda continued, "If you told me a week ago that I'd be here today, on a foreign planet, traipsing through a forest full of slime trees and woodlerms with a giant dragonfly strapped to my back, I would've said you were crazy."

"What's a dragonfly?" asked Larv.

At this, Linda giggled some more.

The Mabitu, who was a good twenty feet ahead of them, suddenly turned around. "Shhh!" it whispered. "We're getting close."

Even through the peanut butter, Larv's newly sprouted hair cell was picking up a sound, which, if he had been from Earth, he would have compared to the sound made by a large group of disgruntled turkeys. As they got closer, he discerned that it was a large group of oodleans, all saying "oodle" over and over again, as fast as they could.

"What in the world is that?" asked Linda.

"This is the cult I was telling you about," said the Mabitu. "They worship the word 'oodle' and they believe that the more they say it, the more likely they are to have a good afterlife, or something like that."

"How ridiculous!" said Linda. Then she asked, "How is it that you know so much about other species?"

"When you can't go out in public without getting mobbed, you have to do something to pass the time alone," the Mabitu explained. "I've spent most of my life studying all of the creatures of the universe—sort of living vicariously through them."

"*All* of the creatures?" Linda asked, amazed.

"All of the sentient beings, I should say," the Mabitu corrected.

"Still, there have got to be millions of them!" Linda exclaimed.

"About eight billion, actually."

Linda couldn't believe it. How long would it take to study eight billion different species? Eight billion different cultures, habits, rituals, biological features? It even knew Larv's life cycle! "How old are you?!" she asked.

"Psh, rude!" the Mabitu joked. "All you need to know is that I look fabulous for my age." It flipped its non-existent hair enthusiastically. As it tossed its head to the side, it noticed movement. "Look!" it said, pointing to the edge of the tree line.

Linda caught her first glimpse of an oodlean. It was wearing a cloak that encircled its entire body with a large Dracula-like collar protruding from the top. The collar was so high that she couldn't see its eyes, which meant that it couldn't see her. The only parts of the oodlean's body she could actually see were a couple of inches of tentacle that poked out from under the cloak. They were even slimier than the leaves.

"We need a better vantage point," said the Mabitu. "This way."

It led Linda up a small hill that overlooked the megachurch, which was more like an outdoor stadium than a church. They hid behind a rock and peered over the edge. There were thousands of oodleans packed tightly into the large field. In front of them was a large bandshell and an impressive-looking sound system. Linda took off her backpack and held it up so Larv could see.

"There are so many of them," said Larv. "How are we going to find the UPT?"

"The UPT came from Nilleby, so it's likely that whoever has it is not an oodlean," said the Mabitu. "They should stick out like a sore thumb." The Mabitu was once again proud of itself for correctly using a human idiom.

The three of them scanned the crowd, searching for a foreigner. It was a real-life game of *Where's Waldo*. Linda could barely make out the individuals on the far side of the field, closer to the stage.

Suddenly, a poorly synthesized church bell effect rang out from the large speakers. The oodleans immediately stopped making their turkey noises and gathered in as close as they could to the stage. Linda could see movement on the stage but could not make out what was happening. Then, a huge screen on the left side of the stage lit up and showed a large rotund oodlean twirl up to a podium. Unlike the other oodleans, who were all wearing black, this one was wearing a white cloak with gold stitching that shone bright in the stage lights. His collar was taller than the rest, but it only went half-way around his head, so three of his seven eyes were visible. The inside of the collar had gold stitching in the shape of the symbol of the Oodle.

"Groodle Schmoodler," whispered the Mabitu.

"Looks like he's trying to be the pope," Linda said.

"He thinks he *is* the pope," the Mabitu replied.

When Schmoodler reached the podium, he opened a large leather-bound book, found his page, and then looked out across his captive audience. "Woodlelcoodlem moodle foodleoodlethfoodlel coodlengroodle-goodletoodleoodlen." His voice was not as turkey-like as the congregation had been. He sounded more like a frog with pneumonia as he spoke into the microphone dangling several feet above the mouth on top of his head. Unfortunately for the microphone, it was in the direct path of the viscous liquid that spewed forth from his cavernous oral cavity. The camera operator was trying desperately to avoid getting the mucous-covered mic in the picture on the big screen, but every once in a while, it popped into frame, and Linda could see the salivary stalactite hanging on for dear life. She looked over at the Mabitu, who had obviously seen it too, as it was making the same disgusted face it had made after tasting the antidote.

"What is with this place and slime?" said Linda.

"God, take a lozenge already," said the Mabitu, referring to Schmoodler.

"I wonder what he's saying," said Linda.

"'Welcome, my faithful congregation,'" the Mabitu translated. "'We are gathered here today to worship the almighty Oodle. Bla, bla, bla . . .' Nothing too interesting."

Linda looked at the Mabitu, awestruck. When it was studying all of the sentient beings in the universe, it learned all of their languages too?! How many languages did it know? Before she could ask, Larv spoke: "There it is!"

"What?" asked Linda.

"Where?" asked the Mabitu.

"The UPT!" said Larv. "I can't see it, but I can hear it. It sounds like it's coming from behind the stage."

"Let's go," said the Mabitu.

Linda slung Larv back onto her shoulders and covered him with her cloak, and they headed down towards the congregation.

# CHAPTER 24

## Troodly's First Day on the Job

Troodly sat in her highjacked escape pod, fidgeting restlessly. The plan was to fly to the wormline and meet with the construction foreman who was to be her new number two. However, she was a very efficient oodlean who could not sit idly in the escape pod waiting for it to take her to the site, so she decided to use the time to call the foreman instead. Because the pod was so small, the hologram of the angry-looking human was projected through the window and appeared to be floating outside the ship. He wore a yellow hard hat, faded blue jeans, and a stained undershirt that struggled to contain his protruding gut. Troodly wondered if he was pregnant, but then remembered that only female humans could carry offspring.

"Who's this?" he demanded.

"I'm Troodly, your new chief engineer." Troodly didn't like to waste time with small talk and pleasantries, so she got straight to the point. At least, she tried to. "I'd like you to brief me on all the details of—"

"Hold on," the foreman interrupted. "*You're* the new engineer?"

"Yes, as I was saying, I need to know the specs—"

"But you're a—"

"Yes, I'm an oodlea—"

"Female!" the foreman interrupted again.

Troodly was no stranger to misogyny in her line of work, but in this day and age, most men at least tried to hide it.

"Astute observation," she said. "Why don't you pretend I'm a man, if that's easier for you, and tell me about the project?"

While the foreman mansplained the project in agonizing detail—even incorrectly detailing the physics of a wormhole to the very scientist who had created the first computer model of one—Troodly multitasked like a boss. By the time he finished talking at her in his slow, condescending tone, she had input the data into her wormhole model, which calculated the space-time dimensions of the other end of the wormhole. Upon seeing the results, a slow smile spread across the top of her head.

Misinterpreting Troodly's smile for confusion, the foreman said, "Miss Troodly, this is very complicated stuff, I suggest you pay closer attention. I'll start from the beginning again."

"That won't be necessary," Troodly responded, ending the call with the swipe of a tentacle. The hologram froze for a split second before disappearing, allowing Troodly to see the offended look on the foreman's prickly face. She didn't often pay attention to the emotional responses of others, but this particular one gave her an unexpected sense of satisfaction.

Shortly after ending the conversation with the foreman, Troodly's escape pod approached the Ellis Wormhole just as the needle on the fuel gauge hit zero. Once she was close enough, she turned off the engine and let the gravitational pull of the wormhole do the work. She would only need to apply a few bursts from the oxygen tank to steer her towards the station on the side of the giant ring that held the wormline open. As she prepared for this maneuver, she thought about the patronizing foreman waiting for her inside the station. The thought of meeting him in person was not a pleasant one. She decided right then and there that she'd rather not. She let go of the controls and sat back as gravity pulled her escape pod into the wormline.

* * *

Troodly popped out of the wormline and plunged into the orange atmosphere much the same way her predecessor, Choodlen, had. The difference was that she was sitting safely in an escape pod. It is true that the escape pod was out of fuel, but luckily, she'd made her decision to enter the wormline before wasting her oxygen bursts directing herself to the station where that dreadful foreman was busy thinking up ways to chastise her for hanging up on him. She now had just enough oxygen left to break her fall, but she would have to be very careful.

She watched the numbers on her digital altimeter decrease rapidly.

10,000 meters.

The numbers in the ones and tens columns changed so quickly she couldn't even read them. The hundreds column ticked by like the seconds on a clock.

5,000 meters.

One of Troodly's tentacle-like appendages hovered over the large blue button that, when pressed, would cause pressurized oxygen to shoot out of the ship with extreme force.

2,500 meters.

While most of her eyes focused on the altimeter, two of them looked out the window, watching the orange sky pass by in a blur.

1,000 meters.

The two eyes looking out the window were temporarily blinded by a bright light reflecting off a metallic surface from the giant trash heap. This caused all seven of her eyes to reflexively blink. When they opened again, the altimeter read 500 meters. In the time it took Troodly to react, press the button, and release the oxygen, she was a mere 100 meters above the surface. Still too far for the burst to have much of an effect. She continued to press the button in short bursts until she could feel the force of the oxygen hitting the ground. She then held the button down, causing a continuous flow of oxygen that created a cushion between the escape pod and the ground.

Continuous, that is, until the oxygen ran out. By that point, she was about twenty meters above the ground, and the pod plummeted down with the full force of gravity. The impact crumpled the pod's landing gear and gave Troodly some minor whiplash, but she was otherwise fine. It was the best landing that could be expected in a fuel-less escape pod. She opened the hatch, jumped down from the pod, and stretched all seven limbs out wide. Her joints creaked and popped, not only from the abrupt landing, but simply from being cramped in the small escape pod for several hours.

She surveyed the landscape in all directions simultaneously. On one side of her was the massive metallic mountain that glittered in the light of whatever star this planet revolved around. On the other side, a wide open plain of orange sand expanded for several kilometers before rising into multicoloured hills. Troodly couldn't make out the details from this distance, but she surmised the multicoloured effect was due to various types of foliage growing on the hills. She decided there was no use trying to get around the trash heap, so she made her way towards the hills. Perhaps she would be able to see more from a hilltop.

The hills were farther than she had estimated. When she was halfway across the plain, they still seemed exhaustingly far away. Orange sand stuck to the slime on her tentacles, chafing with every twirl. Her digestive cavity grumbled, and she remembered the noodles she'd sent that intern to fetch for her—what was his name? Something oddly human-like. Stewart? Shawn? Simon? Steve. Yes, that was it. She wondered what Steve was doing now. How had he reacted when he showed up to her office with the noodles and she was gone? She imagined how long he would spend looking for her before giving up. Judging by how keen he seemed, probably quite a while. Maybe he was still looking for her now. She laughed inwardly at the thought, temporarily forgetting how uncomfortable she was.

Troodly had no idea that Steve had told the president of the PUE that she was a traitor. She also had no idea that the shadow that had swept across the ground in front of her was not a swiftly moving cloud.

# CHAPTER 25

## Schmoodler's Megachurch

Presently, Linda found herself twirling slowly and carefully through a dense crowd of oodleans. Groodle Schmoodler continued to read from his "bible" onstage while the congregation stood transfixed on him. It seemed that his voice, as far from soothing as it was, lulled the crowd into a hypnotic state. This boded well for Linda—had they not been so focused on their reverend, surely it would be much more difficult for her to make her way backstage unnoticed. Looking down, Linda saw a tangle of tentacle tripping hazards that she had to be extra diligent to avoid. Despite her greatest efforts to blend in, when she inevitably bumped into an oodlean, the manners that had been ingrained into her brain from a young age caused her to reflexively say, "Excuse me; beg your pardon; I didn't see you there."

"Shhh!" Larv whispered from the backpack.

Neither Larv nor Linda could see the strange looks they had received from a few of the oodleans. Luckily, the crowd was so large and dense that they were soon swallowed up, out of sight of the suspicious few. The size and density of the crowd were both a blessing and curse, however. In order to avoid bumping into the oodleans, Linda had to twirl very slowly, and because of the slowness of her twirls, she kept losing sight of the Mabitu, who didn't seem to be having quite as much trouble as her. The Mabitu twirled with the skill and grace of a prima ballerina, and in no time at all, it had disappeared into the sea of cloaked tentacles.

"I've lost Mab," Linda whispered loudly.

"That's okay," Larv reassured her, "just keep heading to the back of the stage."

The sound of their voices attracted more unwanted looks, and even a "shoosh" from one of the oodleans. Linda twirled on, vaguely aware of the grotesque, raspy voice bellowing through the speakers. The combination of flinging around in the backpack and the lingering smell of the antidote mixed with peanut butter was starting to make Larv feel rather nauseated.

Soon, the raspy voice was replaced by chant-like singing led by a small choir on the stage. The crowd soon joined in. Trying to fit in, Linda joined in, too. Her warbling soprano voice pierced through the soft hum of the crowd like an unsuspecting foot stepping on a nail.

"Shut up!" Larv whispered, but Linda couldn't hear him over her own voice. He tried kicking her through the backpack instead, but his legs were stuck in the peanut butter.

The chanting of the crowd, which had started out in a very tight unison, started to fall apart. Larv, who had superb hearing, but presently could not see a thing, heard the collapse in synchronicity and knew they were doomed. The oodleans must have noticed Linda's warbling and were now coming after them. Why wasn't she running away? If only he still had the use of his wings, he could fly away to safety and leave this bumbling bag behind. Damn metamorphosis. Larv sat helplessly in his gooey prison and awaited capture.

Larv was unable to see that the musical mishap, shockingly, was not Linda's doing. Some of the oodleans were looking around, confused. Others appeared to be sniffing the air. A large group of them started to shift in the same direction, driven by an unseen force. Many of them had ceased chanting altogether, and those who continued were mumbling like drunkards, totally out of sync with each other. They had regressed back to their turkey-like ways.

Linda saw a bubble float up from the crowd about fifty feet ahead of her. "I found Mab!" she said, not comprehending the significance of the bubble. As she twirled her way towards the Mabitu, she noticed that it was getting easier for her to move around without bumping into people. She credited this newfound ease to an improvement in her own twirling ability. After all, she had been practicing spotting, and it now seemed to be working. What she did not realize was that the actual reason it was easier to move through the crowd was that the crowd was now moving in the same direction as her—in the direction of the Mabitu.

Soon, the chanting stopped altogether. Larv thought this was quite odd. He could hear the pitter-patter of soft, wet tentacles slapping the ground as the entire crowd began to move. Larv was reminded of a typical rainfall on his home planet. First, there are a few drops here and there. Then, the number of raindrops gradually increases until the individual drops can no longer be heard. The sound gets louder and louder until it reaches torrential downpour. In particular climates, this can turn into a full-on monsoon. Larv was hearing a similar progression in the smacking sound of the tentacles. But what did it mean? Were the oodleans running from something? He couldn't bear being in the dark any longer. He had to see what was going on out there. He lifted up Linda's cloak and peeked out. As suspected, he could see that the oodleans had begun moving. It was difficult to get a good look while Linda was twirling. Watching the herd whirl past him made him even dizzier than before. It was worse than the teacup ride at Disneyland North, which had recently been obliterated. Larv didn't know anything about that anyway. He was about to put the cloak back down when something caught his eye. Something in the sky. Was it a pie in the sky? Did he die? He had to wait for another rotation to see it again. Could it be? A third rotation confirmed it. It was a cluster of bubbles. Larv knew immediately what this meant.

"You need to get to the Mabitu, now!" he yelled to Linda.

"I'm twirling as fast as I can, Larv."

"Stop twirling, and just run!"

"But they'll notice us," Linda argued.

"No, they won't. They're after Mab!"

"What? How do you know?"

"The bubbles," Larv pointed. "The antidote is wearing off."

Linda finally realized the direness of their situation. Much like at the lab on Nilleby, she tapped into her inner football player and sprinted through the herd, knocking over oodleans like a linebacker on steroids.

Larv remembered that he had shoved the vial of antidote into the peanut butter and began searching frantically for it. It was difficult for his thin arms to move through the thick substance. The difficulty was amplified by the fact that his arms were getting weaker by the hour due to his forthcoming pupation.

Despite the fact that the mob of oodleans were increasing their speed as the pheromones increased in potency, it wasn't long before Linebacker Linda was at the front of the pack and could see the Mabitu, which had flung off its disguise in order to run faster.

"Mab!" she cried. It looked over its shoulder and saw Linda hurtling towards it.

"The vial!" it shouted. "Toss it to me, quickly!"

Linda reached her hand back, waiting for Larv to place the vial into it like a relay runner awaiting a baton. When she felt nothing, she shouted, "Larv, give me the vial!"

"I'm trying!" he cried. "It's stuck inside the peanut butter!" He continued searching with his arms and legs. He felt something hard brush against his foot. He plunged both arms down and grabbed hold of the vial. He pulled with all his might, but the surface tension was strong.

"Hurry up!" screamed the Mabitu, its voices clashing with each other in anxiety-provoking minor seconds.

Larv continued to tug, but it seemed as though he was pulling himself farther down, rather than lifting the vial up. *The Mabitu's going to get trampled, and it'll be all my fault!* He pushed the thought aside. *Push. That's it!* His feet were now touching the bottom of the backpack. He managed to get under the vial and push it up. The vial made a loud smacking noise as it broke the surface of the peanut butter. The problem now was that he was stuck. "Linda," he shouted, "reach back as far as you can."

Linda was losing steam. The Mabitu was much faster than her (and the oodleans, thankfully), and was far ahead of them. It turned and saw how far away she was. It couldn't risk going back to get the vial. "Forget about me—get the pitch pipe!" it shouted, then disappeared into the woods to circle back to the spaceship. Linda slowed down and tried to catch her breath. The rest of the mob seemed to slow as well. The Mabitu had managed to get far enough away that its pheromones were out of range of their vomeronasal organs.

Linda took the backpack off and opened it up to see only Larv's face poking out through the peanut butter. He was unable to move. The smelly vial was rolling around on his face. Linda couldn't help herself. She burst into a fit of laughter. Larv did not see the humour in his predicament.

"Help me before I drown in here!" he demanded.

"Death by peanut butter," Linda snorted. "I can think of worse ways to go." She put the sticky vial in her pocket, and then began scooping out some of the peanut butter to free the top half of Larv's body. She was careful to leave enough to keep his sensitive hair covered. Neither of them realized that there were now two hair cells that had sprouted, and a third was on its way.

Linda was about to sling the Bag-o-Larv back around her shoulders when she realized a circle of oodleans had formed around them. They had folded down their Dracula-like collars on their cloaks and were eyeing up the two foreigners. For the first time, Linda got a good look at the seven eyeballs that encircled the top of each oodlean's head. With that many eyeballs, it was truly amazing they hadn't been caught sooner.

The oodleans seemed confused, but curious. One of them examined the peanut butter on the ground. Another poked at Larv with one if its tentacles. Linda felt a moist tentacle pat the top of her head, sticking to her hair. *Not again*, she thought. Just when she had managed to get the alien goo from Nilleby out of her hair. The oodlean seemed to be just as grossed out by her hair as Linda was by its slime, and it jerked back its tentacle, taking some hair along with it.

"Ouch!" Linda shouted as several hairs were ripped from her scalp. The oodlean flailed about, trying to remove the hairs from its tentacles.

"Get it off me!" it screeched like a little girl who had walked into a spider web. The oodlean that had been inspecting the peanut butter was too pre-occupied tasting the delicacy to help its friend. The oodlean that had been poking at Larv scooped up some peanut butter and used it to remove the hairs from its panicked friend's tentacle. The hairs stuck to the peanut butter, which the oodlean then wiped onto the ground.

While all this was happening, another oodlean had noticed the plastic tubing under Linda's cloak and gave it a tug. The cloak came off, revealing the fleshy pink-ish alien underneath. The onlookers gasped. They had never seen a human before and began wondering aloud about this mysterious being.

"Where are all of its limbs?"

"They must have been torn off in a terrible accident."

"It only has two eyes! How can it see properly?"

"Is that tiny hole on the side of its head its mouth?"

"How can it eat without food leaking out?"

One of them noticed two droopy lumps on Linda's chest and figured those must have been the stumps of the missing limbs.

"What have we here?" a voice gurgled from the crowd. The oodleans cleared a path for Reverend Groodle Schmoodler. Linda saw the papal outfit twirling towards her and sputtered out the first lie she could think of.

"I'm terribly sorry to have interrupted your service, Reverend . . . er, Father. You see, we are antiquers. We are travelling around the universe looking to collect and trade antiques. We had to make an emergency landing on your planet. If we could just get a few parts for our ship, we'll be on our way."

Schmoodler knew she was lying. He recognized her from the video surveillance footage on Nilleby. Larv, on the other hand, was almost unrecognizable, covered in peanut butter, his wings now frail and shriveled. The only things that gave him away were his big, adorable yellow eyes. Schmoodler decided to humour them. "How terribly inconvenient that must have been for you," he rasped. "Take us to your ship, and we'll see what we can do to repair it."

Linda panicked. She couldn't take them back to the ship or they'd put the Mabitu at risk again. Then, she had an idea. "Thank you for your gracious hospitality. Our ship is just on the other side of the woods over there," she said, pointing in the opposite direction of their ship.

# CHAPTER 26

## A Trek Through the Woods

Linda marched through the oodlean woods, trying not to slip on the slimy leaves and woodlerms that covered the forest floor. At least she didn't have to twirl anymore or worry about tripping over her fake tentacles. Groodle Schmoodler and several other oodleans followed her, munching grotesquely on woodlerms as they dropped down from the treetops. She desperately tried to think of a way to remove herself from this situation. She knew they weren't going to find their spaceship. How long could she go on, aimlessly leading these aliens through the forest? She might be able to outrun most of the oodleans for a short while, but her stamina was not what it once was. Furthermore, Schmoodler, who considered himself above trekking through the woods, rode on a motorized vehicle. Linda figured even if she could outrun it, she certainly couldn't outlast it.

The contraption looked like a cross between a Segway and a Roomba and was obviously designed by oodleans for oodleans. It moved in a twirling motion as it hovered over the ground, leaving enough space for tentacle danglage. It was as though Schmoodler was riding on a Frisbee that someone has thrown in slow motion. Linda giggled at the idea. She then imagined what would happen if the thing cranked up to a faster speed. Would the rate of twirl remain the same, and the forward motion simply increase? Or would the number of rotations per second also increase, causing him to twirl rapidly like a figure skater executing a spin? Would the centripetal force cause his tentacles to stick out, and then eventually send him flying? This image caused Linda's giggle to grow into a chuckle. She didn't notice the twenty-one oodlean eyes that were watching her suspiciously.

Larv moped in the backpack, which now contained half the amount of peanut butter. He had to slouch to keep his sensitive hair cells covered. He was rather uncomfortable. If he wasn't so worried about what Linda would do next, he might have felt a bit of relief given that he was no longer suffering extreme dizziness from her clumsy twirling. He might have also noticed that he could breathe easier without the cloak covering him and holding in the putrid smell of the antidote like an ungodly Dutch oven. The source of the smell was still there, though, as he had made sure to hide the antidote back in the peanut butter to ensure the oodleans wouldn't take it. In their current predicament, he wasn't sure if there was really any point in keeping it. He doubted they would ever see the Mabitu again. Nevertheless, he resisted the urge to toss the vile vial out of the backpack. The oodleans that twirled behind them caught whiffs of the antidote as it wafted by. They assumed the smell came from one or both of the foreigners that they were following, and they muttered amongst themselves about the foul-smelling creatures.

After what felt like hours, they happened upon an open meadow that was similar to the one in which the Mabitu had parked their spaceship. Linda was struck with an idea. It was time to play the old lady card. She jogged to the middle of the clearing and looked around frantically. She ran to the left, and to the right. She turned back towards the oodleans with her most convincing shocked and confused face. "I swear it was right here!" she exclaimed.

"I beg your pardon?" Schmoodler said.

"Our ship!" Linda shrieked. "It's gone! Someone must have taken it!"

A din broke out among the oodleans. Some complained that they had come all this way for nothing. Others pondered who would take their ship, and how. None of them questioned Linda's integrity (recall that almost the entirety of the oodlean species was gullible enough to follow Schmoodler's made-up religion).

"Silence!" Schmoodler bellowed. The oodleans froze immediately. "Are you certain this is the right spot?"

Linda took off the backpack and held it up so Larv could see the meadow. "This was the spot, wasn't it, Larv?" Larv looked around and saw that it most certainly was not the spot.

"Uhhh . . . . don't think—" he started to say.

"Just play along," Linda whispered to him while covering her mouth so the oodleans couldn't see. Larv paused and looked around some more. He wasn't sure what Linda was up to, but he went along with it.

"Oh yes, I'm positive it was right over there," he said pointing across the field. "See, right over there, where the grass has been flattened."

The oodleans followed his gaze. There wasn't really any flattened grass, but they could somehow see what he meant. "Oh yes, right over there," an oodlean said. "There's a divot from the landing gear."

The oodleans scattered across the field, chattering enthusiastically, and somehow finding evidence for the presence of the spaceship. Linda and Larv looked at each other and shrugged.

"Now what?" Larv whispered.

"I haven't thought that far ahead," Linda admitted.

Before they could come up with a plan, Groodle Schmoodler glided towards them on his spinning hoverboard-Frisbee thing. He had entered compassionate reverend mode and expressed his deepest sympathies for the loss of their ship. "When I find the miscreant that stole your ship, I'll make them pay."

"Oh, I'm sure that's not necessary—" Linda began.

"Nonsense! Thievery is not tolerated on my planet," Schmoodler insisted. "Now, where did you say you were heading before you landed here?"

Linda looked at Larv. In all truth, she wasn't quite sure where they had planned to go after this. What was their original plan? Why had Larv made the journey to Earth in the first place? Why had her peaceful, tea-drinking, crumpet-eating existence been uprooted so suddenly? Her sixty-five-year-old mind laboured to sort through the events of the last few days.

Larv saw her blank stare and covered for her. "I'm sorry, Mr. Schmoodler –"

"Reverend," Schmoodler interjected.

"*Reverend* Schmoodler," Larv corrected. "She's had a rough couple of days. Her home planet was recently destroyed."

"Mars?" Schmoodler asked.

"Close," Linda replied, coming out of her daze. "I'm from Earth."

"Ah yes," Schmoodler said. "I heard about the tragedy of your solar system. My condolences."

"Thank you," Linda said. "Now back to your original question." She gestured to Larv. "My friend here needs to return to his home planet Marmalade."

"Molasses," Larv corrected.

"Right." Linda continued: "You see, he is going through puberty, and once he finishes, he won't be able to survive in open air. We need to get him back ASAP or he'll die, like a fish out of water."

"My goodness!" Schmoodler said. "We wouldn't want that, now, would we?"

Linda and Larv shook their heads simultaneously.

"Luckily, you've happened upon the world's leader in intergalactic trade and travel," Schmoodler said. "I have ships travelling all throughout the universe. I'm sure I can find one that will take you to the Molasses Planet."

"That would be just wonderful!" Linda said. "Thank you so much for your generosity, good Reverend."

"Now, let's get out of these dreadful woods and back to civilization, shall we?"

They commenced the long march back to the megachurch from whence they came. This time, Linda and Larv trudged at the back of the pack, several feet behind the oodleans, and bickered.

"I don't trust him one bit," Larv said, "and I'm not going back to the Molasses Planet without the UPT."

"I don't think you have a choice, Larv," Linda replied. "If only you could see yourself."

"I don't care how I look. I feel fine," Larv retorted.

"You can't stay in that backpack forever," Linda reasoned.

Larv pleaded, "If we don't find the UPT, all of this will have been for nothing."

"Who knows how long it'll take to find us a ride," Linda said shrugging. "We could be here for a few days. We might be able to find it before we go, but even if we don't, we have to get you back."

Larv was silent. Deep down he knew she was right. However, he desperately wanted the motile part of his life cycle to have had meaning. What would he be able to do for the PUE once he was confined to the life-saving goo of his home planet? Then again, what could he possibly do while trapped in a backpack? "Even if I do get back to the Molasses Planet in time, where will *you* go?"

Linda hadn't even thought about herself. Earth was gone. Where *would* she go? She shook her head. "I don't know, Larv. I don't know."

* * *

Just as Linda's aching feet were about to give out, they finally reached Schmoodler's outdoor megachurch stadium. All she wanted was a hot bath and a nice cup of tea. A foot massage would be nice, too. Make it a full body massage, actually. She couldn't remember the last time she'd been pampered. Or could she? She recollected a hotel room on Sagana, where her old flame Ryp Comet had once taken her for a weekend getaway. He had magical hands that somehow knew exactly which muscles needed attention. He'd massaged her into a near coma. Oh, to be back there, young and in love. Linda became so lost in this delightful memory that she thought she could smell the scented candles Ryp had lit for ambience. What she actually smelled was the burning incense that had been placed all throughout the megachurch. The oodleans had lit the incense in order to ward off whatever evil spirit had caused their service to fall apart earlier.

Up ahead, a tall, thin figure appeared. Thin is not a strong enough word for its slenderness. Perhaps "wiry" would be a more accurate descriptor. Linda was not paying too much attention to it, as she was lost in her fantasy world. Also, her vision wasn't what it once was, and her glasses had disappeared somewhere on Nilleby. Her subconscious brain registered the blurry outline as a microphone stand that was probably moving because an oodlean roadie had cleared it off the stage and was carrying it to a storage room. As she got closer, however, her subconscious could no longer ignore the fact that the microphone stand was walking around unassisted. Her conscious mind was jolted back to present day, and she registered the fact that this was indeed a living creature, one which was neither human nor oodlean.

"Larv, look at this," she said, standing sideways so that they could both see. They watched as the creature approached Schmoodler and held out something shiny.

"The UPT!" Larv squeaked.

"What are they saying" Linda asked. Larv adjusted himself so that the tip of his hair cell was sticking out of the peanut butter, allowing him to eavesdrop.

"It asked Schmoodler for its reward," he said. "Something about how Nimbulus promised him currency units."

"Who's Nimbulus?" Linda asked.

"I don't know," Larv replied.

Linda marched over to Schmoodler and the wiry being, ignoring the ache in her feet. "Excuse me," she interrupted.

Schmoodler and the living mic stand turned to her and stared, shocked that this pile of pink flesh had the nerve to interrupt them.

"I believe that belongs to me." She held out her hand, waiting for Schmoodler to hand over the pitch pipe.

"I beg your pardon?" Schmoodler replied.

"Mr. Schmoodler—"

"Reverend," he interjected.

"*Reverend* Schmoodler, do you recall that we are antiquers? That artifact is mine. It's an ancient pitch pipe from my home planet. Now that Earth is gone, it's probably worth a small fortune. I'd like it back, please."

Schmoodler looked at her with a blank expression for a moment, and then burst into a fit of uncontrollable laughter. The sudden onset of this fit was like turning on a sprinkler. As he twirled around in place, streams of saliva jetted forth from his mouth and sprayed everyone in a ten-foot radius. Linda instinctively turned around to protect her face and inadvertently put Larv into the line of fire. He struggled to turn around and free his arms from the peanut butter, but he only succeeded to mix the saliva into the backpack and create a solution of peanut butter diluted with spit. Schmoodler's laughing fit stopped as suddenly as it had started.

"Very impressive, Ms. Pumpernickel," he said.

"How do you know my last name?" Linda asked.

"I know who you are. I know all about you. And I know that this is not an antique pitch pipe." He chuckled. "Very impressive story, though. Bravo." Schmoodler slapped two of his tentacles together in applause, splashing more goo at Linda. He held up the UPT. Linda lunged forward in an attempt to snatch it from his tentacle, but he dodged her.

"You greedy, selfish, disgusting creature!" she shouted. "Give that back to me! It's mine!"

Groodle Schmoodler looked directly into Linda's two eyes with all seven of his and dropped the UPT into his abominable gullet, swallowing loudly.

* * *

Back in the actual clearing that contained their highjacked spaceship, the Mabitu waited for Linda and Larv to show up. After nearly being mobbed by thousands of twirling oodleans, it had sprinted all the way here without looking back. What was taking them so long? It waited and waited, glimmering bubbles of irresistible pheromones floating off into the distance. It was only a matter of time until one of them popped in range of an oodlean and led it to the ship.

After what seemed like an eternity, the Mabitu accepted the fact that Linda and Larv were not going to show up. Linda was just too slow and out of shape to outrun the oodleans. Reluctantly, it fired up the engine and launched the small ship into a hover. It expertly maneuvered the ship just above the tree line to the edge of the clearing where Schmoodler's sermon had taken place. It was just in time to glimpse Linda and Larv being marched away by oodleans, thus confirming its fears. The Mabitu deliberated on how to proceed. Linda and Larv had saved its life from the mob on Nilleby and risked their own lives to steal the antidote from the chemist. There was no way it was going to abandon them. All it could do for now was watch from the safety of its spaceship and hope its pheromones would go undetected.

# CHAPTER 27

## T'wonnsi

Troodly was near exhaustion as she trekked through the orange desert, so when she saw a moving silhouette up ahead, she told herself it was just a mirage. The mirage seemed to be pecking at the ground. As she got closer, she saw that it was rather large. It wasn't until it flew away that she realized it was not a mirage. She approached the site where the gigantic bird had been and saw a spacesuit lying on the ground perfectly still. She figured the bird must have taken it from the mountain of garbage. Perhaps it was attracted to shiny things, like a crow.

"Don't move!"

Troodly nearly jumped out of her skin. Had the spacesuit just spoken to her? She must be really dehydrated. She twirled closer to it.

"Don't move!" the spacesuit repeated. "It can't see you if you don't move."

Troodly ignored its warning and continued to approach. She counted seven appendages on the suit. She stood over it and had to bend the top of her head down at an awkward angle to see inside the helmet. She was shocked to see a fellow oodlean. "Who are you?" she demanded, "and why are you wearing a spacesuit in this heat?"

Choodlen saw that Troodly was not suited up and had neither imploded nor exploded. He removed his helmet, moving slowly so as to not attract the attention of the bird. As soon as it was off, he rubbed his face vigorously with a tentacle. "Ahhh," he sighed. "You have no idea how long I've been waiting to do that."

"Why didn't you do it earlier?" Troodly asked.

"I wasn't sure if this planet's atmosphere was suitable for oodleans," he said.

"T'wonnsi's atmosphere is very similar to Oodle's. It's compatible with most carbonate life forms," Troodly explained.

"T'wonnsi?"

"Yes, T'wonnsi. You don't even know what planet you're on?" Troodly asked, sounding unintentionally condescending.

"I do now," replied the oodlean.

"Where's your ship?" Troodly looked around. "Did you crash-land?"

"This is going to sound rather strange to you," he said, "but I've travelled through space-time via wormline. I'm not entirely sure whether I'm in the past or the future."

Troodly put the pieces together. "You work for Schmoodler?"

"How did you know?" Choodlen asked, surprised.

"I also just came through the wormline," Troodly said.

"Are you from the Safety Board?"

"No. I'm ITCo's chief engineer for the wormline."

At this, Choodlen laughed. "You didn't last very long, did you?" He laughed some more.

"What do you mean?" Troodly asked, worried she'd met another chauvinist.

"Until last night, *I* was the chief engineer," Choodlen explained. "That is, until Schmoodler tossed me into the wormline. I'm guessing you met the same fate?"

Troodly understood now. He wasn't laughing at her; he was laughing because he was at his wit's end—and with good reason. He'd been marooned on this planet like a treasonous pirate. "Actually no, I came through voluntarily," she replied. "It seemed like a better option than meeting with that obnoxious foreman."

"Oh yes, that guy is most unpleasant," Choodlen agreed.

Troodly nodded.

"So, how do we get out of here?" Choodlen asked.

"I was going to ask you the same thing," Troodly admitted.

"You mean, you didn't come in a ship?" Choodlen asked, surprised.

"I came in an escape pod. I had a bit of a rough landing. It's no longer functional," Troodly said, matter-of-factly. She did not seem at all worried that they were trapped on this planet.

At this, Choodlen completely lost it. He laughed like a lunatic, rolling around in the orange sand. Troodly waited patiently for him to pull himself together. He continued laughing for much longer than Troodly considered an acceptable amount of time. It wasn't until a shadow swept over him that he stopped abruptly.

"It's back," he said. "Be absolutely still."

Troodly looked up and saw the enormous bird she'd originally thought was a mirage. It glided in a descending circle and then landed clumsily about fifteen feet away from them. It looked directly at them with one of its googly eyes, cocked its head, and then started voraciously pecking the ground. Yes, it was large, but Troodly didn't think it seemed particularly violent.

"It doesn't seem dangero—"

"Shhh!" Choodlen cut her off.

Troodly looked back at the oversized ostrich, which continued to peck aimlessly at the orange sand. "Has it tried to attack you?" she whispered.

"Not exactly, but it hasn't left me alone since I got here. I think I might've angered it."

"What did you do?"

"I landed on it." He described to her how he'd fallen through the orange atmosphere, accepting his imminent death, when his fall was broken by the pillow-like feathers.

"That bird saved your life," Troodly said. "Did you ever consider that maybe it was intentional?"

"Well—"

"Maybe it stuck around because it's fond of you," Troodly suggested.

Choodlen hadn't thought of that, but he didn't want to test it out in case he was correct in assuming that it wanted to eat him.

"I'd rather get eaten by that thing than wait around and die of dehydration," Troodly said. She had a point.

Troodly twirled toward the bird, which was now busying itself preening the feathers on its back. Because of this, it did not see her coming and was startled at her sudden presence. It jumped and let out a loud squawk. Choodlen cringed from a distance. Once the bird calmed down, Troodly continued towards it. It lowered its head to her level, and she reached out a tentacle for it to sniff. It turned its head around two hundred and seventy degrees. Troodly patted the tuft of bright feathers on the top of its head, her tentacle disappearing into the deep plumage. Hours of twirling through the sand had completely dried out her tentacle so it did not stick to the feathers. The bird seemed to enjoy the scalp massage and let out a soft cooing sound. Then, out of nowhere, it grabbed Troodly's tentacle with its beak. Choodlen watched in horror. He knew it. The bird was going to eat them both. Should he do something to try to save her? What could he possibly do?

The bird tossed Troodly into the air and she landed on its back. With two flaps of its enormous wings, it took off. The wind blew sand into Choodlen's face. He coughed and sputtered and watched helplessly as it soared swiftly towards the colourful hills in the distance. Where was it going? Was it taking her to its nest to feed its chicks? He didn't have time to ponder further, as a second bird came out of nowhere, tossed Choodlen onto its back, and flew off after Troodly's bird in one fell swoop.

Troodly was having the time of her life. She couldn't remember the last time she'd let loose and had fun. She had spent most of her adult life worrying about the fate of the universe and doing everything in her power to prevent Schmoodler from destroying it. For just a moment, she forgot about all that. She forgot about the four planets she had accidentally destroyed. She felt the breeze on her skin and allowed two of her tentacles to flap behind her while the other five clung tightly to the golden feathers. She looked down and watched the ground speed by. As her seven eyes gave her a 360-degree range of vision, she simultaneously watched the giant trash heap get smaller and smaller behind them and the colourful plants at the edge of the desert in front of them draw nearer. Soon, she could see that the plants were enormous. Flowers ranging in size from a small car to a house lined the hillside. The brightly coloured blooms included pinks, oranges, purples, yellows, reds, and blues. Was it her imagination, or were some of the flowers opening their petals wider in response to their presence? As if reading her mind, the bird dove down, reached out its long neck, and skimmed its beak across the exposed carpal of one of the larger flowers. It was drinking the nectar. This confirmed Troodly's hunch that it was not predatory.

By this time, Choodlen's bird had caught up to them and Troodly was able to get a better view of the second bird as it rolled its tongue into a straw shape and used it to slurp up the nectar. Behind them, she saw the flower petals close once they had passed.

"Did you see that?" she shouted over to Choodlen. "The flowers open in response to the birds. It's a type of symbiosis! These birds must be pollinators!" Choodlen didn't respond. She looked over and saw that all of his eyes were squeezed shut and he was clinging to the bird for dear life. Troodly laughed. "You're missing out!" she shouted. Choodlen didn't budge.

The birds continued to swoop down from flower to flower, weaving in and out of each other's paths. When their appetites were satisfied, they rose above the massive plants, giving Troodly an expansive view. Choodlen's eyes remained squeezed shut and he missed the picturesque scene. They summited the hill, and Troodly saw a city in the distance. She was both relieved to find a civilization that could help them and disappointed to be leaving the beautiful flower forest.

The city was not the booming metropolis one would find on most overdeveloped planets. There was not a skyscraper in sight. This city was a sprawl of small low-rise buildings and possibly even some single-family homes. For a moment, its primitive designed made Troodly worry that she was much farther in the past than she had calculated. Would their technology be advanced enough to get them back out of the wormline?

As they got closer, she could see that the buildings were constructed using a composite of the orange sand from the desert on the other side of the hill. This gave it a quaint, fairy-tale appearance, like a city made of sandcastles. The buildings, though varying in overall shape, all had rounded edges, a feature that made them seem cartoonish. Closer yet, she saw that the inhabitants were very skilled in their unique architectural style. Beautiful details and sculptures were carved into the sand. Troodly realized then that they were not primitive. They simply did not have the proper resources to build upwards. She had not seen any woody plants in the forest, only flowers with soft, albeit thick, stems. Many of these flowers lined the streets and decorated yards, enhancing the fairy tale image, but decoration was all they were good for. They were much too flimsy to use for construction.

There was one building that was larger than the rest. Although it was no more than five stories high, it stood out from its surroundings. Troodly wondered how the sand conglomerate was strong enough to make a five-storey building that was structurally sound. This building looked new and somehow more modern than the rest. The birds flew towards it and Troodly saw a metallic glimmer against the orange sand. They had taken metal from the giant pile of scraps that had fallen through the wormline! They were a resourceful bunch, indeed. However, Troodly worried that if they continued using the metal to make larger buildings, they would take away from the city's charming aesthetic.

The birds dove down towards the fancy building, which turned out to be a hotel and convention center. Choodlen chose this inopportune moment—they were in full divebomb mode—to open his eyes. He let out an impressively high-pitched scream and squeezed his eyes shut again. He didn't open them until he was sure they had landed. Once they did, he continued to squeeze bunches of feathers with all of his tentacles. He found it incredibly difficult to unclench his muscles and let go. He finally did and slid clumsily off the back of the bird and landed upside down on the hard ground. An upside-down oodlean is a rather comical site, as they instinctively invert their tentacles to prevent their eyes from hitting the ground. Presently, Choodlen's eyes and mouth were inches above the pavement and his undercarriage was thrust into the air. Once this position is assumed, it is quite difficult for the oodlean to right itself. Luckily for Choodlen, Troodly noticed his predicament and came to his assistance.

With everyone right-side-up, they looked around and saw that they were indeed standing near the entrance of the conference center. The birds ran up to a young boy who was loitering on the front steps. The boy seemed happy to see them. He stood up and ran towards one of the birds, arms spread wide as though he were going to give it a big hug. However, right before contact, he stopped suddenly, threw his arms and head forwards, and took small quick steps backwards. It is important to note that this boy was human, or at least rather anthropomorphic in shape and size. The bird mimicked his movements. The bird and the boy then circled around each other, switched directions, and circled back. The boy stuck out his elbows and performed some sort of funky chicken dance move as the bird mirrored him. He then tilted his head to the right and then snaked it upwards. He repeated this motion to the left. The bird copied the movement, but in the opposite direction. They repeated this move as they slowly walked towards each other, until, finally, they met, and the boy threw his arms around the long, fluffy neck of the bird. He then repeated the whole song and dance with the other bird.

Troodly watched in fascination. They seemed to be performing some sort of ritualistic dance. It obviously wasn't a courtship dance, but similar. Maybe it was a friendship dance, or an exercise in building trust? She called the boy over to ask him about it. He was walking up to them when Choodlen grabbed one of Troodly's tentacles and turned her towards the window of the conference center. He pointed inside to where a meeting was taking place and asked, "Is that who I think it is?"

# CHAPTER 28

## Arec Ibo's Unexpected Visitor

Ann Ibo woke up, stretched, and reached for her husband, only to find that he wasn't there. "Arec?" she said in a foggy morning voice.

No response.

She sat up, rubbed her eyes, and found her slippers beside the bed. A silk robe hung from the door. She slipped it on and tied up the sash as she walked down the hallway. She squeezed past the edge of his desk that partially blocked the bedroom door and saw that Arec's high-backed office chair was facing away from the desk. Approaching it from behind, she could see a mound of cartilaginous flesh poking up above the headrest. This was just the tip of the iceberg. The rest of his impossibly large nose was hidden from view behind the chair. Ann watched as the mound rose and fell with each enormous breath that ebbed and flowed from its commodious nostrils. He must have fallen asleep there.

Ann knew that her husband had been having trouble sleeping ever since he'd received the UPT transmission from the larvalux, but hearing about Troodly's treason yesterday had really pushed him over the edge. He'd paced back and forth all afternoon, muttering to himself, and occasionally asking her why he'd been so naive as to appoint an oodlean as the chief scientist of the Protectors of the Universal Environment. Had she been spying on them all along and reporting back to Schmoodler? Had she destroyed those planets and trillions of lives on purpose? The thought sickened him.

Ann leaned over her sleeping husband's chair and gently kissed the tip of his colossal snout. It wasn't gently enough, though, as it startled the slumbering saganite wide awake. "Traitor!" he shouted and bolted upright, nearly nose-butting his wife in the process. He looked around, confused. It took an unreasonable amount of time for him to realize he was in his own living room, next to his awkwardly large desk.

"I'm sorry I woke you, darling," Ann said.

"What time is it?" Arec asked.

"Time for a cup of dizzle," Ann replied.

Arec sighed. "I still can't believe Troodly would do such a thing."

"It does seem very out of character," Ann agreed. "Who knows why she went to work for Schmoodler? Maybe she's up to something else."

Arec shook his head. "If she had some sort of plan to infiltrate Schmoodler, why didn't she tell me?"

"I don't know . . . maybe she didn't want to confront the whole exploding planets disaster."

Ann had a point, but Arec didn't want to give in to false hopes. He simply grunted and began pacing again. Ann left to brew the dizzle, a beverage that contained a chemical three times stronger than caffeine. When she returned, she suggested that he talk to some people and try to find out what was going on. Arec agreed and decided to call Nimbulus.

The holodex rang for an eternity before Nimbulus answered.

"You've done it again," said Ann while it was still ringing.

"Done what?" Arec grunted.

"Called Nimbulus in the middle of the night in his space-time zone."

She was right. Several light years away, a very grumpy Nimbulus was dragging together his bodily particles, a process similar to the re-formation of a shattered T-1000. The only difference was that they were gaseous particles joining together to form a cloud-like body, rather than liquid metal droplets joining together to form a solid, robotic killing machine.

Nimbulus had only been asleep for a couple of hours and was particularly slow to assemble himself. When he saw Arec Ibo's name displayed on his beeping holodex, he was jolted into a more alert state. He assumed Ibo would want an update on his progress collecting UPTs. He answered the call.

"Nimbulus!" Ibo shouted. "Where are you? I can't see you!"

"Turn around," Nimbulus said. Ibo did as he was told, and Nimbulus was shocked to see his two owl-like eyes looking even bigger and rounder than usual. They may have even upstaged his mountainous schnoz. "My God, Mr. President, what's wrong?"

"It's Troodly," he said with audible panic. "She's gone to work for Schmoodler." Ibo's body was vibrating, but it was unclear whether this was caused by his state of panic or the dizzle he was gulping back.

Nimbulus feigned surprise and concern. "You're telling me she blew up four planets and then went to work for Schmoodler?"

"Yes!" Ibo yelped.

Nimbulus tried his best not to sound too satisfied when he said, "My, my. I can't say I didn't warn you about hiring an oodlean."

Ibo was now pacing around his living room office. "Maybe she's spying on him and not us," he suggested.

"Unlikely," Nimbulus replied.

"So, you haven't heard anything about her through your contacts?"

"Not a peep."

"I just can't believe . . ." Ibo trailed off. He looked like he was about to cry.

"Now you listen to me," Nimbulus said in a slightly patronizing tone. "We have to cut our losses. Troodly is long gone, and you must accept it."

Ibo could not accept it. "What if she's in trouble? There is a chance she could be in danger!"

"Do you really think we should spend what little resources we have searching the universe for one missing oodlean on the off chance that she's not a traitor?"

Ibo's bulging, bloodshot eyes darted from side to side as he thought about it. "I don't think we have a choice."

Nimbulus feigned an exaggerated sigh to make his frustration audible. "I'll tell you what. I'll spread the word to my UPT retrieval team to keep an eye out for her."

"Thank you, Nimbulus. I really do appreciate that."

"Anything for the PUE, sir."

Ibo turned to looked back as though something had distracted him, and Nimbulus caught a glimpse of his side profile. He was reminded why, as a mistoform, he could not be in the same room as Ibo—the risk was too great that he could be accidentally inhaled by one of those god-forsaken nostrils. The thought was most unpleasant, and Nimbulus tried to push it out of his mind.

Ibo turned back towards the hologram of Nimbulus. "I've got to go. Someone's at the door."

At that, they both signed off. Nimbulus disassembled himself and went back to sleep, and Ibo and Ann went to answer the door, curious as to who the unexpected visitor might be.

"Maybe it's Troodly!" Ibo said, jittering from overstimulation.

"Don't get your hopes up, dear," Ann replied.

Ibo opened the door and his shoulders slumped in disappointment. Instead of Troodly, he saw an old man—an old human man, perhaps in his seventies. The old man looked up at Arec Ibo's face and his wrinkly eyes widened in alarm at the sight of the dishevelled saganite. He struggled to re-gain his composure.

"WHOAREYOUANDWHATDOYOUWANT!" Ibo demanded.

The old man staggered backwards and dropped his cane, as if blown back by the force of Ibo's voice. He bent over and reached towards the ground with one hand, trying desperately to grasp his cane while his other hand clutched his aching back. The effort was futile. He was unable to reach within a foot of where the cane had landed.

"Let me help you with that," Ann said and rushed to the old man's aid, looking back to glare at her husband for his rude outburst.

"Thank you, dear," the old man croaked as he took the cane and righted himself.

"What my husband meant to say was, how can we help you?"

The old man eyed both of them cautiously. "I'm looking for Arec Ibo," he said.

"I am he," Ibo said, giving his wife a puzzled look. Who was this man and how did he know where they lived?

The old man looked surprised. "So it *is* true," he muttered.

"What's true?" Ibo asked.

Ignoring the question, the old man reached inside his jacket and retrieved an envelope. "I have something for you. A message."

"A message? From whom?"

The old man grinned. "What you should be asking is 'from *when*?'"

Arec and Ann exchanged another confused glance.

The old man chuckled. "It's from Troodly."

At that, the Ibos invited the old man into their home and offered him a cup of dizzle. He took a sip of the potent potable and his pupils instantly dilated. He began talking immediately and did not stop for quite some time.

"When I was a boy, my family travelled around a lot. My father worked for ITCo, you see. It was a strange upbringing, never staying in the same place very long. I was always the new kid at school. I never had a chance to make any close friends. My family actually spent some time right here, on Sagana. This is where I made my first real friend, a fellow human by the name of Snodgester Slayneli. I used to call him 'The Snodgester.' Ah, he hated it when I called him that. He was the smartest man I've ever met—the smartest being of any kind, for that matter."

Despite his gigantic pupils, the old man had a far off look in his eyes. It was that far off look that old men get when they reminisce about the good old days. Arec Ibo wondered when he was going to get to the point. He needed to know what was going on with Troodly. Ann could sense his impatience and put her hand on his to prevent him from interrupting. The old man took another sip of his dizzle, and continued:

"The Snodgester became famous, ya know. You've probably heard of him. His stuff would be right up your alley. He made educational TV shows about the universe. Really great guy. Anyway, we stayed on Sagana for two years. I was devastated when ITCo reassigned my father yet again. I've always loved Sagana, though. I came back here as a young man. I thought about contacting you then, but it would have been too soon. Nothing would have made sense."

Ibo couldn't stay quiet after that mysterious sentence. "What do you mean, 'too soon?'"

"I meant that it would have been too soon to give you this message."

"You're telling me that you've been carrying around this message since you were a young man, and you're only giving it to me now?"

"Actually, I've had the message since I was twelve years old."

Ibo was perplexed. He looked at Ann. "When he was twelve years old, Troodly wouldn't have been born yet."

Ann shrugged.

Ibo continued, "There's no way she could have given him a message. Dammit!" He stood up in frustration. He had gotten his hopes up, but there was obviously some sort of misunderstanding. He looked back towards the old man. "I'm sorry, sir. There must be some sort of mistake."

"Perhaps you should sit down and let him finish," Ann said.

Ibo sighed and sunk into the loveseat beside his wife and waited impatiently for the old man to continue. The old man took his time, sipping his dizzle until his pupils were so dilated that his irises were nowhere to be seen.

"As I was saying, my family moved to a planet called T'wonnsi when I was twelve. This was where I met Troodly. My father was at a meeting with Tyg Schmydler and some of ITCo's other higher ups. I guess they were trying to negotiate some trade deal with this new planet. Having just moved there, I wasn't enrolled in school yet, so I had to go with pops to work. Of course, I wasn't allowed in the meeting, so I was hanging around outside. These meetings had been going on for days. Each day, while I was waiting outside of the convention center, I saw these huge birds that would come by. I passed the time watching the birds. They were nervous around me at first, but very curious. I saw that they greeted each other with a ritualistic dance. I learned the choreography, so to speak, and was able to gain their trust."

Ibo was once again getting impatient. "Where does Troodly come into the picture?" he asked, ignoring his wife's glare.

"Right, right. I'm getting carried away with the details," said the old man. "So, one day, the birds fly down to where I was, but this time, they're carrying two oodleans with them. They looked terrible—like they'd been in an accident. One of them was still wearing a spacesuit. They look into the window of the conference center where ITCo was holding its meeting and that's when she asked me . . ."

* * *

"Is that Groodle Schmoodler in there?"

"Who's Groodle Schmoodler?" the boy responded.

Troodly instantly knew something was off. The boy was young, but not so young that he wouldn't know who Groodle Schmoodler was. Everyone in the universe knew who Groodle Schmoodler was. She pointed through the window and asked, "Who is that oodlean in there?"

"What's an oodlean?" the boy asked.

"He doesn't even know what an oodlean is," Choodlen said. "There must be something seriously wrong with the education system on this planet. Come on, he won't be any help to us." Choodlen started to twirl away.

"Hold on a minute," Troodly said. She turned to the boy. "Do you know what species we are?"

"I think so," he said. "You're ydleans, right?"

"Oh my Oodle," Troodly said.

"So, I was right," said Choodlen. "They're education system is clearly very outdated."

Troodly ignored him and asked the boy, "Who is that ydlean in there?"

"That's Tyg Schmydler. I thought everyone knew that." He lowered his voice and said, "Don't tell anyone I said this, but I don't like him."

"You should meet his son," she responded.

"Son? He doesn't have a son. Trust me, I would know. My dad works for him. He's in there too. That's why I'm out here. I'm not allowed into their super secret meetings."

With that, Troodly's suspicions were confirmed. She was ecstatic. Her plan to save the planets she had destroyed might just work! She looked over at Choodlen, who appeared confused. "Don't you see what's going on here?" she asked.

Choodlen shrugged, "We've landed on a planet of idiots?"

"You're the idiot!" Troodly said. "The wormline sent us back in time!"

Choodlen still wasn't getting it. Troodly wondered how he had managed to work his way up to chief engineer. She continued: "Schmoodler hasn't been born yet! That's his father in there," she said, flailing a tentacle towards the window. "He ran ITCo before Schmoodler. The company's been in their family for generations."

"You mean, we're trapped in the past? How far back? What if they don't have the technology to get us back through the wormline?!"

"Relax," Troodly said. "I ran a simulation on my way here, but I wasn't sure how accurate the results were until now. The simulation estimated the wormline would take us about sixty years in the past, and judging by Schmydler's age, it was accurate. We'll be able to get back."

Choodlen looked panicked. "We better find a ship!" He turned to the boy. "Kid, do you know where we can get a spaceship around here?"

Before the boy could respond, Troodly interrupted, "Not so fast."

"What do you mean? Don't you want to get home?" Choodlen asked.

"I destroyed four planets last week, and then took a job with ITCo. If I go home now, I'll either be killed or arrested."

"That's not my problem!"

"Oh yes, it is!" Troodly rebutted. "Do you really think Schmoodler will want you blabbing about what he did to you?"

"I see your point," Choodlen replied, "but what's the alternative? Stay here forever?"

"We have a unique opportunity here," Troodly said. "We're in the *past*. Maybe we could change the course of history. Maybe I can fix my mistakes—save all those people on Earth and Mars."

"That would mean we would have to stay here until last week . . . our time—uh, the present time on the other side of the wormhole, I mean," Choodlen stammered. "I'm not staying here for sixty years!"

"That's not necessarily true," Troodly said, eyeing the bird whisperer.

"What's going on? Why are you looking at me?" the boy asked.

"Perhaps you would be willing to help us out," Troodly said.

"What do you have in mind?" asked the boy, surprised that someone his age could be helpful to adult scientists.

Troodly explained, "I need you to give a message to my future self."

"What? You mean you want to send me through a time portal or something?"

"No, nothing like that. I'm going to give you a letter. All you have to do is deliver it in sixty years from now, minus a week or so."

"You're saying that you want me to keep this letter until I'm—" the boy took a moment to do the mental math, "—seventy-two years old?"

"Precisely!"

"I don't know . . ." the boy hesitated. He knew firsthand that twelve-year-old boys aren't the most reliable. He lost things all the time, especially given how often his family moved. How could he take on such a big responsibility? What if he lost the letter?

"Listen," Troodly persuaded, "If you do this, you could save billions of lives." She told him all about the disaster that she had caused in the solar system and that, if he were to deliver this letter, he could prevent it from happening. He would be a hero.

Whether or not it was intentional, Troodly had said exactly the right thing to a twelve-year-old boy. He imagined himself in a superhero uniform with a mask that only covered his eyes, and a cape billowing behind him as he flew around the solar system saving people, one-by-one. He did not consider the fact that he would be a seventy-two-year-old hero and not look as good in spandex as he was imagining.

He agreed to take on the hero's responsibility of carrying a message for sixty years. Troodly ended up writing him not one, but two letters: one addressed to herself, and one addressed to Arec Ibo, the president of the PUE. She knew he would have learned of her decision to steal the escape pod and work for Schmoodler by now, and he was likely extremely confused about her motives. Furthermore, he might be able to send a ship to rescue her and Choodlen from this planet. Before she handed him the letters, she asked, "You said you don't like Tyg Schmydler, right?"

"That's right," the boy said, looking around to make sure no one was listening.

"Tell me why not," Troodly said.

He spoke quietly, but with purpose. "First of all, all he cares about is making money. He doesn't care who or what he harms in order to get it."

"The woodlerm doesn't fall far from the tree," Choodlen mumbled.

"Huh?" the boy asked.

"Ignore him," Troodly said flatly. "Please, continue."

The boy obliged. "One of my teachers told me that his company is destroying the environment with all the emissions from their giant spaceships. She also said something about how transporting so much matter from one planet to another can, like, put them off balance or something? I think she called it de-tuning. But worst of all, I hate how badly he treats my dad. He's always making us move. As soon as one planet starts feeling like home, my dad gets transferred to another. And I hate how my dad is turning into one of them. All he talks about anymore is money, and he agrees to all of the transfers so he can make more money. He says it's 'for the family,' but we don't care about all that money. We just want to live in one place." The boy looked up and was surprised at himself for spilling all his feelings to two complete strangers. "I'm sorry, I shouldn't have said all that."

"Why are you sorry?" Troodly asked, legitimately confused about the apology.

The boy shrugged and stared at the ground.

"You said exactly what I wanted to hear," Troodly said.

"I did?" he said, looking up.

"Yes. You've got the correct political mindset."

"I do?"

"*And* you're familiar with Sagana. You will make an acceptable messenger."

"I will?"

"Unquestionably," Troodly replied. Then, in a rare moment of sincerity she said, "As you get older, you will sometimes feel frustrated about the way the universe works and the greedy people in charge. When that happens, I want you to remember this moment. Remember that there are beings out there trying to save the universe. Remember that you are the one we entrusted to deliver these very important messages."

"Messages?" the boy asked. "You mean, there's more than one?"

Troodly handed him the letters. "This second letter is for Arec Ibo, President of the Protectors of the Universal Environment, or PUE. He is a good saganite. He has dedicated—*will* dedicate—his life to preventing universal de-tuning. We need his help to get back home. Deliver it on this day in sixty years, not sooner."

"Why not sooner?" he asked.

"Because if he receives the message sooner, he might travel back in time and rescue us before we've had the chance to meet you."

The boy looked puzzled at first, but Troodly saw the gears turning as he wrapped his mind around the time travel paradox. "Ohhh, I think I get it," he said.

"Remember, deliver this letter to me first," she said, pointing to the letter in his left hand, "and then make your way to Sagana to deliver this one to Arec Ibo," she said, pointing to the letter in his right hand. "Do you understand?"

"Yes ma'am," he answered solemnly, as the importance of his task really sunk in.

"Now if only there were something we could do about that situation," Troodly said, looking through the window at Tyg Schmydler.

# CHAPTER 29

## A Pair of Prisoners

After witnessing Groodle Schmoodler swallow Aunt Norma's pitch pipe—UPT, whatever the heck it was called—Linda's inner bull resurfaced for the third time in the past few days. Or was it weeks? So much had happened since leaving her peaceful existence on Earth that Linda had no concept of how much time had passed. All she knew was that the raging beast inside her had charged at Schmoodler and tackled him with almost enough force to dislodge the UPT from his digestive cavity. *Almost.* It was, however, more than enough force to dislodge Larv from the backpack full of peanut butter and send him flying. He crashed helplessly to the ground and watched in horror as one of his hind legs floated down and landed gently beside him. As gruesome as it sounds, Larv did not feel any pain from the dismemberment, as this was part of the natural process of his metamorphosis. The horror came from the knowledge that his ability to live outside of the Molasses Planet was quickly coming to an end. Up until this point, he had been more or less successfully living in denial of his cruel fate.

Presently, Linda and Larv found themselves locked in a metallic holding cell aboard one of Groodle Schmoodler's ships, which was headed for the Ellis Wormhole. Schmoodler had made them an offer they couldn't refuse—literally. They weren't given the option to refuse. He would let them go if they successfully completed the "safety test" for his wormline. In other words, he was going to send them through and see if they could a) survive, and b) find their way back. No matter the result, it was still a win for Schmoodler. If they made it back alive, he could report to the safety committee and get them off his back. If they didn't, then he was rid of two annoying environmental activists who were trying to destroy his business. Linda and Larv were going through that wormline whether they liked it or not. So, there they sat, locked in the holding cell awaiting their doom.

"Maybe the wormline will lead to the Molasses Planet," Linda said, trying to be optimistic.

"Maybe it'll lead to a black hole and kill us instantly," Larv responded.

"Come on, Larv. That kind of negative thinking isn't helpful."

"It's not negative," Larv said without expression. "I'd rather die quickly than wait for more of my limbs to fall off."

It just so happened that Larv was still in possession of the limb which contained his holodex. Its sudden beeping startled him. The lens was still partially covered in dried up peanut butter crusties, but it was clear enough to project a blurry 3D image of Arec Ibo.

"Mr. President!" he squeaked, feeling hopeful for the first time in a while.

"Agent Larvalux," Ibo responded. "I have news regarding Troodly. She's not a traitor, like I told you in my previous report. I repeat, Troodly is *not* a traitor!"

"That's good, but listen—" Larv began.

"We need to send a rescue mission to retrieve her. Your last report mentioned you had acquired a ship, and your location is the closest to hers. Your orders are to put the UPT retrieval on hold until you find Troodly." His voice was militant in its nasality.

Blurry though the image was, Larv could see President Ibo's massive pupils, which were giving his nose a run for its money. "Sir, I'm afraid I won't be of much help in Troodly's rescue."

"What do you mean?" Ibo asked frantically.

"Sir, we've been taken prisoner by Schmoodler. We're locked in a holding cell on his ship. Look." Larv pointed the camera of his holodex around the room so Ibo could see. Linda waved as it scanned past her.

"My God," Ibo said. "My rescue team needs rescuing."

"Yes, we do!" Linda chimed in. "He's going to send us through the wormline! He's using us to test it out, like guinea pigs!"

"What's a guinea pig?" Ibo asked.

"It's a cute, fluffy little animal on Earth. People keep them as pets . . . well they used to anyway. I guess they probably don't exist anymore."

Ibo turned around and Larv could hear another voice coming through the transmission. It was Ibo's wife, Ann. "Did you say he's sending you through the Ellis Wormline?" she asked.

"That's correct," Larv replied.

"That's great!" she replied.

"What do you mean?" Larv asked. "We could die!"

"Troodly went through the wormline!" Ann explained. "She's alive!"

"Huh?" Linda and Larv said in unison.

Arec and Ann explained how Troodly had gone through the wormline and landed on a planet sixty years in the past. They described the message they had received from the old man written by Troodly's current self sixty years ago.

"But how did the old man live long enough to give you the letter?" Linda asked.

"Weren't you listening?" Larv said, frustrated. "He was only twelve when Troodly gave him the letter."

It took several attempts to get Linda to understand, and it is uncertain whether she ever fully did. Regardless, Linda and Larv were instructed to go through the wormline (as if they had a choice), and then find Troodly on the other side. Ibo would send a rescue operation to retrieve all of them, but it may take a while. He wasn't sure how he would get a ship past Schmoodler's crew at the opening of the wormline.

* * *

Two giant birds were circling around the heap of metallic trash on T'wonnsi, searching for shiny knickknacks to decorate their respective holes. Twice already, Herman[6] had tugged items out from the middle of the heap, causing mini avalanches of clanking metal. The second time, Sherman[7] became rather irritable when he was nearly struck in the head with a sharp object. He had shouted obscenities at Herman and instructed him to only take things near the top of the pile. It had been about ten minutes since

---

6 *Struthio twonnsinia*: Empire *Carbonata*, Domain *Eukarya*, Kingdom *Animal*ia

7 *Struthio twonnsinia:* Empire *Carbonata*, Domain *Eukarya,* Kingdom *Animalia*

Sherman was nearly impaled, and he had just started to relax again when suddenly he heard a loud noise followed by a shrill "SQUAWK" from Herman.

Sherman instinctively dove down to avoid another avalanche. When no avalanche came, he flapped his great wings to make up the lost altitude and positioned himself alongside Herman. "Wot was that all about?" he asked.

"Bloody 'ell, it's 'appened again!" shouted Herman.

"Wot's 'appened again?" asked Sherman.

"Sometin's landed on me back! Dis one's 'eavier than the last," said Herman.

"Gave me quite the startle, that squawk o' yours," Sherman complained.

"Foreign objects landin' on me back gave *me* quite the startle!" Herman responded, obviously annoyed at Sherman.

"Alright, alright, no need to raise your voice then. All I'm sayin' is you needn't squawk so loudly next time. Nearly gave me a 'eart attack."

This made Herman even more annoyed. "It's an involuntary reflex, ya twit! I can't just turn it down."

"I'm not asking you to turn it down. Maybe just dial it back a bit."

"Dat's the same fing!"

"No it ain't. Turnin' down is turnin' down. Dialin' back is dialin' back."

"You're a bloody twit!"

"Right then, let's have a look." Sherman gave his mighty wings a flap and positioned himself slightly above Herman so that he could identify the object that had fallen from the sky onto his back. "Good lord!" He exclaimed. "Wot are the chances?"

"Wot is it?" demanded Herman.

"You've got anovuh alien on your back, I reckon."

"An alien? Is it the same as the last ones?"

"Oi don't fink so. Dis one seems to 'ave less legs."

"Where are all these bloody aliens comin' from?"

"Oi 'aven't a clue."

"Well Sherman, wot do you fink we should do wif it?"

"Oi reckon we take it into town, like we did wif the othahs."

"You're tellin' me you want to turn around and fly all the way back there?"

"Got any bettah ideas?"

Herman did not have any better ideas.

"Then it's decided. Besides, we can get some more nectah on our way." This idea seemed agreeable to Herman, and so the two of them veered left and headed back towards the city on the other side of the flower forest.

* * *

Clinging to the back of the giant bird, Linda heard Herman and Sherman's entire conversation, but to her, it sounded like a jumble of squabbles, squawks, and croaks. She didn't understand their language and had no clue what was going on. She couldn't stop thinking about Schmoodler laughing at her as she was sucked out of the hatch of his ship into the vacuum of space. The image stuck with her as she had tumbled helplessly through the wormline, bouncing off the polystyrozene walls until she was so dizzy she had passed out. The next thing she knew, she was in a free fall through an orange atmosphere. She had noticed she was wearing a backpack and thought that perhaps it was a parachute, so she had reached back and felt around for a rope to pull. She grasped onto something and gave a tug, only to realize that she'd just pulled off another one of Larv's legs. How had she forgotten the backpack with Larv and peanut butter? Wormline travel must have taken a toll on her already questionable mind. Next thing she knew, she had struck the soft, feathery back of the giant bird with considerable force. She was actually quite amazed that she hadn't killed it—or at the very least broken its back. But the bird seemed to be fine after some squabbling with its friend, and so Linda held tight and hoped for the best.

On very rare occasions, hoping for the best turns out in one's favour. It had worked twice in Linda's life. The first time was when she somehow managed to pass a math test in grade school that she had not properly prepared for. The second time was when she'd auditioned for her choir on a whim (it didn't take long for the director to realize the fortuity of Linda's success at the audition, as well as her own grave error in judgment in accepting Linda into the choir). The present situation became the third time that Linda hoped successfully. The bird took her and Larv directly to where Troodly, Choodlen, and the young boy were loitering outside the conference center. Troodly had just finished explaining to the boy where and when to deliver the two letters when Linda appeared.

"Excuse me, miss. You wouldn't happen to be Troodly, would you?" she asked.

Troodly looked surprised. "How did you —"

"I'm Linda, and this is Larv." Linda turned around to show her the dishevelled contents of her backpack. "Arec Ibo said we might find you here."

Troodly looked at the boy, then back at Linda, then back to the boy. "That was fast," she said to the boy. "Nice work!"

A wide grin spread across the boy's face as he realized that his future self was successful in delivering the letters. Linda looked at the boy and felt an overpowering sense of familiarity. "Have we met before?" she asked him.

"No, ma'am. I don't believe so," he responded.

Something about the way he spoke also seemed familiar to Linda. It was a strange accent, indeed, but she couldn't put her finger on it. She shrugged it off.

"Where's your ship?" Choodlen chimed in.

"What ship?" Linda asked.

"You said that Arec Ibo sent you here. You must be here to take us home, right?"

"Not exactly," Linda replied. She recounted her and Larv's capture by Groodle Schmoodler and how he'd forced them through the wormline. "It was pure luck that President Ibo called us when he did," she finished.

Choodlen's heart sank. He had been sure their rescue mission had arrived. "What are we going to do now?" he cried.

"I guess we'll just have to wait patiently until the real rescue mission gets here. At least they know that we're here now," Linda said, trying to console him.

"There's a better way we can pass the time," Troodly said. "Let's go somewhere we can talk."

They found a café not too far from the conference center and sat at a table in the back. The server asked for their drink orders. Linda refused to order anything after the episode at Garrick's Teahouse on Nilleby.

"I'll have an orange pekoe tea," the boy said.

"What did you just order?" Linda asked.

"An orange pekoe tea," he said. "It's a type of black tea made from the leaves of—"

"I know what it is," Linda interrupted. "They have actual, *normal* tea on this planet?"

"Yes, of course," the boy responded. "My dad says it's a big trade hub. That's why ITCo is having their conference here."

Linda was surprised that this quaint sandcastle city was a trade hub, but she happily believed the boy. She turned to the server. "On second thought, I'll have the orange pekoe as well."

Once the server had left to get their drinks, Larv chimed in weakly from the highchair that Linda had placed the backpack on. "What do you mean, ITCo is having a conference here?"

"This is what I brought you here to talk about," Troodly said. "Groodle Schmoodler's father is right over there in that conference center."

"His father?" Linda asked, surprised. "Isn't he a little bit old for conferences?"

"He is old in present day," Choodlen explained, "but remember, we've travelled back in time."

"Schmoodler hasn't been born yet," Troodly added.

"But we just saw him not two hours ago!" Linda argued.

"That was before we went through the wormline," Larv reminded her.

"Oh balderdash! I can't keep track of all this time travel mumbo jumbo," Linda said in frustration.

"The point is," Troodly said, "we're currently stuck in the past for the foreseeable future." Troodly ignored the puzzled look on Linda's face and continued. "We have a unique opportunity to do something useful . . . something that could make a difference to the future of the universe."

"Like what?" Larv asked.

Troodly thought for moment, then said, "ITCo was around before Schmoodler was born, obviously, they're having a meeting as we speak. And yes, Tyg Schmydler is greedy and corrupt, but we're not far enough in the past to do anything about that. We could, however, prevent the family business from continuing beyond Schmydler. We could put a halt to their family tree, so to speak."

"You mean, you want to kill Schmoodler's father?!" Linda shrieked.

"Shhh!" everyone else said, looking around to make sure no one else in the vicinity had heard.

"Are you crazy?!" Linda whispered. "I hate the Schmoodlers as much anyone else, but I'm no murderer!"

"No, I don't want to kill him," Troodly said, "but maybe there's something a little less violent we can do to prevent Schmoodler's birth."

The server arrived with their drinks, and everyone was dead silent. "Is everything okay here?" the server asked.

"Just fine, thanks," Linda replied, a little too enthusiastically.

"Is there anything else I can get you?" the server asked.

"No!" Choodlen snapped.

The server eyed them dubiously and walked away. Linda eyed her tea just as dubiously. She leaned over and smelled it. It smelled like orange pekoe tea. There was nothing she wanted more than to sip the steaming brew, but she was hesitant. She watched the young boy take a drink from his cup without concern. She observed him for a few minutes and saw that he was unaffected by the beverage. She finally decided it was safe and lifted the warm mug to her mouth. Just as the liquid was about to reach her yearning lips, she caught a whiff of an odour so offensive it made her gag. She looked down at her cup, but the odour was not coming from there. It came from her left, where Larv was sitting in his backpack. He was holding the vial that contained the antidote to the Mabitu's pheromones.

"Put that vile thing away!" Linda said. "I can't believe you still have that."

"I have an idea," he said.

"What on Earth are you talking about?" Linda asked.

Larv held up the vial as high as his feeble forelimbs would allow, and said, "We could use *this* to prevent Schmoodler's birth."

# CHAPTER 30
## The Shockwave

Somewhere outside the opening to the Ellis Wormline lurked a small spacecraft piloted by the Most Attractive Being in the Universe. The Mabitu had followed Schmoodler's ship all the way from planet Oodle and watched in horror as Linda and Larv were tossed in. Presently, it was debating whether or not to follow them in. The ship had left, but there were most certainly workers stationed in the maintenance structures attached to the sides of the portal. Would it be able to fly through without them noticing? Even if it did, what would happen inside the wormline? Where did it lead to? *When* did it lead to? Would its small spacecraft be destroyed? What were the chances that Linda and Larv were even alive? These were impossible questions to answer, and it was an impossible decision to make. The Mabitu flew back and forth indecisively.

As it circled around, contemplating its next move, the Mabitu suddenly saw—or heard—or felt—a strange, yet hauntingly familiar, sensation. The Mabitu had felt the same sensation once before in its incalculably long lifespan. It was centuries, maybe even millennia, ago, but the Mabitu recognized it immediately and with an abysmal sense of certainty.

*The shockwave.*

That's what the Mabitu called it, for lack of a better term. It was reminiscent of the shockwaves shown in films about atomic bombs in that it looked like a clear ripple passing by. The ripple expanded in all directions as far as the eye could see. Much like an atomic bomb, the Mabitu had the sense that this ripple destroyed everything in its path. But unlike a bomb, it then reassembled everything instantaneously. It was a difficult sensation to describe. All the Mabitu knew for sure was that it was exceedingly unpleasant, and that the universe had never been quite the same since. It had felt the shockwave pass through its perfect phosphorescent body, and then it had noticed the changes to the universe that followed. The Mabitu recalled seeing a blue AntiPro™ logo plastered to the side of a ship, but it was ninety-nine percent sure their logo had been red before. This and other subtle, yet seemingly inconsequential, differences had the Mabitu doubting its own memory. However, it wasn't long before it had noticed more substantial discrepancies. For example, the leading manufacturer of artificial atmosphere had changed from NitroGen to its previously obsolete competitor, AtmosHere. This shift, although more or less trivial in the grand scheme of things, was disappointing, as the Mabitu found the forced puns of the AtmosHere ads to be quite intolerable—for example, "An air of certainty" and "We don't make airors." It was also disappointing to those who had invested heavily in NitroGen and had since gone bankrupt.

The Mabitu had discovered the most extreme divergence from pre-shockwave time when it travelled to a planet only to find that it was inhabited by an entirely different species than before. It was a rather troubling experience, as the pre-shockwave species was one of the few in the universe that was immune to its pheromones. The post-shockwave species was not, and the Mabitu was forced to take off without refueling. This resulted in an extended stay on a nearby moon, where it had to make an emergency landing and wait for a fuel drum to be delivered. The Mabitu had yet to encounter the pre-shockwave species since the pre-shockwave time, and occasionally wondered if they even existed at all anymore. The thought disturbed the Mabitu, who assured itself that the universe was an enormous place, and they surely inhabited a different planet now.

There were countless other examples of disparities between the pre- and post-shockwave universes that the Mabitu could not explain. It hypothesized that the shockwave had vaporized everything in its path, and then put it back together—only it didn't put everything back together exactly the same way it was before. There were a few atoms out of place here and there. It was as though the fabrics of space and time had been ripped at the seams, and then sloppily stitched back together. And the most distressing thing was that no one else seemed to notice. Actually, no. The most distressing thing was that it had just happened again.

# CHAPTER 31

## The Plan

Back on the other side of the wormline, Larv held up the odiferous vial of pheromone antidote as the small café cleared. The server approached their table and began gagging and retching. When she managed to regain control of her spasming pharynx, she firmly asked them to leave. By this point, the damage had been done. The entire café was filled with the noxious fumes. A potential patron opened the door to enter, and then jumped back outside as though he had been pushed by an invisible force.

"Give me that thing!" Linda demanded. She grabbed the vial from Larv and shoved it back beneath the surface of the peanut butter. His arm made the illogical decision of staying attached to the vial, rather than his thorax. Linda, Larv, Troodly, Choodlen, and the boy evacuated the establishment along with the last few customers. Choodlen found a nearby trash can and casually emptied the contents of his stomach. The business would remain closed for cleaning for a further two weeks.

When they were all safely breathing clean air, Larv explained his intentions with the vial. "If this antidote is strong enough to quash the Mabitu's pheromones," he said, "then maybe it would be even more effective on another species."

"What's your point?" Linda asked, clueless.

"My point is, if we can somehow contaminate Tyg Schmydler with the antidote—"

"Then we could prevent Schmoodler's conception," Troodly finished his sentence. "Larv, that's actually a good idea." She paused for a second, calculating in her mind. "Schmoodler was born just over fifty-nine years ago, which means . . . he's going to be conceived some time in the next two weeks."

“That makes no sense whatsoever,” Linda interjected.

Troodly ignored her and continued to think out loud: “Would the antidote last long enough for a two-week margin of error . . .”

“It didn’t last very long for the Mabitu,” Larv said. “Is there a way we can make sure to contaminate him immediately before conception?”

“Oh, that Mabitu,” Linda mumbled under her breath, “always bragging about its ridiculously fast metabolism. We get it already, you’re naturally thin.”

“What did you just say?” Troodly asked.

“The Mabitu has a fast metabolism,” Larv replied, able to easily hear all of Linda’s mumblings.

“Much faster than an oodlean’s,” Troodly said. “So maybe it would work. If we can get Tyg Schmydler to swallow some of that antidote, his body will take several days to evacuate it completely.”

Choodlen chimed in. “As long as Schmoodler’s projected conception lies within the period of pheromone flatulence, it won’t happen. *No one* could procreate with that smell lingering.”

“It’s a long shot,” Larv said, “but it just might work.”

Linda, who had finally clued in, asked, “But how on Earth do we get him to drink the antidote?”

* * *

Not three hours later, Linda exited the bathroom of the suite they had rented in the very hotel hosting the ITCo conference. They had managed to convince the concierge that they were part of the conference and to put all of the room charges on ITCo’s tab. It wasn’t difficult given that two of them were oodleans and the boy’s father was an employee of ITCo. “Do you know who my father is?” Linda had heard him say. “His name is—” Someone sneezed so loudly that Linda didn’t quite catch the name of the boy’s father. It sounded sort of like omelette, which had made her chuckle. *We’re with Mr. Omelette’s party*, she’d thought.

“How do I look?” Linda asked as she modeled the stolen maid’s uniform for the rest of them. As luck would have it, the hotel was run by humans, which meant that Linda was the only one who could blend in disguised as an employee. It was up to her to carry out the plan—to deliver the payload, so to speak. The fate of the universe lay in her clumsy, pudgy little hands.

"A little older than the other maids working here," Choodlen started to say.

Troodly slapped a tentacle over his mouth. "That'll do just fine," she said. "Now you'd better hurry. The conference is about to adjourn for the day." She handed Linda the vial, which she had cleaned of peanut butter, and ensured was sealed properly to avoid another café disaster.

Linda placed the vial in the pocket of her apron. "Wish me luck," she said, and then headed down the hall towards the elevator. The plan was to follow Schmydler back to his room and offer him room service. She would recommend the strongest drink on the menu—an extremely pungent selection from Garrick's line of high-end exotic liqueurs called Spü (yes, the same Garrick that made Linda's tea back on Nilleby). The description on the back of the bottle read as follows:

> *Made from the fermented remains of crustaceans from the sulfurous seas of Sagana and aged three millennia inside the shell of a mummified cochlean, this undignified liqueur is not for the faint of heart. Only the most refined pallet can appreciate the complexity of flavours that burst forth from the bottle immediately upon uncorking and continue to wreak havoc on the senses long after consumption. Harsh notes of peat, seaweed, skunk, and durian colour this delicacy, ensuring a flavour experience not soon forgotten.*

The description more or less matched the smell of the antidote, so, in theory, Linda would be able to pour the vial into Schmydler's drink unnoticed. It wasn't much of a plan, but it was the best they could come up with in the limited amount of time. Their success relied solely on Linda's ability to upsell the revolting beverage. She figured she could play to his ego—tell him only the manliest of men could handle it. If he was anywhere near as narcissistic as his son, he wouldn't be able to pass up the challenge, would he?

Linda reached the lobby and followed the sign that led to the conference room. She peeked in the window and saw that the meeting had finished. The attendees were slowly starting to gather their things and trickle out. A few lingered behind and mingled. She spotted Schmydler talking to a female oodlean. It was difficult to tell with oodleans, but he appeared to be laughing. The female leaned in and touched his tentacle with hers. Were they flirting? Was that Schmoodler's future mother? Linda realized her window of opportunity may be much narrower than previously estimated.

After several more minutes of overly enthusiastic chatter and salacious tentacle touching, Schmydler left and twirled his way to his hotel room. Linda followed, trying to stay a good distance back so as to not raise suspicion. She saw an abandoned housekeeping cart in the hall and started pushing it, hiding herself behind tiny bottles of shampoo and lotion. The hiding was completely unnecessary, as Schmydler had no idea who she was. Nonetheless, she stealthily followed him behind the cart all the way to his penthouse suite. She waited a few minutes after he entered, and then tentatively knocked on the door.

"Housekeeping," she called, in a weird, falsetto voice. She cringed at herself.

Schmydler opened the door. "I believe you have the wrong room," he said. "Mine has already been made up."

Linda paused for a moment, and then said in the same falsetto voice, "Yes, but I forgot to refill your shampoo," she said, and pushed her way past him.

"You realize oodleans don't have any hair, right?"

Linda let out a loud, fake, high-pitched laugh, reminiscent of a man trying to impersonate a woman. "Of course, dear, but it's hotel policy to refresh all toiletries every day," she lied. She was surprised how quickly she was able to think on her feet. She grabbed a shampoo from the cart and strode across the room.

"Bathroom's that way," Schmydler said, pointing in the other direction.

"Oh my!" Linda bellowed. "The other suite is a mirror image of this one." She turned around and found the bathroom. She was surprised to find that it was outfitted with a round oodlean toilet, which resembled a bird bath with a hole in the middle. She placed the shampoo on the counter and made a fancy little tower with the body wash and lotion bottles. She looked around the room and spotted a menu sitting on the dining table. "Can I offer you room service?" she asked, still sounding like Mrs. Doubtfire.

"No thank you, I've got dinner plans," he responded.

"How lovely!" Linda enthused. "A date?"

"Actually, yes," he responded. "How did you know?"

"I can always tell when love is in the air. It's a gift."

"Right . . ." Schmydler was obviously weirded out by Linda's display. She decided to switch gears and do her best friendly grandmother act.

"You seem nervous, poor dear! How about a drink?"

"I don't want to show up to a date drunk," he said.

"Oh, but surely an oodlean of your status wouldn't want to appear nervous either," Linda improvised. "Why not just one little drinky poo, to take the edge off?"

Schmydler hesitated. "Alright, twist my rubber tentacle."

Linda flipped through the drink menu. "Might I suggest our signature liqueur?" she said, pointing it out to him.

"No thanks, I'll have a Scotch on the rocks."

"Oh, but you must try some Spü! It's a rite of passage. Only the most refined pallet can appreciate the complexity of flavours." She began to read the description of the revolting beverage, but Schmydler wasn't having it.

"Scotch will be all," he said. "Now if you don't mind, I'd like some privacy."

"Of course," Linda mumbled, "Not everyone can handle such an exotic choice." Unable to think of another lie, she placed the menu on the bed, open to the Spü page, and left the room, defeated.

# CHAPTER 32

## Ibo's Rescue Mission

On the other end of the wormline, Arec Ibo was busy preparing the PUE's rustic spaceship for a rescue mission to retrieve Linda, Larv, Troodly, and Choodlen. He was lost in thought when a tentative "ahem" caught his attention. He turned to the entrance of the control room and saw Steve, the intern who had first alerted him to Troodly's apparent desertion. When Steve had learned that Troodly wasn't a traitor after all, he had begged Ibo to join the rescue mission. It was the least he could do for accusing Troodly of such a heinous act. Ibo had reluctantly agreed to let the young oodlean tag along.

"How can I help you?" Ibo asked.

Steve gulped. Ever since boarding the ship and meeting President Ibo face to face, his nerves had gotten the best of him. His initial enthusiasm had quickly turned into trepidation as his anxiety manifested in his lower intestine. Presently, he could feel a gurgling sensation in his gut that told him he needed a toilet, and he needed one soon.

"Uh, sir . . . I can't seem to open the door to the, er, restroom," he sputtered.

"Ah, yes," Ibo replied. "The door is a bit tricky. It's an airlock, you see. So the, uh, wastes, can be flushed directly into the vacuum of space without compromising the rest of the ship. I'll show you in a minute."

Steve hesitated. But another, more intense, gurgle urged him to say, "Sir, I need you to show me right now."

"Right, then," Ibo said, and led Steve to the facilities.

Once the intern was settled on his porcelain throne, Ibo returned to the control room and decided to call up Nimbulus. Although grumpy at times, Nimbulus often provided much needed practicality and level-headedness.

Could he call it level-headedness when a mistoform does not have a head? Ibo shrugged to himself and sent a video request on his holographic transmitter. Within seconds, a cloudy three-dimensional shape appeared before him. It wasn't cloudy due to bad video quality—it was simply what Nimbulus looked like. The condensation point of a mistoform is approximately -100°C, and that's just to get it into a liquid state. It is unknown how cold it needs to be to solidify one, but some astrobiologists believe their freezing point to be near absolute zero. This hypothesis has never been tested due to obvious ethical concerns and alien rights infringements. Some have even proposed that frozen mistoforms would yield the most beautiful crystalline structures and that beings from across the universe would pay handsome sums to see such a display. Alien rights activists had to fight absurdly hard against space tourism tycoons to prevent that from coming into fruition.

"Can you hear me now?" Ibo shouted at Nimbulus' hologram. Nimbulus gestured that he could not. Eventually, Ibo figured out how to unmute himself, but by this point, Nimbulus had gone from mildly unimpressed to barely holding himself together. Technically, he was always barely holding himself together, being a gas and all, but that's beside the point.

"No need to yell, I can hear you more than I care to," Nimbulus said to the giant nose floating in his office. Ibo's camera did not have a wide enough angle to capture the rest of his body. Either that, or he was standing much to close to it.

"Nimbulus, you won't believe what just happened!" Ibo said, still shouting. "I just spoke with an old man who came from the other side of the wormline, only on the other side, he's a young boy."

"What are you talking about?" Nimbulus grumbled.

"Troodly's alive! She made it to the other side of the wormline, as did Linda and the larvalux."

"She what?!" Nimbulus choked, unable to hide his shock.

"Yes, it's wonderful, isn't it?" Ibo said. "They have travelled sixty years into the past. Troodly sent a message with the young boy, who waited until he was an old man to deliver to me. She's not a traitor after all!"

"How can you be so sure?" Nimbulus warned.

"She's been pretending to work for Schmoodler to keep tabs on him." Ibo smiled with delight under his gigantic nose.

"How do you know it's not the other way around? She could be a double agent!" Nimbulus insinuated.

"I just *know*, Nimbulus. Besides, she would have sent a help message to Schmoodler, not me, if that was the case."

Exasperated, Nimbulus pointed out, "She could have sent one to him, too."

"I don't think so," Ibo doubted. "Anyway, I wanted to tell you that I'm heading to the Ellis Wormline on a rescue mission to get her and the others. While I'm gone, you'll be in charge."

"Sir, I don't think that's a good . . . wait . . . me? In charge?"

"Yes, of course, you're next in the line of command." Ibo chuckled at Nimbulus' reaction. He seemed surprised. Maybe he was just nervous to take on the responsibility.

Then, Nimbulus' agitation suddenly faded, and he relaxed and said, in a much more agreeable tone, "Well, sir, if you insist."

"I do. Now listen, I'm leaving as soon as the ship is fueled up and ready to go. I should arrive in about two hours, assuming our tachyon drive doesn't malfunction again. I'll update you when I find them."

"Safe travels, sir," Nimbulus said, and then ended the call.

* * *

Nimbulus let out a sigh of relief. President Ibo hadn't seemed to notice that his image was purposely distorted to prevent him from seeing his location. He was not in his regular quarters. He gathered himself together as best as he could and floated down the metallic corridor of the luxury space yacht to find Reverend Groodle Schmoodler, CEO.

"Nimbulus, what I can I do you for?" Schmoodler asked from his stool in the very same viewing lounge where he had met with Choodlen before tossing him into the wormline a day earlier. Was that only yesterday? So much had happened since then. He had given a riveting sermon on planet Oodle, captured the weird pink earthling and the larvalux, and then sent them for a ride through the wormline, as well. Would Nimbulus be next? He laughed inwardly at the thought. The wormline, originally intended solely for the largescale transport of goods, was becoming quite useful for the disposal of certain inconveniences.

"Reverend, I've just got off the holotran with President Ibo."

"Why did you have to ruin my good mood by mentioning that throttling little weasel?" Schmoodler opened a can of boodleoodler, dumped the entire contents into the top of his head, and belched loudly. Particulate from his esophagus sprayed up in an aerosol cloud and diffused into Nimbulus' gaseous body, causing him to absorb some of the alcohol second-hand.

"You'll want to hear this," he said.

Schmoodler waved a tentacle in a hurrying motion. "Go on, then. I haven't got all day."

"Everyone who went into the wormline is alive," Nimbulus announced.

At this, Schmoodler perked up.

"They've landed on a planet sixty years in the past. Ibo is heading up a rescue mission to get them out."

"That meddling bastard! No wonder his nose is so big. He's always got it poking into everyone else's business." Schmoodler grabbed a bowl of woodlerms and voraciously began stress eating. He didn't bother to finish chewing a mouthful before choking out, "What about Troodly? I hired her to replace Choodlen. Can we get her to close off the wormline temporarily?"

"Reverend, Troodly went into the wormline voluntarily. She's working for Ibo."

"WHAT?!" Schmoodler shouted, spraying woodlerm guts all over the room, several partially chewed chunks flying straight through Nimbulus. "That good for nothing, back-stabbing, little b—"

"If we leave now, we can intercept them outside the wormline," Nimbulus reassured.

Schmoodler ignored him. In a desperate attempt to save his colossal ego, he said, "I always knew she was one of them. That's why I used my superior power of manipulation to get to her to go through the wormline."

"Of course, Reverend," Nimbulus pretended to agree.

"I have an idea. If we leave now, we can intercept them outside the wormline."

"Good plan," Nimbulus said, holding back his frustration that his boss was taking credit for his idea.

"That's why they pay me the big bucks," Schmoodler said, condescendingly. After a moment's pause, Schmoodler snapped, "What are you waiting for, nimrod? Tell the captain full speed to Ellis! Close the door behind you!"

# CHAPTER 33

## Linda the Maid

Sixty years in the past, Linda was hiding in a custodial closet down the hall from Tyg Schmydler's penthouse suite. She had yet to come up with an alternative plan to get the antidote in the wealthy oodlean's gullet as she had been temporarily distracted by thoughts of what her five-year-old self was doing at this very moment. Was this around the same time she had climbed onto the kitchen counter to steal cookies and then fell and broke her wrist? Or was it closer to when she had gotten butter all over her hands and then chipped her tooth when she tried to do a cartwheel? What would happen if she ran into her younger self?

She forced herself to snap out of it and looked around the closet for inspiration. Perhaps she could pour the antidote into a shampoo bottle. No, Schmydler had said himself that he didn't have hair and wouldn't use shampoo. Maybe the body wash? There was no guarantee he would use it before his date, and certainly no way to tell if the smell would last on the surface of his skin. Oodlean skin constantly produced mucus, and there was a good chance the antidote would be cleared away before it served its purpose. She had to get it into his system somehow. Could she inject it? Risky, yes. Maybe she could dress up as a nurse and make up some excuse for giving him a shot. There'd been an outbreak of some sort of virus, and he needs a vaccine immediately. It wouldn't be the first time she'd dressed up as a nurse. There was that one time with Ryp Comet when she—never mind that. She needed to focus. Now was not the time to drift into another Linda Land fantasy. What if Schmydler refused the vaccine? He would wonder why he was the only one getting it. Besides, where would she find a syringe? Bad idea.

She began rummaging around in the closest again when the door suddenly swung open. Linda let out a startled yelp.

"There it is!" the maid exclaimed. "I've been looking everywhere for this. Did you take it?" She was referring to the stolen cart.

"Uh, no," Linda said. "It was here when I came in."

The maid looked at her suspiciously. "Are you new? I don't recognize you."

"Yes," Linda said. "First day."

"Here, this'll help with the first day jitters," she said, tossing Linda a sample-sized bottle of whiskey from the minibar stock. "Don't drink it all at once," she joked, and then hurried away with the cart before Linda could say a word.

That was a close call. She was lucky the maid hadn't realized she was an imposter. She looked at the bottle of whiskey in her plump little hand. Maybe she could try an adapted version of the original plan—mix the antidote with the whiskey, and then anonymously send him a drink while he was out for dinner. He would think it had come from one of his admirers.

She heard a door open down the hall and peeked out. It was Schmydler. He had on a new suit, tailored perfectly to fit all seven tentacles. He was heading out for his date. There wasn't much time. Linda closed herself in the closet, opened the minibar whiskey, and drank half. She hadn't shot straight liquor in years and was surprised at how smoothly it went down. After a slight hesitation, she held her breath, opened the antidote vial, and poured it into the whiskey bottle to top it up. She then made sure the vial, which still contained some antidote, was securely sealed before leaving the closet and letting her breath out. Her little hands worked so quickly that she was easily able to catch up with Schmydler. Behind her, another maid opened the door to the custodial closet and immediately wretched. Linda, locked on to her tentacled target, did not look back.

# CHAPTER 34
## Ellis Interception

Also locked on target was Groodle Schmoodler's gas-guzzling luxury space yacht, which raced towards the Ellis Wormline at tachyon speed. In order to travel safely at such high velocity, Nimbulus had to shove himself into a gas cylinder, which was then strapped securely to the wall. The cylinder Schmoodler provided him with was on the small side, and Nimbulus was under an uncomfortable amount of pressure. He felt like a genie cramped inside a lamp. At such a pressure, he might just become one of those crystals and wind up on display in some sicko's museum.

As suddenly as it began, the ship jolted out of hyperdrive. Nimbulus could feel the cylinder strain against its straps at the abrupt deceleration. One of Schmoodler's minions opened the valve and a hissing sound accompanied Nimbulus's release. He made his way to the viewing lounge, where Schmoodler already sat, chuckling to himself.

"Would you look at that hunk of junk!" he exclaimed, pointing to the sad-looking PUE spaceship out the window. "How does that thing even fly? It's got to be at least ten years old. What would that make it? A model 14?"

"Model 13, actually," Nimbulus replied. "President Ibo doesn't believe in perceived obsolescence the way most do. He says he'll keep flying that thing as long as it gets him from A to B."

"That's something only poor people say," Schmoodler said, feigning sympathy. "It's so sad that he'd rather make up excuses than contribute to the economy. I suppose we should put him out of his misery."

* * *

Aboard the PUE's tin can, Arec Ibo gazed out the small circular window that resembled a porthole. The model 13 spacecraft was identifiable by its circular windows and round edges. But then again, the models alternated between round edges and sharp edges with each generation. There was no functional purpose for the changes. They were purely stylistic. Those who purchased the newest model needed everyone else to know it. It was an absurd display of status and needlessly wasteful. One of Ibo's mandates as president of the PUE was to educate youth on how much stuff was wasted in the universe and the dangers of waste materials being improperly disposed of. He thought about his life's work and the apparent futility of it all as he watched the construction crew busily working on the wormline.

"We didn't approve the construction permit," he said to no one in particular. "What does Schmoodler think he's doing? Just because he's rich, he thinks he's above the law!" His irritated voice was higher pitched and even more nasally than usual. "All his money won't matter when he's finished destroying the universe."

Ibo's grumblings were interrupted when a young orderly approached. "Uh, sir, I think you better come see this." Ibo followed the orderly to the porthole on the other side of the ship, where he saw the large, gleaming luxury yacht. It was a model 24 with sharp edges and larger rectangular windows. It must have been pre-ordered, as this model had not been officially released yet.

"There's the raging narcissist himself. He must be here checking up on his illegal construction project. Why, I oughta give him a piece of my mind!" As if on cue, the nearly obsolete two-dimensional video monitor beeped, indicating an incoming call. The software was just barely compatible with Schmoodler's holographic transmitter. Ibo accepted the call, ready to chew him out, but was surprised to see Nimbulus on the other end of the line.

"Nimbulus? Where are you? What's going on?"

"I'm aboard Schmoodler's yacht," he replied.

"What are you doing there?"

"I'm being held hostage. Schmoodler caught me rounding up the UPTs. He destroyed them all."

"That good for nothing, slimy piece of—"

"I need permission to dock," Nimbulus interrupted. "He said he's willing to turn me over to you in exchange for your word that you won't stop his wormline construction."

"You've taken it too far Schmoodler!" Ibo yelled at the screen, hoping Schmoodler was listening in. "You'll never get away with this!"

"Please, just agree and let us dock," Nimbulus pleaded, "or else he's going to put me back into that God-awful cylinder."

"Permission granted," Ibo growled through clenched teeth. He was fuming.

* * *

The Mabitu had been circling around the opening to the Ellis Wormline when it saw the other two ships approach. It hid under one of the construction stations and hacked into the other ships' communication systems. It was able to capture most of the conversation between Ibo and Nimbulus. It watched as the docking bay of the larger ship extended towards the smaller ship until it made contact. There was now a tube bridging the two ships. The Mabitu had a bad feeling. It hacked into the PUE's flight recorder box in order to eavesdrop on what was happening inside.

* * *

After the docking bay finished pressurizing, Ibo opened the hatch. "Nimbulus, thank goodness you're okay," he said as the mistoform floated down the corridor toward him. He was followed closely by Groodle Schmoodler and another oodlean. "What are you doing here?" Ibo asked. "You're not welcome on my ship."

"Doodlen, go disarm the defense system while Nimbulus shuts off manual drive," Schmoodler said, ignoring Ibo.

"Hey, what do you think you're doing?" Ibo protested. "Nimbulus, what's going on?"

Nimbulus ignored him and floated straight to the command console. Two more oodleans boarded the ship and handcuffed Ibo and the rest of his crew before they had a chance to react.

"President Ibo," Schmoodler spat, "I'm sick and tired of you meddling in my business. Your little non-profit project is over. No one cares about your made-up stories of universal de-tuning. All you do is slow down business for the rest of us."

"Universal de-turning is a scientifically proven phenomenon, and you know it!" Ibo spat.

"Scientifically proven? You mean because of these?" Schmoodler said, dumping out a bag full of Universal Pitch Transmitters. One of Schmoodler's cronies appeared with a sledgehammer and, one by one, proceeded to smash each and every UPT. "There goes your proof," Schmoodler said, and then burst into a fit of moist, maniacal laughter.

* * *

The Mabitu listened in horror as Schmoodler's cronies cuffed Ibo and his crew to the zero-gravity handrails inside the PUE ship. The sound was a bit muffled from the flight recorder on the outdated ship, but it was pretty sure it heard Schmoodler say that he was going to send them into the wormline, too. With their manual drive shut down, they wouldn't be able to maneuver a safe landing on the other side. The gravity of the planet would pull them in, and they would smash to the ground. The ship, and all those inside it, would be obliterated. In such a state, they certainly would be not able to rescue Linda and Larv. The Mabitu was their only hope. A chemical that was functionally equivalent to adrenaline surged through the Mabitu's system, releasing a swarm of bubbles from its effervescence. The bubbles spread out in all directions, popping in a glorious, glittery display as they hit the ship's inner surfaces. Struggling to see through the pheromonal nebulosity, the Mabitu steered its ship to the opening of the wormline, took a deep breath, and flew in.

# CHAPTER 35
## An Act of Desperation

On the other side of the wormline, Linda sat at the bar of the fancy restaurant where Tyg Schmydler was wooing his date in a disgusting display of overt affection. She could see their tentacles brushing up against each other under the table as Schmydler boasted about himself and his fortune. There was nothing subtle about his intentions. She knew tonight was the night. This was her only chance to prevent whatever it was that oodleans did to make baby oodleans. She had no idea what that might look like, and she didn't want to know. All she knew was that she had to get the antidote into him as soon as possible. She browsed the drink menu and ordered the most exotic sounding drink she could find. When the bartender wasn't looking, she poured the contents of the minibar whiskey in, and then politely asked a server to deliver it to Schmydler.

Linda watched with bated breath as the server took the martini glass filled with swamp water over to Tyg Schmydler's table. She couldn't hear what they were saying, but she could see they were having quite a discussion. Schmydler's seven eyes darted around the room suspiciously. His date appeared to be encouraging him to have a taste. The server stood there impatiently. The restaurant was full, and he had many other customers waiting on him, but he dared not walk away from Tyg Schmydler. Linda could see his nose begin to wrinkle as the fumes from the antidote broke the surface tension of the drink and drifted violently up his nasal passage.

*What is that awful smell?* the server thought. He felt a burning sensation rise up the back of his throat. *Don't gag, don't gag, don't gag,* he willed himself. *Not in front of the richest being in the universe.* At last, he couldn't take it any longer. The server, trying his best to appear calm and courteous, placed the drink on Schmydler's table and mumbled, "I'll be back in a moment to remove it if you don't want it." He then dashed into the kitchen and barely made it to the dish pit before expelling the acid that had crept from his throat into his mouth.

Linda snuck closer to Schmydler's table so she could listen in.

"I think it's nice that someone sent you a drink. They must admire your work," Schmoodler's future mom said.

"Maybe so," Schmydler replied. "But someone in my position—incredibly rich and powerful—must be careful. For each admirer I have, there are least as many who'd like to see me dead."

"What a shame," his date replied. "They must be so jealous of not only your wealth, but your intelligence and your dashing good looks," she flirted.

"Tell me more about my good looks," Schmydler said.

*Did he really just say that?* Linda thought.

"Let's just say I wouldn't want anything to happen to you before I get my tentacles all over your glistening body."

*Gross!*

"Well then," Schmydler said, "I guess we'd better get the check and get out of here."

"If only the waiter would come back and get rid of this poison," his date said.

"I know how to get his attention," Schmydler said, and knocked the drink right off the table, shattering the glass and spilling dark liquid all over the floor. Linda gasped in horror. The two oodleans laughed while kitchen staff rushed out with dish rags to absorb the beverage. Schmydler paid the bill without leaving a tip and started to get up.

There was only one thing left to do. Without hesitation, Linda marched over to Schmydler and, in an over-excited voice cried, "Tyggy! There you are! Why didn't you call? I had such a wonderful time last night."

"Who the hell are you?" he said.

Linda giggled flirtatiously. "Don't act like you don't remember me, big boy." She winked.

"What is going on?!" Schmydler's date demanded, glaring at him with all seven eyes.

Schmydler was silent. He was wracking his brain trying to figure out where he recognized this human from. Had he gotten drunk last night and engaged in interspecies relations? It wouldn't be the first time. He didn't think so, but she did look awfully familiar. Either way, he did not want to ruin his chances with his current date. "I'm sorry, Miss, you must be mistaken," he said and began twirling toward the exit.

In a final act of desperation, Linda poured the remaining contents of the vial into her mouth, grabbed Tyg Schmydler by the tentacles, pulled the top of his head down, and kissed him. She looked up just in time to see the would-be Mrs. Schmydler storm off in a cyclone of anger.

* * *

Back in the hotel room, Troodly, Choodlen, and the ever-deteriorating Larv anxiously awaited Linda's return. She had been gone for hours. The boy had gone home for supper. Choodlen had given up his nervous pacing and was now snoring loudly on the bed. Troodly remained perched silently on a stool, where she had been since Linda left. Only her eyes moved, as though she were carrying out calculations in her mind. Larv tried to imagine how Troodly or Choodlen would carry him in the backpack designed to fit a human body. Oodleans didn't even have backs. If Linda did not return, they would have to figure something out. He was quickly running out of limbs, and his body had started to flatten. Pretty soon, it would turn in on itself to form a tube, curl up into a spiral, and then harden. Once that happened, he would no longer be able to survive outside of the Molasses Planet, not even in a tank full of peanut butter. He was slowly coming to terms with the fact that he would not make it back to his home planet in time. If Linda could do this one thing and they were able to save the universe from Groodle Schmoodler, then his life will have had a purpose. But the longer it took Linda to return, the less he believed that would be the case.

There was a knock. Choodlen snorted and groggily opened three of his eyes. Troodly bolted upright and twirled swiftly to the door. She peered through the peephole and let out an exasperated sigh. She opened the door and the young boy entered. No Linda.

"Have you eaten?" he asked, matter-of-factly. He looked around the room. "Still not back yet, huh?"

"No," Troodly replied, "to both your questions."

"I brought you some leftovers," he said, placing some to-go containers on the table.

Choodlen got up to investigate the human food. He opened the lid of one container and found small green plants that looked like miniature trees. "Which part do you eat?" he asked.

"The whole thing," the boy said. "It's crunchy, see?" He chomped loudly into one to demonstrate.

Choodlen shrugged and popped one into his mouth. "Interesting," he said, and then opened another container. This one contained deep fried balls of lab-grown meat product covered in a sweet and sour sauce. He ate several of those before moving onto the last container, which contained noodles. He held the container over his head and dumped most of it directly into his gullet without chewing. There was something about oodleans and their noodles.

"Hey, save some for Troodly!" the boy said.

Before Troodly had a chance to indulge her hunger, there was another knock on the door. This one was a lot more violent than the last. "Let me in!" Linda shouted.

Troodly opened the door and Linda burst through, making a beeline for the toilet. After getting violently ill several times, she grabbed the mini tube of hotel toothpaste, squeezed the entire contents into her mouth, and then washed it down with at least a gallon of water directly from the tap. "Sorry," she whispered breathlessly.

"Are you okay?" Troodly asked. "What happened?"

Once she caught her breath, Linda told them everything, including how she had transferred the antidote from her mouth into Tyg Schmydler's.

"Whoa, that's brilliant!" the boy exclaimed.

"Disgusting!" Troodly grimaced.

"Way to take one for the team," Choodlen said.

Larv smiled weakly. *She did it!* he thought.

"How will we know if it worked?" the boy asked.

* * *

"Schmoodler! Think carefully about what you're doing!" Arec Ibo pleaded. The cold metal of the handcuffs dug into his wrists painfully.

"I have thought about it, Mr. President, and I've concluded that I should have done it much sooner!"

"Think of your followers!" Ibo urged. "They think you're a reverend."

"I *am* a reverend!"

"What would they think if they found out you were a murderer? What would that do to their faith in Oodlism?"

"They'll think whatever I want them to think. That's enough out of you!" One of Schmoodler's cronies stuffed a sock into Ibo's mouth and wrapped duct tape around it.

"You'll never get away with this, Schmoodler!" Ibo said in a perfectly clear, albeit nasally, voice.

"How is he still talking?" Schmoodler asked.

"My nasal passage is intimately connected to my oral cavity," Ibo began.

"It was a rhetorical question!" Schmoodler snapped. He turned to his accomplices. "Come on guys, let's get out of here."

And that was when things got weird. Before Schmoodler made it halfway across the docking tube, *poof!* He disappeared into thin air. Arec Ibo blinked and turned his head sideways so that the mountain between his eyes wasn't obstructing his view. He didn't trust what he had just seen with his own strigine eyes. But seconds later, Schmoodler's luxury space yacht also disappeared. The rest of his crew, Nimbulus included, were immediately sucked into the vacuum of space through the gaping hole where their ship had been docked. A deafening woosh filled the cabin of the PUE ship as all of the air was sucked through the docking bay door. Any loose items expeditiously made their way out the door, too, smashing into anything or anybody that was in their way. Ibo was narrowly missed by the business end of a particularly pointy pencil.

Luckily for Ibo and his team, they did not join the outpouring of matter, as they were handcuffed securely to the ship. Their luck would run out very soon, however, if the cabin pressure decreased to a critical point. Ibo strained to breathe, but all of the air was pulled out of his lungs before any oxygen made it into his bloodstream. He had to act fast, before he lost consciousness. He spotted the large red emergency button on the console within arm's reach. Ibo's henchmen had made sure his hands were unable to move from his sides, but they had overlooked one thing: he was a saganite. With immense effort, he lifted his head and his monstrous nose inched forward. Summoning all his strength, Ibo tapped the button with the tip of his tremendous snout and closed the airlock seconds before the cabin lost enough pressure to kill its occupants.

Once the cabin repressurized, the door to the ship's toilet opened and out twirled Steve, the oodlean intern. He had spent more time in the restroom than out since boarding due to intestinal distress. He had wondered whether it was just nerves or if he had eaten tainted noodles. Since the restroom door was an airlock, it was made of very thick, sound-proof metal, and so Steve had not heard any of the commotion. Needless to say, he was rather stunned to find the rest of the crew in shackles, most of them passed out or barely conscious. He twirled over to Ibo and ripped the duct tape from his mouth, taking several rogue nose hairs with it.

"Ow!" Ibo yelled as he immediately snapped back to full consciousness.

"Sorry, sir!" Steve slurred.

Ibo winced in pain. His head throbbed and his ears popped from the pressure change. "What the hell happened?"

"I don't know, sir," Steve slurred. "I went to the toilet and when I came out, you were all handcuffed."

"I mean after Schmoodler handcuffed us," Ibo said.

"Schmoodler?" Steve asked.

"Are you telling me you've been in the toilet since before Schmoodler boarded us?"

"Uh . . . I guess so?" Steve was embarrassed about his digestive struggles and silently prayed no one would use the toilet any time soon. The smell in there was less than optimal.

Another crew member came to. "What happened? Where's Schmoodler?"

"I don't know," Ibo responded. "He just disappeared into thin air, and so did his ship."

"What about the rest of his crew? Nimbulus?"

Ibo shrugged, and then squinted as a bright light suddenly shone directly into his eyes. The light was reflecting off of something outside the window. "What's that light coming from?"

They all looked out the window in time to see the most beautiful crystalline structure float past. Its luminescence made the most brilliant diamond seem dull in comparison. A light from the ring structure surrounding the opening of the wormline hit the crystal at just the right angle to reflect a thousand tiny rainbows all over the interior of the ship.

"It's so shiny!" Steve slurred, awestruck. Then, just as quickly as it had appeared, the crystal floated out of sight. Steve hurried over to the window and strained to catch one more glimpse of the shimmering gem before it disappeared.

"Steve," Ibo said.

"It's sooo beautiful!" Steve slurred.

"Steve!" Ibo said, louder.

"We should follow it."

"STEVE!" Ibo shouted, jolting the intern from his trance. "Our ship is being pulled into the wormline. You need to get us out of these handcuffs."

# CHAPTER 36

## The Mabitu to the Rescue

The Mabitu was through the wormline and did not witness the sudden vanishing of Groodle Schmoodler and his ship. However, it could have sworn it felt *another* shockwave. Or was that just what travelling through a wormline always felt like? Maybe. But it could not shake the feeling that its atoms had been disassembled and reassembled for the second time that day. It wondered if mistoforms felt a similar sensation every time they woke up and thought of how unpleasant that would be. It tried to ignore the disconcerting feeling and instead focused on finding its friends. It saw two large birds in the distance and wondered if they were sentient beings. Its best chance was to follow them and hopefully they would lead it to a civilization. There were no notable landmarks or roads in the vast expanse of orange desert, only a giant pile of trash that the Mabitu took note of so that it would be able to find its way back to the wormline.

* * *

"Oy, Sherman!" one of the birds said.

"Yeah, mate?" the other replied.

"Oi fink der's somefing followin' us."

Sherman looked back briefly and spotted a ship behind them. "You reckon?"

"Dat's wot oi said, ain't it?"

"Alright, alright. No need to ruffle your feathahs. How long's ee been back there?"

"'Ow would oi know? Do oi look like oi got a rearview mirrah attached to me 'ead?"

"Den 'ow do you know ee's followin' us?"

"Oi don't know, oi said oi *fink*."

"Wot's the big deal anyway? Ee's probably anovuh lost tourist or somefing."

"As long as dis one doesn't drop outa the sky onto me back. I'm still recoverin' from the last."

"Let's just ignore 'im and get some food from the little man. I'm 'ungry!"

"'Ow about some nectah?"

"Oi ain't in the mood for more nectah. Oi fancy dose fruits the little man gives us."

* * *

The Mabitu was right. The birds led it straight to the sandcastle city. It would have to be very careful to avoid another mob scene, like the one on Nilleby. It set the ship's controls into low altitude cruising mode, which allowed it to hover slowly between the orange sand buildings as it scanned for any sign of Linda and Larv. It would not be able to open the hatch or get out to question anyone, otherwise its pheromones would escape. The concentration of pheromones inside the ship was dangerously high, as the Mabitu had been sealed inside for several hours steadily releasing bubbly glitter bombs. The second it opened the hatch, the pheromones would pour out and attract unwanted attention. It decided the best course of action was to systematically glide up and down every single street in hopes that they would be outside. It kept a watchful eye on the fuel gauge as the digital needle wavered precariously above the empty mark.

After several hours of no luck, it stopped outside a café, as it recalled Linda's proclivity for tea. However, as it strained to see into the windows, it noticed the "closed for cleaning" sign posted above the open door. It continued around the next corner, and something caught its eye. The two birds it had followed into town were standing on the ground voraciously pecking at what appeared to be mangoes. As it approached, it noticed a pile of discarded mangoes that were covered in holes. It watched the birds curiously as they bored holes into the mangoes with their pointy beaks and sucked up the juices through their straw-shaped tongues. It continued past the birds and spotted a human boy on the other side. The boy held out a mango to one of the birds, which immediately pecked it out of his hand and went to town. If there was a human here, perhaps Linda wouldn't be far. Experience taught the Mabitu that members of the same species tended to gravitate towards each other. It looked at the fuel gauge and decided it would be a good idea to turn off the engine and stake out the area until it could figure out what to do next.

It watched the boy laugh at the goofy birds, with their awkwardly long necks and tufts of fluffy orange feathers on the tops of their heads. They allowed the boy to pet them in exchange for more mangoes. One of the birds slurped up the insides of an unripe mango and hopped back in surprise at the sour taste. It stuck out its hollow tongue and shook its head vigorously in an attempt to expel the juice. The boy doubled over laughing at the ridiculous display. The Mabitu found itself laughing along with him, its three voices ringing out in a euphonic major triad. But the triad soon turned minor, as the Mabitu thought about its life without the antidote, and how it would always be on the outside looking in. Although, in this particular case, it was on the inside of its ship looking out. Either way, the same principle applied. It was not free to interact with most other creatures, and the loneliness was harrowing. All it could do was watch others from afar and laugh along vicariously.

Once the birds had had their fill of mango, they began some sort of ritualistic dance. Their heads bobbed up and down, then side-to-side, then made increasingly larger circles. The boy faced the birds and mirrored their actions. His much shorter neck required him to use his entire upper body to make the larger circles. The Mabitu laughed at how awkward the boy looked. It must have been a parting ritual, for as soon as it was over, the birds took off. Their absence revealed the entrance to a hotel lobby that was previously hidden from the Mabitu's view. The boy was about to enter the hotel when suddenly the doors burst open and two security guards tossed out two oodleans. The guards went back inside and returned shortly after to toss out a third unwelcome guest. The Mabitu would have never guessed that this third guest would be Linda, but indeed it was, and on her back was a fourth. Poor Larv sloshed around inside the backpack of peanut butter, unable to sturdy himself with his one remaining appendage. The Mabitu powered up the ship, shot across the street, narrowly missing vehicles that approached from both directions, and opened the hatch.

"Linda," it shouted. But Linda was too busy yelling at the guards to notice.

Larv, of course, heard, and tapped furiously on Linda's back with his weak leg. "Linda, forget about them! Turn around!"

Linda turned and saw the open hatch of the ship. She saw the Mabitu at the exact same time the pheromones reached the security guards. All three of them bolted towards the hatch. Before the guards could reach it, Linda activated full minotaur mode and tackled them to the ground. Troodly and Choodlen watched, stunned. "Get on that ship!" she yelled to them. Troodly and Choodlen did as they were told. Linda struggled over the toppled security guards and continued towards the hatch. Just as she was about to climb in, a hand closed around her ankle, and she fell face first. She removed the backpack and threw Larv into the ship. She kicked her legs, frantically trying to escape the grasp of the crazed guard. The boy came to her rescue and pried the guard's fingers away. Linda and the boy both jumped into the ship and the Mabitu closed the hatch.

Relieved, Linda said, "That was a close one." But then she turned and saw Troodly and Choodlen going after the Mabitu. They were not immune to its pheromones.

"Help!" it screeched, dodging a tentacle.

Linda sprung into action. She grabbed two of Troodly's tentacles and tied them around the base of a chair. The boy, who was pre-pubescent and unaffected by the pheromones, followed Linda's lead and grabbed Choodlen. With great effort, the two of them managed to tie a struggling Choodlen around another chair.

"Why did you let those things on the ship?" the Mabitu cried.

"Nice to see you, too," said Linda as she gathered Larv up off the floor and shovelled him into the backpack.

The Mabitu just glared.

"Relax, they're on our side," Linda said.

"Speak for your self."

"The female is Troodly," Linda explained. "She's the head scientist of the PUE. And the male is Choodlen. He used to be Schmoodler's chief engineer until he was tossed into the wormline."

"So, we're helping one of Schmoodler's employees?" the Mabitu accused.

"Former employee," Linda corrected. "He's on our side now. And besides, he designed the wormline. We might need his help getting back out."

"Fair point," the Mabitu said with a sigh. "I guess they can stay." The Mabitu turned to the boy. "What about the little human?"

"Oh, that's . . . um . . . " Linda turned to the boy. "What's your name? Something Omelette?"

"It's *Comet*," the boy corrected. "Ryp Comet."

"Come again?" Linda said. She knew she was getting old, and her hearing wasn't what it used to be. There was no way he had said what she thought he had.

"Ryp Comet," the boy repeated.

"That's funny, I thought you said Ryp Comet," Linda chuckled.

"I *did*."

Linda stared blankly at the boy. Her stomach launched itself into her throat. *Could it be*? She did some mental math, which took entirely too long, and figured he was the right age. It slowly started to make sense. When they'd first met on Sagana, they had felt like they had already known each other.

"Linda? Are you okay?" the Mabitu asked.

"Huh? What? Oh, yes. I'm fine," she sputtered, unconvincingly. "Ryp has been a tremendous help to us, but he'll not be coming with us. He lives in the here and now. I suppose we should take him home, huh Ryp?"

"Yeah, I guess," Ryp said. "My dad's probably wondering where I am."

"We need to get the eff out of here," the Mabitu said looking out the window.

A large crowd had formed around the ship. They heard a loud bang coming from the ceiling. Someone had climbed on top. The Mabitu pulled the directional controls up and raised the ship above the crowd. It eyed the fuel gauge nervously. "Hey kid, you wouldn't happen to have any rocket fuel at home, would you?"

* * *

Linda spent the short trip to Ryp Comet's childhood home lost in thought. Would this young boy really become her lover in fifteen years from now? Would their current encounter change the course of the future and prevent them from meeting? Would his older self recognize her younger self? Would it make things weird between them? The whole situation was entirely too strange. Thinking about it turned Linda's already-foggy brain into full fledged pea soup. By the time they arrived, she had decided one thing: she would not mention anything to young Ryp. The less he knew, the less likely it would affect his future. Furthermore, she could only imagine how scarring it would be for a young boy to be told by an old lady that they would be lovers some day. She couldn't do that to him.

"You can land in the driveway, right there beside my dad's ship," Ryp directed.

The Mabitu obeyed. "Where's the fuel?"

"I'll go get it," Ryp said. He slipped out the hatch quickly to avoid releasing too many pheromones and ran inside the house. The Mabitu was doubtful. How could a small boy carry enough fuel to fill this ship's tank? The boy returned with nothing but a hose and a remote controller.

"What's he doing?" the Mabitu asked.

Linda shrugged.

"Come over here and I'll whisper it to you," Troodly said seductively, still struggling to untie her own tentacles.

The Mabitu ignored her coaxing and continued to watch Ryp as he used the remote to open a small hole on the side of his father's ship. He unscrewed a cap inside the hole and shoved the hose in. "Oh no he isn't!" the Mabitu said in disbelief. "What a little badass!"

Linda still hadn't figured out what was going on but watched with curiosity. Ryp carried the other end of the hose to the Mabitu's ship and looked up to the cockpit. The Mabitu pressed a button to open the fuel tank and pointed to the right and down. Ryp followed the Mabitu's gestures and found the intake. He put the free end of the hose into his mouth and started sucking.

Linda cringed. "Don't drink that!" she shouted.

As the fuel reached his mouth, Ryp removed the hose and shoved it into the fuel intake pipe, coughing and spitting. Only then did Linda clue in. "He's siphoning the fuel from his dad's ship?"

"You better believe it," the Mabitu said, amused.

"But won't his dad need it?" Linda asked.

"Not as badly as we need it."

"Where did he learn how to do that?"

"Does it matter?"

Linda watched her underaged, future lover with an odd sense of admiration. When the fuel stopped flowing, Ryp removed the hose and closed both gas tanks. The Mabitu opened the hatch just a crack so they could thank him and say goodbye.

"Nice work, kid," the Mabitu said.

"It was a pleasure meeting you, young Ryp," Linda said, struggling to hold back tears.

"It was nice meeting you guys, too!" Ryp said. He casually turned to go, and then stopped, as something had just occurred to him. "What . . . what if I never see you guys again?"

"Don't worry about that," Linda replied. "If it's meant to be, then we'll meet again."

"You really think so?"

"I know so," Linda said with a wink. "You take care of yourself now."

"I will." Ryp looked at the two oodleans tied to their chairs. "By Troodly! Bye Choodlen!" They didn't respond, as they were still fixated on the Mabitu.

"Don't worry," the Mabitu said. "They'll remember your goodbyes as soon as they're out of pheromone range and regain their senses."

Ryp didn't fully understand, but he nodded anyway and stepped back to allow the Mabitu to close the hatch. The engine fired up just as Ryp's dad opened the door of the house and shouted at his son.

"That's our cue," the Mabitu said, and took off.

* * *

Within half an hour, they reached the giant pile of trash and began their ascent.

"I don't see the entrance to the wormline," Linda said.

"No. They haven't built a ring around this end yet. To be honest, I'm not really sure how to find it," replied the Mabitu.

"I'm going to have to wake them up," Linda said, referring to Troodly and Choodlen who had struggled themselves into a stupor.

"Do you have to? Maybe we can fly around a little and try to find it ourselves."

Linda gave her best teacher glare. "Mab, we need to get out of here."

"But—" the Mabitu protested.

"Now!" Linda insisted.

"Fine." The Mabitu gestured for Linda to go ahead and wake them up.

Linda marched over to Choodlen and slapped him into consciousness.

"Hey, what was that for—" he trailed off as a bubble landed on his nose and burst into a shower of sparkly pheromones. He stared at the Mabitu and started struggling to free himself again.

Linda slapped him hard.

"Ouch!"

"That's enough!" Linda said sternly, blocking his view of the beautiful, glowing creature with her lumpy pink body. He tried to lean over to look around her, and Linda slapped him again. "How do we find the entrance to the wormline?" she demanded.

"I'm not telling you," Choodlen taunted, growing increasingly drunk on pheromones. "I'll only tell that gorgeous, glimmering—"

WHAP! Linda slapped him again, even harder than before. The smack of her hand against his moist skin made a satisfying sound. "You will tell me, and you will tell me now!" she demanded, more sternly this time.

"What is it you want to know?" Choodlen had already forgotten the question.

"What does the entrance to the wormline look like?"

"What does love look like?" he said and then tried to glimpse the Mabitu again. Linda raised her hand and Choodlen flinched. "Fine! I'll tell you, just don't hit me again."

Linda lowered her hand. "I'm all ears."

"That's good, cause you're gonna need them." Choodlen giggled drunkenly.

"Enough with the nonsense," Linda scolded. "Tell me how to find the wormline or I'll slap you silly."

"No nonsense. You won't be able to see the opening to the wormline. You have to *hear* it."

"What are you talking about?" Linda said.

"Follow your ears," Choodlen whispered.

Linda was about the slap him again when Larv's voice weakly whispered something from the backpack. Linda had forgotten about Larv, who hadn't said a peep since they boarded the ship. She kneeled down beside the backpack and looked at her pitiful pal. She tried her best to hide the shock on her face upon seeing his deteriorated appearance. She hoped she hadn't made things worse by tossing him onto the ship. "What did you say?" she asked gently, and then bent over the bag to hear his response.

"I can hear it," he whispered. Larv was fairly certain what he was hearing was the wormline. It was a windy, wooshing, fluty noise. In fact, it sounded like a roomful of people simultaneously blowing into empty bottles of varying sizes. Linda could hear no such thing, but she was not a cochlean. She trusted Larv. "Go that way," Larv whispered, pointing with his big round eyes, which had faded from bright yellow to a dull ecru.

Linda translated the directions for the Mabitu, who steered the ship to the outermost limits of the orange atmosphere. Ahead of them lay the black expanse of outer space speckled with the pin hole lights of distant stars.

"He says to turn just a tiny bit to the left and up," Linda instructed.

"That must be it!" the Mabitu said excitedly.

Linda rushed to the front and looked out the window. "Where?"

"There!" The Mabitu pointed directly ahead.

"I don't see anything."

"Exactly!"

"Huh?"

"There's a patch right in front of us with no stars. Just blackness. That must be it."

"See? What did your old pal tell you?" an inebriated voice said from the back of the ship.

The Mabitu rolled its eyes and said insincerely, "Thank you, Choodlen."

"Come over here and thank me," Choodlen teased.

"In your dreams," the Mabitu mumbled.

Linda chuckled.

"It's not funny," the Mabitu said. "I literally just threw up in my mouth." It tried its best to ignore Choodlen's advances and continued to guide the ship towards the void. The ship entered the wormline and was immediately spat back out. "What happened?"

Choodlen giggled and said, "Come over here and I'll—"

"Do not finish that sentence!" the Mabitu snapped.

Choodlen giggled some more. Linda started towards him, hand raised.

Choodlen winced. "No, don't!" he said, pathetically. "Once we enter the wormline, we'll be going against the peristaltic force. You'll have to gun it."

The Mabitu realigned the ship with the opening of the wormline. "Sit down and strap in," it said to Linda. She made sure Larv was secure and then took her seat. The ship entered the wormline and immediately shot into hyperdrive. Within seconds, they shot out the other end, narrowly missing the side of the ring structure. Everyone let out a collective sigh of relief and then cheered.

"We made it!" the Mabitu said, surprised.

"You did it, Mab!" Linda said, unstrapping herself and hugging the glimmering captain. She had never touched the Mabitu before and was surprised by the way it felt. The sensation of the Mabitu was almost as indescribable as its appearance. It was like hugging a soft, fluffy kitten, but there was no hair, only radiating beams of light. It made Linda's skin tingle in a soothing way, like she had just applied icy hot joint cream. The Mabitu couldn't remember the last time it was hugged in a non-threatening way and was surprised by how comforting it was to be pressed against Linda's soft, plump body. It let itself relax and even closed its eyes.

# CHAPTER 37

## Reunited

When it opened its eyes, the Mabitu saw the PUE ship in the distance and suddenly remembered what it had witnessed before venturing into the wormline. "Ibo!" it exclaimed.

"What?" asked Linda.

"Arec Ibo," the Mabitu clarified.

"Who?" asked Linda.

"The president of the PUE," Larv chimed in.

"Oh. Nose guy?"

"Yes!" exclaimed Larv and the Mabitu in unison, Larv's voice turning the Mabitu's major triad into a dominant seventh chord.

"What about him?" Linda asked.

"Before I went in the wormline to get you, I saw his ship out here," the Mabitu explained. "He was being boarded by Schmoodler. I think Schmoodler was going to kill them!"

"We better go check on them then!" Linda said.

The Mabitu spun the ship around three hundred and sixty degrees but did not spot Schmoodler's yacht. "Looks like Schmoodler took off." They approached the PUE ship. "Linda, you'll have to request permission to dock."

"How do I do that?"

"Press that button there. No, *not* that one. Up. Left. Too far. Yeah, that one."

Linda pressed the button, and the ship automatically called the nearest vessel. A giant nose appeared on the monitor. "President Ibo!" Linda yelled at it.

"Ms. Pumpernickel, what a pleasant surprise. Whose ship is that?"

"Long story," Linda shouted, glancing at the Mabitu, who gestured that she didn't need to shout.

"Are you alright?" Ibo asked, turning his head so that one of his wide eyes could search his screen.

"Yes, we're just dandy," Linda said to the eye.

"Blink twice if you need assistance," Ibo said suspiciously.

"What do you mean?" Linda blinked.

Ibo stared at her intensely until she blinked again several seconds later. "Message received, loud and clear," he said.

"No! I . . . that was just me blinking. It wasn't a secret message. I'm perfectly safe."

"What a relief," Ibo said, stepping back from the screen. "Did you find Troodly?"

"Yes, sir."

"Excellent work! May I talk to her?"

"Um . . . she's, uh, indisposed at the moment," Linda said, looking back at the pheromone-crazed oodlean tied to the chair via her own tentacles.

"Is she okay?" Ibo asked.

"Oh yes, of course. She'll be fine," Linda assured him.

"She'll what?"

"Never mind. We have much to discuss. Permission to dock?"

Ibo was hesitant. Linda was acting rather strange, and the last time he gave a ship permission to dock, he ended up in handcuffs.

"Let me see your ship," he commanded.

"How do I do that?" Linda asked, searching her screen for some sort of clue.

"Take your camera and scan it around the room."

Following the Mabitu's gestures, Linda removed the camera from the console and pointed it around the room, quickly scanning past Troodly and Choodlen.

"Stop,!" Ibo shouted. "Who's the other oodlean? Is Schmoodler there with you?"

"What? No! Of course, not. That's just Choodlen. He's harmless."

Ibo squinted at the oodleans on his screen until he was satisfied that neither of them was fat enough to be Schmoodler. He looked around the rest of the room and did not see any weapons or handcuffs or burley henchmen. "Very well. Permission to dock granted."

Larv on her back, Linda had to drag Choodlen and Troodly, one at a time, kicking and screaming, through the docking tube onto the PUE ship. The Mabitu stayed behind for obvious reasons, sealing the airlock before any bubbles could drift into Ibo's ship.

"What's wrong with them?" Ibo asked of the oodleans.

"They'll be okay, just give them a minute," Linda said.

"Right . . . well, it's a pleasure to finally meet you in person, Ms. Pumpernickel."

"Same to you, Mr. President." Linda heard a whisper coming from behind her. "Larv says hi." She turned around so Ibo could see the disheveled cochlean in the backpack.

Unlike Linda, Ibo was unable to hide his reaction to Larv's condition. "Good God!" he gasped, as he noticed Larv's left eye starting to droop.

Linda quickly turned back around to glare at him and put her finger to her lips.

Ibo got the hint. "Good to see you, young larvalux," Ibo said. "Thank you both for all you've done. The PUE will not forget all your help. We were just about to head through the wormline to find you, but we had a slight delay. You won't believe what happened."

"Try me," Linda said.

Ibo told her all about how Schmoodler had boarded them and handcuffed them, and how Nimbulus was working for Schmoodler all along. "And then, poof! He disappeared into thin air, and so did his ship!"

"Oh my Oodle, it worked!" Troodly said, now free from the effects of the pheromones.

Linda turned to her and said, "Welcome back."

"I don't want to talk about it," Troodly said, clearly embarrassed about her uncontrollable behaviour in the presence of the Mabitu.

"It never happened," Choodlen added.

"What are you all talking about?" Ibo asked. "What worked?"

"We, uh, kind of did some meddling," Linda said.

"What sort of meddling?" Ibo asked.

"Oh, you know," Linda said, trying to downplay it. "Just the kind that changes the course of history, no big deal."

Ibo turned to Troodly. "What is she talking about?" he asked.

"We went back in time and stopped Schmoodler's birth from happening," Troodly said matter-of-factly.

"Technically, we prevented his conception," Choodlen corrected.

"You did *what*?!" Ibo asked in disbelief. "How?"

"You explain it to him," Troodly told Linda. "I've got something else to look into." Troodly twirled toward the console and started typing purposefully.

"TROODLY!" a voice bellowed excitedly. "I'm so glad you're okay. I am so, so, so, *so* sorry—"

"Not now, Steve," Troodly brushed off the excited intern.

"You remembered my name!" Steve said, and then twirled away in response to the shooing motion of one of her tentacles.

* * *

The Mabitu waited on its ship. Alone again. But at least there was no imminent risk of molestation. Bored, it gazed out the window, which now faced back towards the wormline. It noticed a squiggly line on the side of the ring. Or was it a Z? It was a Z, and it looked like a logo. It was not ITCo's logo. What would the Z stand for? Maybe it was the construction company, but the Mabitu doubted that Schmoodler would allow the construction company's logo on his wormline. He was much too egotistical for that. The Mabitu used the ship's external telescope to zoom in on the Z. Underneath, it read "Zomana." It had never heard of Zomana before. It searched the entire ring, but nowhere could it find any evidence of ITCo. Something was very wrong.

* * *

Back on the PUE ship, Arec Ibo stared at Linda in amazement. "You mean to tell me that the Mabitu is real?"

"As real as you and I," Linda replied.

"Can I meet it?" Ibo asked.

"Absolutely not," Linda asserted. "It stayed on its ship for a reason."

"Oh come on, I won't attack it. I can control myself," Ibo pleaded.

"I thought I could, too," Choodlen chimed in. "Trust me, you cannot."

"May I continue?" Linda asked.

Ibo nodded and Linda dove back into her long-winded explanation of every single detail of what had happened in the last few days. She surprised herself with her ability to remember everything so vividly. She was in the middle of telling a cringing Arec Ibo about how she'd spat the Mabitu's antidote into Tyg Schmydler's mouth when Troodly interrupted.

"I'm not a murderer!" Troodly shouted, staring at the monitor.

"I beg your pardon?" Linda asked.

"The solar system! It's back! Earth is intact!"

"It is?" Linda said, rushing over to the screen.

"He did it! The boy did it! He delivered the message to my future self and prevented me from destroying the planets!"

"Ryp saved Earth!" Linda shouted excitedly. "The ladies from chorus are okay . . . I can go home," she realized, suddenly overwhelmed by emotion.

"That's wonderful news," Ibo said. "But I have just one question about the whole Schmoodler situation."

"What's that?"

"If Schmoodler never existed," he pointed out the window to his left, "then why is the wormline still there?"

# CHAPTER 38

## The New ITCo

The Mabitu attempted to contact the PUE ship for the third time. "Pick up!" it shouted in frustration. In its boredom, it had hacked into their communications system again and was eavesdropping. On the fourth attempt, President Arec Ibo finally answered.

"Oh wow, I see what you meant about the effervescence," Ibo said to Linda.

"Yes, just wait until you see one of the bubbles," she replied.

"Is that one right there?" Ibo said, pointing at the screen.

"I do believe it is. Wait for it . . . " The bubble popped, releasing a shower of sparkles like a mini fireworks display.

"Wow!" Ibo said, staring at the screen in awe.

"*Hellooo*," the Mabitu said, annoyed. "I'm right here!"

"Hi Mab," Linda replied. "Sorry we're taking so long. Lots to discuss."

"Why didn't you tell me about Schmoodler?" the Mabitu asked.

"What about him?" Linda asked.

"Oh, I don't know, maybe that you *erased him from history*?"

"I hadn't told you?" Linda asked, genuinely surprised.

"No! Did it slip your mind?" the Mabitu asked sarcastically.

"I suppose it did," Linda said in all honesty. "So much has happened, I can't keep track of who knows what." Linda knew the real reason it had slipped her mind was because her mind had been preoccupied with thoughts of Ryp Comet.

"Is there anything else you neglected to mention?" asked the Mabitu.

Linda thought for a moment. "I don't think so."

"You don't *think* so?"

"Hey, what's the big deal anyway? The universe is better off without him."

The Mabitu took a deep breath and tried to prevent its voices from sounding too dissonant. "This is not the first time someone has messed with the space-time continuum. It's happened twice before that I know of. It always results in all sorts of changes. Some are barely noticeable, but others . . . others can be disastrous."

Linda and Ibo exchanged concerned glances. "How so?" Linda asked.

"I don't know the full extent of it. I'm the only one who seems to notice when it happens. The last time it happened, an entire species disappeared, or at least I haven't been able to find them since. It creates a sort of butterfly effect."

"With Schmoodler gone, the universe is saved from de-tuning!" Ibo said. "We should be congratulating Linda and Larv and Troodly and Choodlen, not reprimanding them."

"Look out the window," the Mabitu instructed.

"The wormline?" Ibo said. "Yes, we noticed it's still there."

"Thank goodness for that," Linda said, "or else we would've been stuck on that orange planet in the past. You think it's a bad sign?"

"Look closer." The Mabitu transmitted the zoomed-in image of the foreign logo.

"Zomana," Ibo read aloud.

"Is it ZO-ma-na or zo-MA-na?" Linda asked. "Or zo-ma-NA?"

"Either way, it's not ITCo," the Mabitu replied.

"What's your point?" Ibo asked.

"I looked it up. Zomana was ITCo's biggest competitor. Without Schmoodler to take over the family business, ITCo fizzled out once Tyg Schmydler retired. Zomana gained control of the market. Zomana is now the leading intergalactic trade and travel corporation."

"Zomana is the new ITCo," Troodly said.

"Exactly."

A deafening silence filled the room as the implications of this new information sank in, bringing a sense of hopelessness along with it. Everyone, even Linda, recognized the futility of the situation. If it wasn't one money-hungry magnate, then it would be another, and on it would go until they succeeded in destroying the universe.

After several silent moments of mourning the fate of the universe, Arec Ibo sighed. "I guess that means our work with the PUE is far from over."

"But what can we do?" Steve the intern lisped. "All the UPTs are gone."

"I guess we'll have to make new ones," Ibo said, "and hope that we can get some solid evidence for universal de-tuning before it's too late." The president looked around the room at his supporters. They needed him right now. As demoralized as he felt, he needed to be their leader. He needed to be optimistic for them. "You've all done so much for the PUE. I'd like you all to continue working with us. Steve, your enthusiasm will take you far. You're no longer an intern. You're promoted to my personal assistant."

Steve's eyes widened and he looked like he was about to cry. "It would be an honour, sir," he lisped and then twirled faster than a tornado to the restroom.

Ibo looked at the rest of them. "I won't blame you if you want to leave, but I'd love to have you all working with me. What do you say?"

Everyone agreed to continue working for the PUE in some capacity. They would have to sort out their roles later. In the meantime, they had one priority.

"Our first mission is to get this larvalux back to the Molasses Planet before it's too late," Ibo said. He bent down to Larv's level and said, "We'll be counting on you to be one of our new master listeners once your metamorphosis is complete. You'll be stationed at the base of your own listentower and paired with a larvalux assistant. How does that sound?"

Larv smiled weakly in agreement.

"Wonderful!"

The Mabitu, who was still on the monitor, spoke up. "I volunteer to take Larv home."

"Thank you," Ibo said. "We'll find a way to compensate you for your time and fuel."

"I don't want money," the Mabitu said. "I want you to help me find a new antidote."

Ibo agreed to the Mabitu's terms. "We've got two of the most brilliant scientists in the universe working for us," he said, acknowledging Troodly and Choodlen. "I'm sure they're up to the task."

"It would be the least we could do after . . . well, you know," Choodlen said, looking ashamed.

"I'm going with them!" Linda blurted. "Come on now, we'd better hurry." With Larv securely strapped to her back, she prepared to re-board the Mabitu's ship.

# CHAPTER 39

## The Molasses Planet

It took two days to reach the Molasses Planet, located near the outside edge of the Nasus Galaxy. They could have arrived sooner, but Larv's fragile body could only handle short bouts of tachyon speed. After the first day, Larv lost his one remaining limb and developed a pronounced indent running along the front of his body. On the second day, the indent became the hollow center of his now tube-shaped body. His eyes could no longer open, and the left one was dangling by a thread. His skin was covered in cilia and his elongated body no longer fit properly in the backpack, so Linda kept him comfortable by continuously smearing peanut butter over the exposed hairs cells.

They arrived in the nick of time. The ship broke through the cloudy outer atmosphere, and they saw the thick brown goo that covered the entire surface of the planet. They were greeted by a young female larvalux agent who Arec Ibo had contacted during their trip and had agreed to work with Larv. She led them to their new post at a listentower, which contained a small platform upon which the Mabitu expertly landed the ship. Linda and the Mabitu carried Larv out the hatch and gently released him into the molasses.

As soon as he entered the goo, Larv's body began contorting uncontrollably. Linda gasped. "Is he okay?"

One by one, a group of adult cochleans rose to the surface and surrounded Larv. They formed a circle and moved slowly clockwise.

"What's going on?" Linda asked, watching the strange ritual.

"Shhh, just watch," said the young female larvalux.

The movement of the adults created a whirlpool in the molasses. The current gently pushed and pulled Larv's body, forming it into a perfect

Fibonacci spiral. His metamorphosis was complete. The adults sunk back down below the surface, leaving a circle of air bubbles in their place.

"Larv, are you okay?" Linda called out.

The young larvalux shooshed her. "Just whisper, he can hear you."

"Sorry," Linda whispered.

The young larvalux hovered above adult Larv, whose voice was not loud enough for Linda to hear, and translated: "That was close."

"Oh Larv! I'm so glad you're okay," Linda whispered.

"You can't call me that anymore," Larv said through his translator. "I'm no longer a larvalux."

"You'll always be Larv to me," Linda whispered. "I've only known you for a little while, but I feel like we've been friends for a long time." Linda started tearing up.

"It's been an honour working with you both," Larv said.

"You, too," Linda choked.

The Mabitu said, "I'll have to come visit here often. It's one of the only planets that's safe for me."

"You'll get your antidote, I know it," Larv said. "Take some molasses with you. It contains some unique compounds that Troodly and Choodlen might be able to use."

The Mabitu retrieved an empty peanut butter jar from the ship and scooped up the thick, dark liquid. "Thanks, Larv."

"I hope it works," Larv said.

"Me too." The Mabitu looked over at Linda, whose face was brighter pink than usual. "We'd better get going," it said. "This atmosphere isn't great for humans."

Linda nodded. "Larv, I'm going to miss you, old friend."

"I'll miss you, too."

"Take care." Linda burst into tears as the Mabitu led her back inside the ship.

She continued to sob for the next three hours straight as the Mabitu drove the ship aimlessly. When she finally quieted down long enough, the Mabitu asked, "Where to?"

Bleary eyed and puffy faced, Linda looked up. She was taken off guard by the question. She honestly hadn't thought about her future in this new timeline. Finally, she said, "I guess I'd better go check on Earth. I wonder if my house is still where I left it."

"I wouldn't get my hopes up if I were you."

"I know, I know. The truth is, I don't think I really care about my house that much. I just turned sixty-five years old, and I've only just begun to realize there's more for me out there, out *here*, than the material things in my house. But I would very much like to check on my chorus, Daisy, Aunt Norma . . . " Just then, a strange thought occurred to Linda. "Mab, will I find another version of myself in my house? You know, assuming Schmoodler's non-existence made it so that I never left?"

"No, I don't think it works like that." The Mabitu contemplated for a moment. "Actually, I couldn't say for sure. I've never run into another version of myself, but then again, the universe is a big place."

"Let's go knock on my door and find out. If it's not too much trouble, that is."

"I've got nowhere else to be," Mab said.

"Me neither," Linda replied.

"Then it's decided," declared Mab. "Next stop: the Milky Way."

* * *

As Linda and the Mabitu approached Earth, they encountered several astrobarges orbiting the once blue planet, which had long since turned a smoggy gray. Some were preparing to depart at tachyon speed; others were waiting their turn to land. The high volume of traffic was hazardous to fly through and the Mabitu had to concentrate hard to avoid a collision. Linda gazed out the window, wondering if it had always been this busy. She scanned the advertisements plastered sloppily all over the immense vessels like paper maché. There was that same AnitPro™ ad with the stick-thin gwishank model. Some things never changed. On the side of a smaller, private vessel was the gaunt face of a human woman with messy hair and a dirty face which accentuated her striking blue eyes. She looked so familiar, but Linda couldn't place where she recognized her face from. Large letters spelled "This is the face of a slave." *Slave?* Linda thought, puzzled. There aren't any slaves on Earth. That was abolished centuries ago. She read the caption at the bottom of the ad: "Thousands of human farm workers die each year from treep-related incidents. Boycott AntiPro until working conditions improve and farm workers are paid a livable wage."

Linda pointed the ad out to the Mabitu. "Something's not right," she said. "Treep isn't grown on Earth by humans."

"It wasn't *before*," the Mabitu replied.

"Before what?" Linda asked.

"Before you tampered with space-time. Have you forgotten about that already?"

Linda did not admit out loud that this fact may have indeed slipped her mind momentarily. Instead, she shrugged and looked back at the ad, which wasn't really an ad at all. It was a protest. She had seen posters protesting the consumption of AnitPro™ due to its health risks, but never one protesting the working conditions of its harvesters. She scanned back up to the slave woman's burning blue eyes. Like the sun rising on a dwarf planet, the realization dawned on her abruptly.

"Petunia Petals!"

"What?" the Mabitu asked. "Is that some sort of figure of speech?"

Linda doubted herself and continued to study the face on the poster. It was definitely her, minus the voluminous hair, professional make-up, and shoulder pads. Yes, Linda was certain of it. But . . . Petunia Petals, a farm worker?

"Earth to Linda!" the Mabitu shouted, waving a glowing hand in front of her face until she snapped out of her trance.

"That woman on the poster," Linda said pointing. "Her name is Petunia Petals, or at least it was. That probably wasn't her real name anyway. Probably a stage name."

"Who is she?" the Mabitu asked.

"She's a celebrity. A journalist with her own television program called *Earth's Hour*."

The Mabitu looked at the poster, then back to Linda. "Not anymore."

# EPILOGUE

Several lightyears away, the ornian CEO of Zamona stood in a corner office on the top floor of a large building that acted as the headquarters of AnitPro™. He looked out the window at the bustling metropolis below, two sets of arms folded in front of his thorax.

"What do you think, sir?" asked the occupant of the swanky office from behind his large mahogany desk—real mahogany, imported from Earth after all the trees were cut down to make room for the treep fields.

The CEO turned to face his fellow ornian, trying not to stare at the stump where his hand used to be. "Well, Snyeild, I must say, I like what you've done with the place."

"It sure has changed a lot since we were younger," Snyeild replied.

"Indeed it has." The CEO turned back to the window and Snyeild got up to join him, his legs clicking along the polished marble floor.

"That building over there, that used to be where our huts were," he said, pointing with one of his three good arms.

The CEO followed his gaze, squinting. "My goodness, you're right!" He looked to the left of the huts. "And that road over there. That must have been paved over the old dirt road that the transports took to the treep fields."

"Good memory," Snyeild replied.

"How could I forget?" the CEO mused. "The monotony of riding those transports every damned day."

"I'm glad those days are far behind us," Snyeild said.

"Yes. We've come a long way," the CEO replied.

Snyeild nodded in agreement. "Another drink?" he offered.

"Please."

"Feeling adventurous?" Snyeild asked with a glint of mischief in his eyes.

"Always," the CEO said, grinning.

Snyeild used his second set of arms, which still had both hands, to open the cabinet behind his desk and pulled out a tall, slender bottle etched with an intricate design that swirled around the name of the liqueur scrawled across the label in an elegant font: "Spü." He uncorked the bottle and the potent aroma of its contents wafted across the large office. Stifling a cough, he poured the pungent brown liquid into two crystal tumblers and passed one to his boss.

"Appointing you president of AntiPro was the best decision I've ever made," the CEO of Zamona said.

"Don't make me blush," Snyeild replied. Incidentally, he was actually blushing. Not from the compliment, but from the effort of choking back the foul liqueur.

"No really, Snyeild. Your idea to outsource the treep harvest to Earth was brilliant." The CEO took a sip of Spü and turned to hide his grimace.

"Did I ever tell you how the idea came to me?" Snyeild asked.

"I do not recall," admitted the CEO after stifling a gag.

"Well, after what happened to my hand, I wanted to get as far away from that stuff as I could," Snyeild said, indicating his missing hand.

"No doubt!" agreed the CEO.

"But then it dawned on me—instead of *me* moving away, why not move the *treep* away?" He took another laboured sip of his drink, proving to his boss that he was among the manliest of men. "And then I thought, if humans like the stuff so damned much, they can bloody well grow it themselves!" The two of them roared with laughter. "I got lucky when it just so happened that Earth's soil was so well-suited to the crop."

"Yes, well, your luck is my luck," the CEO said, clinking his glass against Snyeild's, forcing him to choke back another sip of the masculinity-testing beverage.

"So, how are the kids?" Snyeild asked after he recovered.

"They are doing just fine," the CEO replied with a smile. "Both broods. In fact, I've got grandchildren on the way."

"That is wonderful news." Snyeild said, raising his glass for another toast. "Congratulations!"

"Thank you, old friend," the CEO replied, and then forced himself to gulp down the remainder of his repugnant drink.

Printed in Canada